FOSSIL LIGHT

FOSSIL LIGHT

a novel in films

Dennis Kennedy

β
Blackrock Press
Dublin

Book and cover design Valerie Reid
Cover photo © Ted Jones

ISBN 978-1-3999-6206-3

In memory of my grandmother
Bridget Ronan
who made the trip

I dreamed I fell asleep on the bank of a lake in the west of Ireland. The grass was warm from late-afternoon sun, though the earth was damp. You're too old for this, Dan, I thought, your ancient bones will rattle. I was clutching a camera, my grandmother's Kodak Brownie, my talisman. I heard a shout from the water. A man in a boat. Somewhere above my head there was a movie camera fixed to a tree. I could hear it whirring, filming not my life but another life. When I woke the stars were out in a black sky. They wouldn't give enough light for the camera. It's fossil light, I thought, light that reaches me from long-dead stars. I was still dreaming. The camera continued to run.

PART ONE

Delia's Picture Show

1886–1948

1

Now that the old woman was dying they were running scene by scene, the clips she'd always remembered and those she'd suppressed. Not in that flash people talked about, it was a slomo of her days, projected by some force outside her. Or inside her, what did it matter, it wouldn't stop. What's life but waiting for the last bed? With sheets if you're lucky, not a ditch in the bog in Connemara like her Da or a basement floor like her James. Was she preparing for judgement, announcing it in the newspaper? No judge, though, no obit, she just marked them item by item like a note for the grocer, milk, Wonder Bread, Fleishman's oleomargarine in a squeeze bag to blend the colour. Not in time, in some other order, unconstructed or dismantled. Her face was burning up.

She saw the wall opposite, nothing but the flocked wallpaper, green and faded pink flowers James had stuck up crooked and she made him do it over. But the lines still didn't join and the bugs were coming out with too many legs on them. Scorpions crawling up and down the wall in formation like the English soldiers in Castlebar and large grey lizards and green striped snakes, not garter snakes but something long and fat, black tongues flicking.

Here is where they went, she thought, all them snakes Paddy drove out. Snakes eating lizards, lizards eating insects, insects eating what? Running out of the fireplace which was boarded shut and up to the ceiling, coming over toward her head. She screamed *míolra!* which is vermin, and they scurried back and somebody said something she couldn't hear, her daughter Mary, married to the doctor with the German name she never remembered who didn't know shite and stood there next to her.

Mary bent over and stroked her face with a cloth and she dropped back again on the pillow, her loose grey hair sticking to her forehead and filmy grey eyes.

*

Little Dan stood by the door holding a Brownie Six-20 at his chest. He looked down into the viewfinder, framing. It kept him out of the rawness in the room, seeing it in the small groundglass rectangle: sunlight coming in the window, relatives round the bed, the mirror over the fireplace throwing light on his grandmother's face. He'd been told to stay near. He wondered what she was thinking, her eyes darting on the ceiling. She looked . . . he didn't know that look. In their afternoons he'd never seen her face like that. He wanted to capture it, though he was too young to know why or what it meant. He clicked the shutter, then pressed in the little silver key on the side and wound it forward until it stopped, ready for the next shot. He loved the box camera, its simplicity and its magic, though he couldn't say why to that either, but he knew it wasn't a toy. It was an adult thing, a memory machine.

*

The old woman looked at the ceiling. But was this Huron Avenue or the house on Cohoon Street? Or was it the farm cottage? With plaster crumbling inside and out and the roof leaking, on the rise right in front of Loch Measca, what the English call Lough

Mask, where the water would flood up to the door in a winter storm, the ground soaked for weeks and the grass not keeping the wet under the sod and the damp inside where the turf fire couldn't drive it out. In their room, the five children and the sixth who died and then the seventh too, that was me, the clothes hung on nails in the plaster and damp as well so you'd put them by the fire in the morning and Caty once put the best dress too close, scorched it she did and got a smack from the Mam.

Only the two rooms with a curtain between and the privy outside and the doorless barn and a rickety lean-to. The Da and Mam in the main room which was the kitchen and not enough chairs and the deal table scrubbed with pumice every night. A bed in the corner they brought close to the fire on bad nights but it would go out and you couldn't cut turf in that weather so what was had was in the shed but that was all till spring and you'd need it for the kettle and the cooking. Da was called Seán or was it Séamus, she couldn't remember, he was always the Da to her. The Mam was Máire, that's Mary like her own daughter, so many Marys in the village you couldn't but she was the Mary Higgins that was, when that was.

Then I was there, Bridget or Bridgie by name and everybody called me Delia since there were other Bridgies near, some also Moran like ours or Morehan or Morahane because few wrote anyway and spelling was for the priests and the gombeen men. The place was called Churchfield, a field but no church because it burned a hundred years ago, or hundreds, and for a child an hour's walk to Tourmakeady where was the shops, if ha'pence was to be had in the house for a loaf, or the Mam would bake brown bread in the big iron pot-oven on the fire with soda, but maybe it wouldn't work at all, it'd be a hard lump of black and I'd be blamed for not tending though I was the littlest. And it wouldn't go far with all of us, but there was the buttermilk with the tatties if the cow was happy and gave out enough for the three houses that shared her and the Da got the most because he worked the hardest and sausage on Sunday.

That I would do as well, the milking, and Méabh she'd sometimes stamp and catch my toes and it hurt bad for days. I called the cow Méabh, that's said Maeve, like the queen in the old stories, though the others called her Aisling, that's dream, because she was sleepy. If there was little milk there was always plenty of water. It wasn't a desert that place, no for God's sake no, Mayo was water on all sides, the sea or the lochs or the bog. If you could sell water we'd be richer than the high king of Connacht ever.

She'd heard people say how beautiful it must be there on the edge of the loch in green hills, but for her it was only wet, the fog coming in from the lake and the damp down the hills. Work all day for a few potatoes and a bit of cabbage, when do you stop and stare? The mud clinging to your bare feet and splashing your legs under a thin dress.

The snakes crawled up the wall again and up her legs and she batted at them, and the insects buzzing like a swarm of bees around her head on a hot August day. It was a hot August day in the bedroom but she shouted Lay a fire to her son John, the one they called Skip, but she might have said it in Irish and her children knew not of the old ways because she never spoke of the old ways, the Hunger. They'd never had to stir a turf fire or eat a blackened potato for their tea, what with that big furnace in the basement and the shops full even during the war if you had the ration book. John carted the coal from the street in a wheelbarrow and a baby barrow for his little Danny to help and pushed it through the window down the coal hole. That was not cutting turf in the windy bog and bringing it on your back the miles to the house. They wouldn't believe her, they'd think the old woman was on one of her rages.

The moon on the water, the rattle of bones on the hill.

But she remembered it, that's sure, every bit of it, and the terrible hour when the banshee cried down the hillside and the Da was hurt there the next day when his loy slipped and he cut his foot bad and it got septic and buckled under, and the eldest brother John took over the farm. Seán the Mule, they called him, because he'd won the mule from Pádraic McAnna in a bet at the races and went everywhere with it because he feared McAnna would kill it just for spite. Lucky, he named it, Ámharach, till one night we heard it bray like the banshee and in the light it was dead in the barn because it had been sick even when he won it, not ámharach at all. We couldn't eat it and then Seán was the mule and carried the farm things hisself.

Then one day, that one day when he said, Ye're too young to be of help and what with the Da sick and the Mam pining I can't do it all meself so some must go off. For the money. There's no work here west or east so it's England for little Willie, and we'll send ye girls over the great sea when we can. That was harsh, even for him, but many were going, some had gone since the Hunger, whole families one after the other, a chain of going and sending back for others to go so those still behind could feed. We had uncles in a factory in the Boston states and an aunt in service for the Bostoners and somebody in Ohio. OH-HIGH-OH, a grand name, some red Indian name it must be, with a great wide river, so they said. But Nellie and Caty, they didn't think it would happen with the cost of the passage though they wanted it bad, anything other than that life and maybe then a man to be had. They'd leave the Mam in a flash and the brother even faster.

The old people would say that on a good night you could stand at the top of Croagh Patrick and see the lights of Boston but they was after telling tales because it took weeks and bad things could happen to a girl on the ship, Nellie said, but what that was I knew not.

*

Dan clicked the shutter again as Doc Joe bent down to take the old woman's pulse. That'll be a classic portrait, Joe thought, doctor and patient, hand in hand. There wasn't much left of her, the heart slow and intermittent. She wasn't thin, in fact she looked heavier, but her skin was drawn tight like parchment and scaly despite the moisture on her face and the plastered white hair. And the right leg was gone from the knee. Diabetes mellitus, leading to gangrene of the foot. Skip called it the dropsy and said she got it from not getting up in the night to piss. A folk notion of uraemia Joe had heard before. By the time he was called in the oedema was so severe there was nothing for her but the chop. He could smell the gangrene as soon as he came through the front down downstairs. They were all gagging – why had they waited to call him?

He was always called in too late. What they said behind his back was true, that he wasn't much good since the war and they used him because he didn't charge the family. His hands shook in the morning but he could take another swig from his silver flask, and he wasn't a surgeon any longer so it didn't much matter. He was a shellshock doc with a dying clientele. His office was on the first floor in the 1800 block of Vine Street, close to his father's butcher shop, waiting room, consulting room, storeroom, but he had no interest in expanding and no heart for collecting from his Over-the-Rhine patients, the old German district declining like him after the war. Sometimes they brought him a live chicken or a torn paper bag of turnips. He sent Delia to Saint Mary's for the operation, some young cutter delighted with the work, but he knew the trauma would only hasten the end. She'd been home three days and was disappearing into the sheets.

He set her hand down. He looked at her children, just his Mary and Skip, Ed was still at work, and Skip's Gert and little Danny at the door, half-in, half-out, standing ankles crossed in shorts, entrechat, holding an old Brownie. Joe shook his head. He took another drink and handed Skip the flask. It was a memento from Italy, sterling with the lion stamp and a hinged cap, beautifully curved for the hip pocket, given to him by a grateful Brit captain who'd served in Africa and was hit in the gut at Anzio. Jesus, even his dick was shot off. A family heirloom, Major Joe, he said in a cut-crystal voice, One I won't be passing on. He died the next day. There was a monogram on the face, CST. No one in the field hospital knew what it stood for, since the initials didn't correspond to the officer's name, but there it was, fine engraving inside an oval, its provenance another casualty of battle.

Doc Joe was a casualty too, he knew, infected in Italy and now a carrier of the disease, its pathology hidden. Maybe the meaning of all that time was hidden, not available, lost in the attempt to force sense onto those millions dead, all the propaganda and the frantic righteousness and the hatred of the Hun and the Jap and the crowing over victory. Disease makes sense, it has a purpose, but all that made no sense, the whole European theatre of war. He laughed at the thought of it being a play. He took the flask back and put it in his pocket, warm and dependable.

Gert at the doorway started to cry, though he couldn't imagine why, since the bitch in the bed had been brutal to her since she came to live with Skip on Huron Avenue. The old woman called them krauts, Gert and the Doc, and hated the idea that all three of her children had married Germans. Nothing to do with the war – he knew she didn't care one bit about the war with her sons not in it. Hell, half of Ireland would have invited Hitler to invade that sodden little island just to ruin Britain for good. For her it was simply that he and Gert and Ed's wife Louise weren't Irish. Mixed marriages, she called them, even though all of them were Catholics.

Joe was older than Mary by a dozen years and had been married before, so the old lady resented him making her daughter second choice. Mary had lived in the house during the war with their son Michael, and Peggy the Red, who was somehow related to the old bitch's dead husband, as well as Skip and Gert and Dan and Tuffy, and who knows what else, chickens in the fucking cellar. Hell, even Tuffy was a kraut, a schnauzer. When is a schnauzer a snoozer, Cliff would say to Danny, and answer, When he's sleeping, thinking that was clever. Cliff was cheery, though, at least when drunk, which was most of the time, though who was he to talk. Cliff was another kraut, married to Peggy, in France in the war drinking Bordeaux from the bottle in bombed-out cellars when they pushed the Germans far enough to rest for an hour. Joe hadn't been here on Huron to see that crowd of women and children in the house since he was busy chopping off boys' legs and stitching up chests, all hopeless, like bright tulips wilting on the first hot day of spring. Skip was lucky out of it, even if he crawled down in the sewers or whatever he did and had to come home at night to his old bitch of a mother.

It was already 1948, two years after he was discharged and came back to Cincinnati, like the thousands of other soldiers crowding Union Station. Doc still didn't know what to do with himself. Last in war, last in peace, last in the hearts of his countrymen. Like the poor sods who got planted in France and

Italy. Just as he didn't know what to do about the old lady, other than let her die, which was going to happen anyway. Still vain about her age, trying to brush her hair, asking for face powder in the hospital – hell, she'd been lying about her age for decades, getting younger as she got uglier, and she'd never been a beauty. That downturned cut of a mouth, thin exacting lips, black stare.

He knew his dislike of the old woman was illogical. For all her nastiness if it weren't for her there would have been no Mary for him and thus no little Michael and, because these things define us backwards, no him either.

*

Years later, when Danny had become a filmmaker, he'd see his grandmother in 1930s black and white, sharply photographed with depth of frame, not sepia or sentimental, with a male narrator you could trust, Olivier or Fonda. She was young, the voice would begin, with a touch of her own west of Ireland in the vowels. Too young many said, and to travel only with other girls was risky even if they were older. And to send all the family at one go to the unknown, what was the point of that? Those many years later Dan wondered if Delia had seen it that way, like one of the pictures James took her to at the Lyric downtown when they were courting. Or more like a dream sequence? She told him that the old women tried to frighten her, giving out to her brother for dispatching his sisters like they were chickens. Willie already in Liverpool, the others dead at birth or soon after, only Seán to be left behind without his mule. The old women had practice scarifying, with Churchfield and Trean and Garranagerra and Tourmakeady and Cappaghduff and all the rest around, town and village reduced by those going, who was counting. The west falling free since the Hunger despite the highest birth rate in Europe. But her mother went along with it, though she was crazed with grief still and not responsible, the two years after her husband was sent underground, high on the hill. On still nights she heard his bones rattle, she said, shouting at the wind.

The old women succeeded for she was frightened, and though Caty and Nellie were kind and careful with her, her fear would last the journey and beyond. What did she expect at the end, a place whose name she couldn't quite remember? Cin-cin, like a double sin. At age ten, when her world had been bordered by bog and loch, the rhythm of light and water, potato patch and the annual pig. Perhaps she imagined a something in that somewhere, perhaps not, but at the start it was fear that shook her and that she could not shake, uprooted, cast away. Through her long life she never forgave that first violation, the loss of the soil, birthright of the lake on the long summer evenings, hers to keep for just the looking at it.

They owned little so there was little to take. What they had with them were clothes in a rough wooden chest her brother nailed together like a coffin, rope handles at the ends, *Ellen Moran to New York and Cincinnati* in black, put there by Cathal the Paint from Ballinrobe, because he owed Seán money. Who rowed himself across the lough in a tiny boat with his paint box and long brushes and his ragged grey dog for company. Ellen chosen for the address because she was the eldest, eighteen years to Delia's ten. Sweet Nellie, who mothered her and raised her, and Caty who didn't care much but was strong, they were the three. The priest said it, he'd read it in a book for the Irish who were leaving, they'd need heavy coats for the snow in the Ohio states but those were cheaper and better to buy there if they had some money for it, and if they hadn't they could with luck save it before the winter. The box stored in the hold for the voyage. On board they each took a large bag made of old rugs, but Delia's was canvas so it would be lighter since she had smaller things.

Seán the Mule cut a new blackthorn and gave it to Nellie, sized to her height. It had a fine knob at the top, not a shillelagh but strong. To keep you safe on the ship, he said, and after as well.

At the American wake, scrounged out of the passage money from some uncle or cousin in a place called Lawrence in another place she couldn't pronounce – how many places were there, she wondered – the keeners started again. The sound was horrible, like her father's death, and her mother now begging her not to go, forgetting she'd agreed to it all along. All three of her girls at once was crushing and she had to blame them somehow. O mavourneen, why do ye break the heart of me who birthed ye, she cried, half in Irish, half in sobs, Will you leave me alone with the death itself calling every day? Her sisters ignored it and stood outside with the boys they liked, who thought they might get a kiss or more in the high feeling before they left. They might have got it from Caty but Nellie knew boys are like that and had a sharp tongue and they went away disappointed. While Delia had to stand by the Mam and listen to the wail. When she closed her eyes on her wedding night she heard it still.

And she heard it on the road in the jaunty car all the winding miles to Claremorris with the soft rain on her new hat and new shawl and her new shoes pinching. She wore little cloth slippers made by Nellie once to a wedding, but never real shoes of leather and she didn't like them, children didn't wear shoes at all, her feet making wails themselves till she took them off. She would have thrown them to the ground but Caty stopped her. Seán the Mule followed them on foot on the track the two miles to Tourmakeady, getting further behind, then dropped off with a wave but no word, to see the feed merchant. Nellie turned to watch him go with tears in her eyes but Caty stared straight ahead. Delia didn't know her feelings, aside from the fear held in her chest like a stone in her new shoe.

The driver pulled up at the station in Claremorris with a shout of Ho, people scampering along the edge, not knowing to stand or go, anxious they were on the wrong platform, back and forth like a ball on a tether or the pig in the yard. When the black engine came in it was a monstrous thing dripping oil and water and smoke and steam like a great kettle on the fire, making a sound never heard in her small life, but strangely calming. Not about the going but about the trustworthiness of the thing, the Great Southern and Western. The rush to board with the box in the guard's carriage and then such speed as she'd never thought of, with the men leaning out the windows smoking and eyeing the three sisters, Nellie huddled with her on the wood bench, third class, Caty staring back, challenging any one of them to speak. Tuam, Athenry, Ennis, Limerick and over the wide wide river, Mallow and Cork, names she'd heard but thought impossibly far, and she was passing them all in an afternoon, exciting her with a moving picture of dizzy space. She'd never considered space before, except looking at the loch at sunset, and she barely understood now, but aware of a thing on her shoulder like a devil whispering.

Queenstown was even more alarming, a mass of people dressed all ways and porters with giant barrows shouting as the train pulled in, right along the long dock that seemed to push halfway out the sea through the still harbour water and above it gulls screaming louder than the porters. She could taste the salt and feel it damp on her face. Nellie thought they could save the thruppence by carrying the box themselves once it was on the platform but only porters could take it on board so they followed the man and his barrow loaded with other chests, most of them finer made, and watched him load it. He tipped his hat to them with a smirk. As he rolled his cart away she heard him say, Muttons and a lamb to the slaughter.

What does he mean, Delia asked, but Nellie pretended she hadn't heard and nudged her forward. They scrambled up the gangway, everybody behind pushing, so there'd be no turning back. Almost at the top someone shoved hard and she dropped her bag and cried out. The bag was suspended on the ramp, about to fall all the way into the water, and she saw in a flash everything that was in it, her change of clothes, a little hat, some biscuits, a water bottle, her tin cup and plate for the journey. Teetering on the edge of the gangway, the bag opened at the top and a small rag doll fell out, no bigger than her father's hand, thin strips of red linen for hair, painted face, a tiny skirt. Her mother made it for her years ago and she slept with it still. She watched it drop in slow motion all the way to the water, a fearful long time. As the bag itself was about to go, a barefoot skinny boy behind her caught its wooden handle. He gave it back to her, smiling the while. She nodded to him and muttered thanks. Her heart was racing. The doll floated below. Her sisters had gone ahead and didn't see. She held the bag tightly to her chest up the gangway.

*

Gert looked through the screen of the back door and saw Danny in the yard playing with Tuffy. He'd left the camera on the kitchen counter. What would I do without him, she thought, I'd rather leave him than him leave me. She must have spoken out because Skip said, Who's thinking of leaving? She turned but didn't answer, a little smile on her face. It was a sweet face, beautiful skin, not pale, soft hazel eyes, fine cheekbones and a welcoming mouth. Skip felt weak when she smiled, but held the weakness inside, not showing anything on his face except afternoon whiskers. The world – well, the world was beyond and this woman was here but always lightly absent. He looked out the window at his son, the reason for a hurried marriage, and wondered at the turns of life. He lit another Lucky Strike. Gert was gone, as quickly as cobweb blows away.

She had wandered upstairs, feeling a little weak from the climb, one steep flight in this old house. She stopped at the window at the top, before the corridor turned to the right, and looked out on the side yard. The squirrel tree, occupied by Billy; she fed him peanut butter on saltines, and he'd take them up to a crook in a branch and nibble the peanut butter off with his teeth and tongue, delicately, holding the cracker in his forepaws before he let it drop. He preferred crunchy, but Danny would only eat Skippy smooth. She'd call to the squirrel from below, Here, Billy, Billy, and Tuffy would bark. They seemed to have an arrangement, Billy and Tuffy, like America and Russia with their bombs and planes. Out the window she saw the leaves showing the first signs of turning. What kind of a tree was it? It was a towering thing, squeezed by the narrow space between this house and next one. Maple? When she asked her mother-in-law about the tree, the old lady shouted at her. It's my tree in my yard of my house, she said, and you've no need to bother it with your squirrels. Now she was in the next room, the shouts dying with her.

Gert was used to people shouting at her, youngest of three, picking up after her brother and sister. Before her mother-in-law there was her father, a stubborn German, cold as their house in winter and unforgiving as the bare floorboards or Hitler in heat. He did little work, surviving on his Kentucky cronies, low-level ward politicians like the water board or the rationing commission, expecting the German connection would be enough so he wouldn't have to do real work. That was funny, Gert thought, considering the war against Germany. But Germans were here first, before the Irish. The Irish went to the police in Cincy, the Germans went to farming in Kentucky, or government.

Real work frightened her father, so he'd sent his lame wife to work in the store on Short Street when they ran short, acting like a lord in a Rhineland castle but drinking beer from a bucket from the saloon next to the store. Shouting at them. Gert wouldn't talk back to him, because they'd all had the back of his massive German hand. Otherwise, he was a quiet man. Aside from that, Mrs. Lincoln, the joke went. Tall, stooping over as he aged.

They were from Covington, right across the river from Cincinnati, the wide Ohio, North-South divide. Her father was Johan Luganmann though he dropped an N and called himself John. She was Gertrude Anna Luganman. You're Gertrude, little Danny said, you don't like Trudy so you're Gert and Dad is John but called Skip and I'm Daniel but called Dan. We're a three-family and we live with Gran who is Bridget but called Delia.

Skip was Delia's youngest son. In 1940 he brought Gert to live here in his mother's house on Huron Avenue. Skip would shout too, but only when he was drunk and that wasn't so often in those days and beer was all he'd take. Hudepohl, brewed on Clifton Avenue, or Wiedemann's from Newport. Whiskey, but only if he could get it. He'd a drop taken, Delia would say in her green-sodden voice from over the sea, and he'd forget I own the house so I'd knock the sense into him because James his father, God rest him, was too gentle to do it, so. The *so* from the west of Ireland, so. Gert saw her do it once with her blackthorn stick with its knobby end she'd brought on the ship with her accent long ago. Gert gasped and Delia told her to close her kraut mouth or she'd knock her as well.

Gert never understood why there was such a thing as shouting. It put her stomach in motion and her gut in suspension, worms crawling in circles through her intestines or that night dread that woke her sometimes when Skip snored and turned over and she was lost in a room catching her breath.

*

The ship was huge, frightening in the way the black locomotive was not, especially with the horn blasting in bunches of three melancholy notes, so deep you'd feel the vibrations before you heard the sound. Warnings of departure or disaster. She was the lamb. How did it stay afloat, the size of it? The superstructure stood high above the main deck, the deck high above the water, the masts higher than all. White Star Line, *SS Germanic* on the stern, Liverpool under it. Built in Ireland, Caty said, by the Protestants in Belfast. Delia had never been near a Proddie, though she was told that once in Tourmakeady, when she was four, she'd seen Captain Boycott, the agent of Lough Mask House, before Parnell drove him out of Ireland for the snake he was, according to her Da, and the Da was not a Land Warrior. We have enough patch as it is, and an honest landlord, he said, but it was not patch enough for Seán the Mule so she was climbing the steep wet gangway, slipping in her shoes. She worried that the ship might be ungodly, like one of the Prod churches they stole from Catholics and she crossed herself as she crossed the rail.

There was no time to think of such things as they hustled below. Steep stairs the sailors called ladders, four turns, then a final long descent, one older woman bouncing on her bum the last few yards, yelping at each bump. Her man picked her up, red-faced and out of breath. Again Delia felt the pressure of feet behind, making her nervous when she needed to be cautious in her tight shoes.

Some of the berths were already taken with English and German emigrants; the ship stopped in Queenstown only a few hours for the Irish before the long passage, so there was a scramble to find the best spaces. They had been given a numbered berth but no one was paying attention. Caty took charge and found a large berth on the lowest rank of three, big enough for all of them if Delia scrunched in the corner with their baggage. She spread out the two thin mattresses they had carried, rolled in the handles of their bags, and two light blankets. It was crowded but cosy, with a curtain to draw across. She found comfort in being crowded, since she was used to that at home, used to the sweat and smell of her sisters, and some of her fear retreated. There was a screen of boards, once-painted and now worn from the touch of many hands, that half-hid six ranks of berths. There was no fresh air, just one small porthole above the top level, its glass fixed and ancient, dulled by salt water. Little light.

The smell. Farm smells she knew, and the sharp-sour turf fire, and dead fish on the loch, but this was human. Accumulations of hot feet, seasick stomachs, stale mouths, urine and shit. The Moran girls were gagging. Their mother had given them hankies with dried herbs sewn in, their names embroidered in green, Ellen Ita, Catherine Anne, Bridget Columba. But nothing could defeat the assault to the nose. They vowed to spend their time walking in the open air.

Up they went, at the harsh call of a sailor. Bring your tickets and papers, he shouted, in an accent she'd not heard before. The crush again on the ladders, people still carrying their bags against theft. Their own money was divided in five places: small leather purses with leather thongs Nellie and Caty wore around their necks under all their garments with thirty shillings apiece, two gold sovereigns each in a strong string belt around the waist, also under the clothing, and some loose silver and copper Nellie had in a cloth bag pinned under her outer skirt which bounced as she walked. This was for the voyage, the rest for arrival in New York and the onward journey, seven pounds five shillings and some pence in all. It seemed an enormous sum to Delia, who was too young to carry any of it.

On deck two officers in white uniforms and hats with gold braid stood in the weak sun. The ship was already underway, moving slowly under tug out of the harbour. They were checking tickets again, one by one. Passengers had been vetted on shore for signs of disease and their names, ages, and nationalities carefully entered in a large log. The shipping company was responsible for documents; immigrants rejected in New York for health or politics were sent back at the firm's expense. Sad groups of sallow-looking Poles and Russians often made the return journey, even poorer than before. There were Irish and English as well who were returned for tuberculosis.

Let me stand with youse.

It was the lad who had caught Delia's bag on the gangway. He wore an oversized shabby wool jacket, black trousers belted with ragged rope and turned up twice at the cuffs, a soft cap, a dirty white shirt without collar. His hands were grimy and he was too thin for his tall frame. He looked about twelve or thirteen. He slid in next to Delia, behind her sisters. Have ya yer docket, he said.

She held it tight in her hand.

S. S. GERMANIC
Liverpool – Queenstown – New York

Thursday, 26th March, 1886
Third class
Child under ten, half fare, £2-12/6

White Star Line
J. Scott & Co. Agent, Queenstown

She had turned ten in January but looked younger. She wanted to say this but the boy spoke again. Lemme have 'er, I'll give 'er back later.

Why do you want it?

They'll let ya stay with yer wans there if ya say ya lost it. He stretched for it and she pulled away. She'd had many cautions about the dangers of shipboard and boys. She liked him for helping her but something was not right.

Come on, won't cha, jus a minute, as he reached again.

She bumped into Caty, who saw what it was and said, And who's this barefoot jackeen? She smiled at him as if he were a cute dog. Off, now, she said, there's no bone for ye here.

He looked at them and spit out, Ya fookin culchies, yer all the same, and ran to the back of the queue, the soles of his feet making sucking noises on the deck.

Caty said, Give me the ticket, I'll hold it, so.

Delia didn't like giving it up but was already afraid the officer would question her age. What did he want, she asked.

He's a stowaway without a ticket and he was trying to steal yours. Though I doubt he'd pass for ten, even if he is skinny as a cuaille.

What will happen to him, then?

I suppose they'll put him ashore in a boat. I heard it happens all the time.

Delia looked over the rail at the unfinished spire of Saint Colman's Cathedral, receding in the mist enveloping Queenstown. She thought of the boy's smile when he caught her bag, his crooked pure white teeth, his eyes alight with mischief, and she hoped they wouldn't find him.

2

Danny came upstairs with the camera just as the doorbell rang. In his grandmother's room he looked again through the viewfinder and saw her face relax. She turned and smiled at him in her crooked way.

The snakes were gone, her mind was clear. She was back at Loch Measca when the Da died, and on the table they laid him for the wake. After the priest said the words and rubbed oil on his forehead and hands and feet and they set out the porter from the shebeen and the poitín they couldn't afford and the neighbours came, all the people from Churchfield and beyant, and Willie came back from Liverpool though he was late, and all crowding into the room and out on the step in front and some across the mud track to the edge of the loch to smoke their pipes, for the Mam wouldn't allow it in the house for the smell that lingered.

The keeners began the olagón and soon the Mam was chanting along in Irish.

Why did he die tonight when he never died before?

Why did you leave us? Had you not ever a comfort heart could wish?

Blaming the dead for being dead. She told her son John about these keeners and their dirges and he made up a joke about Paddy and Mick who pick up the dead Fintan from his wake and walk him down to the pub between them for a last pint until he falls off the stool and they blame the barman for his death and the barman says, He pulled a knife on me, he did. Told it in all the bars in Dutchtown and they bought him drinks on it.

Delia cursed the Da dying long ago and the brother that sent her away and the hunger and the mud. The children around her and their children not knowing what it was then and the memories die with her. She clenched her teeth and hit her fist on the mattress. It made no sound.

Memory was private to her. Not even with her husband did she share those Mayo days, and he didn't know them either, born in America though his own father was Tipperary, Rody he was, and now that memory was all that was left she wanted it public. I'll tell the stories, but no words came out, only dark breath and a groan in the throat. Hush, Mary said, as if she were the mother, not the daughter, Lay back quiet now.

She heard the hush behind her and saw in the corner of her eye a black figure coming forward, another smiling ghost like James her father and James her husband, her dead making visits to say things she didn't understand, as if they were in the water after a shipwreck and whispering through bubbles of salt. Then she saw it was the priest, the Irish one whose name was actually Mick and thank God not the pastor Monsignor Schengber, that old kraut.

It's Father Mick, Mom, Mary said as she got up. The priest said hello to Dan and told him not to take pictures. Gert was setting up a little crucifix and two candles by the bed, a Catholic kit for death. The cross was its lid with a snap catch and under was storage for candles and a white cloth and the magic water, all that holy mystery. Gert stuck the cross upright in a slot in the base and the candles in brass-lined holes to each side. She was having trouble with the match, then Father Mick was saying since she couldn't speak could she make a sincere act of contrition in her head and God would forgive her sins and he started it, O my God, I am heartily sorry for having offended thee. Little Ed used to say Hardly sorry, which was true in her case. The priest made the gestures and mumbled as they do at confession, Ego te absolvo, eggo baco. I can speak, she tried to say, But I'm busy right now with a list.

I'm offering her Viaticum, the priest said, taking pleasure in the Latin word, and took a host from a little pixie gold thing like a locket and held it up and broke off a piece because she couldn't swallow much and they said any part of it was the whole though why any Christ would want to be in that piece of dry nothing she never understood. She wouldn't open her mouth. Delia, this is Viaticum, he said, Holy Communion for the journey. I'm not going anywhere, I've already been. Then Mary gave her a drop of water which she needed and the priest stuck in a tiny bit of the thing, like stiff blotting paper, and she wondered if it counted when they force fed you.

He unpacked his little leather case. Extreme Unction, he said, and held up a little glass vial. It was sticky and had a crack down the side. He looked at it in alarm. Damn, he said, the oil of chrism leaked out. Do you have some oil I can use?

I've got castor oil, Doc said.

I've got Pennzoil, Skip said, thirty weight.

Olive oil or salad oil, please. I will bless it.

Gert came back with a bottle of French's salad dressing from the Kelvinator super-automatic. She shook it and it clouded up. The priest looked at the bottle, orangey-red, viscous. Don't you have something you fry with?

I use bacon dripping, Gert said, we get the best bacon from the Jaegers. The Jaegers were Doc Joe's parents who ran the German butcher's shop on Republic Street. Gert was crying again, so Father Mick said nothing. She brought up a coffee can filled with solid drippings. He looked troubled but blessed it. Eggo baco, corpus porkus. He stuck his thumb in the can, made a face and began, Delia, per istam sanctam unctionem, and smeared it on her eyelids, ears, nostrils, lips, hands, and feet, all the organs of sin, she thought, except the most important one.

Take it easy, greasy, you've got a long way to slide.

Dan clicked the shutter.

Prayers were lost on her. Not that she didn't believe, she was too Irish to deny God or the priests and the church, but at Mass the Latin made her sleepy, as if her mother were singing a lullaby in Irish and she dozed next to her by the fire.

*

It was still called steerage class, as in the age of sail, when the lowest grade of passengers were in a hold through which the steering cables passed. Every Irishman knew stories of those days during and after the Hunger, when the crossing took at least six weeks and could take fourteen in bad weather. Shipwreck, bad food and water, abuse, cholera and typhus: some emigrants from Munster or Connacht found rest in a shrouded dive into the cold Atlantic. Steam changed it all, bigger ships, better accommodation, the crossing less than two weeks. The *Germanic* looked magnificent in full wind, her two stacks billowing white smoke, sail assist from three masts square rigged and a jigger at the stern.

They were in the third day, used to the food if not the smell, able to walk on the open deck and chat with other Irish. A woman named Clara was on her way to a marriage arranged by an uncle in San Francisco. Her intended had emigrated from Kerry decades before, was now over fifty and still single. He'd made easy money running saloons during the silver strikes in Nevada, wasted it on drink and gambling and whoring, and was now determined to set up a proper restaurant and a family. Clara's father, a successful Catholic farmer, was providing a cash dowry. She was a bit chubby to Delia's eyes, warm and friendly. Her hair was light brown, her eyes the same, the autumn of a walnut shell.

Aren't you afraid he'll treat you poorly, Nellie asked.

Clara smiled. I'm more afraid he'll be ugly. Uncle Teddy wrote he's a decent-looking man, but you never know, do you? And me Da, he wanted me gone. She showed a tintype she'd been sent, a portly figure standing stiffly in a dark velvet jacket and large knotted tie and pearl stickpin, not much hair, thick moustache. The image was faded and had been bent in the post; it could have been a decade old, or more.

Clara had strong Kerry talk. Mayo people thought Kerry people stupid, but Clara seemed intelligent and was often reading a book. She made a joke of most things, thought it an adventure to be going alone to the end of the earth to a man she'd never met. She'd been advised to take a top berth, though she didn't know the advantage. She was two rows away from the Morans and suggested the girls should shift upwards to an empty one, to be near. But the bulkhead curved inward and the space got narrower as it rose so they stayed on the bottom shelf. Besides, Caty thought there was something wrong with Clara's account. If her father had money, even a little, why wasn't she in second class? It would be rude to ask so to her sisters Caty whispered, She's no great catch, that one, and sure she's over thirty or I'm the Archbishop of Armagh and Primate of All Ireland. How can the man expect children? Delia knew Caty was a little jealous. They too were going to the unknown, but with only hard work ahead and no man.

The noon bell rang for dinner. Long tables of rough planks were lowered from overhead into the narrow space between the berths. Other narrow planks were set on iron supports to make benches. There were hundreds of passengers in steerage who scrambled each time to find places as if at musical chairs. Late-comers had to stand or sit on the edge of their berths. Some people complained about the food but there was plenty of it, cooked in huge kettles in the forward galley and brought by stewards in large buckets. No cloths or napkins. Your own tin plates and mugs and cutlery. Soups and stews with potatoes and great loaves of coarse bread. No fresh fruit, few vegetables. The meals were greasy with gristly beef or pork, but the Morans didn't mind; having meat every day was entirely new to them.

Washing up was unpleasant. A big barrel on deck for the scraps, which smelled no matter how often it was emptied over the side, then another for washing the plates and utensils, filled with cold seawater. By the time Delia got to it in the queue, grease and scraps were floating throughout, a secondary stew ready salted. Fresh water was reserved for drinking and there was precious little of it unless you could bribe the stewards. They didn't ask much, but on shipboard everything had a price and it was too high for the Morans.

By the fifth day the dinner benches were empty and most emigrants were moving only between their bunks and the sick-up basins on the floor. An Atlantic storm formed deep swells running from the north, rolling athwartship. Even some sailors took to their hammocks. The hatch to the open deck was battened for safety, and the air below became stagnant, so heavy you could feel it crawl on your skin like the feet of ants or spiders. The girls soon discovered why upper berths were preferable, as people above them sometimes didn't make it to the basins in time. Nellie rigged up an extra blanket as a tent inside the berth to protect them; she had to clean it twice a day if she was able. She and Caty could keep nothing down but a few dry biscuits. The water supply mysteriously became more limited and they were dehydrated. You could buy fruit from the crew: sixpence an apple, a shilling an orange, exorbitant, and the price went up as the storm lasted.

Delia's appetite held. Since almost no one else was eating dinners, a friendly steward took her to the galley, which made things easy for him and got her briefly out of fetid steerage. There was fresh air from a ventilator. Most of the crew were English, though the cooking was dominated by Italians. They filled her water cup but wouldn't give her extra for her sisters. They laughed at her accent and she laughed at theirs. They asked her to speak some words in Irish. She lost her native shyness and sat on a stool in a corner of the small steamy room to repeat the tale of Fearghus Dubhdhéadach or Blacktooth, high king of Ulster and some say of all Ireland, as much as she remembered of it, learned from her mother on grey winter afternoons. How he gained the throne by battle and lost it. Treachery subverted Tara in the time of the heroes. She spoke by rote and when a cook they called Johnny asked her to explain the tale in English, she could only say that Fearghus was a great Irishman of long ago whose sword was magical and whose voice still today was captured in the leaves of the forest.

Why then aren't the Irish still great today, Johnny said in a sarcastic Italian voice.

Delia knew the answer, having heard it many times at home.

Because the English ruined the land, she said, and all the cooks laughed.

Since no one was permitted on the weather decks, there was little to occupy her. Nellie would normally tell her a story, or make up one about their new life in Sinsinsi, which she made into a wondrous place, but her sisters were too sick to talk. Clara, who was green with vomiting, lent her a book but it had only a few pictures, line sketches of a city skyline, and the words were too hard for her to follow for long. Returning from the galley she slipped and fell as the ship rolled, hitting her head on the woodwork. As she got up and tried to clear her head she thought she saw the young lad from Dublin dart around the corner of the last berth, still barefoot and even skinnier. She walked aft but didn't find him and was about to return to her sisters when a thin arm reached down from a middle shelf and tried to pull her up. She shouted in alarm as the boy stuck his head through the curtain. Shhh! he said, climb up. She caught her breath and surprised herself by not hesitating. He'd created a cosy space for himself in a disused berth with broken boards.

What're you doing here?

Shhh your hole, they'll find me. Youse anytin to eat? I'm fearful hungry.

She'd just had her dinner but carried nothing. You been hiding the while?

Almost nicked the first day, but it's a fearful big boat and there's secret spots, engines, lockers, and then I found this place. No one looks here, all the way to the end. What's your name? I'm Fergus.

She laughed at the coincidence and gave her name as Bridgie. My sister called you a stowaway, she said. Where're you going?

We're all for New York.

We're for the Ohio states.

Jobs?

I think in service. There's a cousin there to fix it.

What's the place?

Can't pronounce it. You?

Fergus looked away, then back at her. Don't know, don't care. I get through inspection on shore, I'll do anytin. Anytin's better than Gardiner Street.

Where's that?

He looked at her strangely. North Dublin, where'd ya tink?

Have you run away from home then?

I've no home, he said. Dublin's a jax.

She tried to imagine traveling alone, no protection, no money or relatives at the end, a tremble through the back of her skull. But she wanted details; she wanted a story to entertain her. How will you get off the boat not caught?

She saw in his eyes that Fergus had yet to figure that out. Bridgie, he said, me Mam was a Bridgie.

Is she in Dublin then? Did she want you to go?

She died.

Me Da died. What of yours?

Drunk, dead, who knows? Gone. They all fookin die, he said, and turned his head. She wanted to reach out and stroke him or touch his hair but he was dirty and ragged and she thought she'd not. I'm fearful hungry, Bridgie, he said again, I can only get what I steal at night.

We've no food but the dinners. He showed his disappointment and she considered the problem. My sisters're not aitin now, they're sick. Maybe I could get their dinners, so.

Don't tell 'em, they'll turn me in.

Delia didn't think they would, but with Caty it was possible.

They need water, though, she said. We can't get enough.

Ya'd think it was the wine of Jaisus, the way they keep it. But let it to me. I'll do for youse, and we'll trade, like at the horse fair. He spat in his hand the way he'd seen the horse traders do at Smithfield on Sundays, and they shook. She wiped her palm on her skirt, and he laughed.

So that evening, as the wind began to die and the ship became steadier, Delia brought a plate of soup and cold potatoes to Fergus in his secret berth, with plenty of bread. He reminded her of a piglet just off the teat, gorging anything on the ground that might be food. She giggled a little at his manners and he smiled back at her, his mouth dripping soup. He would have blessed her, or kissed her, if he knew to do either. And true to his promise, he had two glass bottles of water, rags for stoppers.

How'd you get these?

They've an open barrel of water in second class with a ladle. You have to be there at night, no one's watching. I nicked the bottles afore. He looked straight at her and smiled his little knowing smirk.

What will they do if you're caught?

He took his thumb, greasy from the soup, and drew the dirty nail rapidly across his throat, ear lobe to ear lobe, grinning the while. But they won't catch me, he said.

*

The room filled with the mantra of the rosary, Hail Mary, Hairy Mary, endless like the clicking circle of beads, then the priest left. Someone had set a black rosary on her hands. The silver cross and chain were twisted loosely in her fingers like a lace hankie used once and forgotten. When he arrived on the street Ed had seen the priest's black Chevy parked next to John's coupe and knew it was serious. He came to the side of the bed. Mom, he said, tears in his eyes. She managed to look at him. Mom, again, and took her hand. He tugged at the rosary but she tightened her grip, a talisman against the snakes.

Buachaill, he thought she mouthed, her name for him as a child, meaning Boyo. He put her hand down, still holding it, and she pressed the beads into the sheet.

How is she, Doc?

Joe gestured with his open fingers vaguely, turning his wrist. What he hated most in his job was the refusal to accept the inevitable, families asking for something to be done, ease suffering, another operation, magic medicine, as if there were a cure for fading away. The war taught him how powerless doctors are but this family around a deathbed, none of these people were in the war, what did they know of the persistence of death? How it knocks you on your ass, pushes you into the mud and doesn't let go.

Even if he'd never liked the old woman, Joe was a member of the family. Delia tried to talk her daughter out of marrying him and gave in only as Hitler approached Poland and Mary approached thirty. Thought it was her last chance. He liked the rest of them well enough, ordinary people trying to make something for their families after the war. He also liked this house, it was a comfort for him, the dining room, the narrow porch in front with the hanging swing, open space in the back. You could walk the Huron backyards up to Hugh Brummer's and drink beer, telling lies with pretzels. Hugh liked to joke about the war, stories he'd heard in France about fat Göring and crazy Hess. Hitler has only got one ball, he sang to Colonel Bogey's March, learned from the Brits, Göring has two but they are small. But Joe wouldn't talk about the war.

Ed was in his work dungarees, smelling of copper wire and

electrical burn. A pair of snips protruded from the large front pocket, its snap undone. He'd got the message when he returned to the car barn on Mitchell Avenue after a morning repairing transformers on the Vine-Norwood line. He asked a friend to drive him to the house; he didn't own an automobile as he could ride the trolleys free and had a frugal disposition. His two children were an expense, both great feeders. The girl once ate an entire jar of Hellmann's mayonnaise with a tablespoon, followed the next day by a stick of unsalted butter, and she never got sick.

He took Joe aside and asked if there was any hope. Joe put a hand on his shoulder. He wanted to say Corragio, as he heard the Italians tell the wounded, like in Verdi, but just shook his head.

Ed turned sharply and walked towards the bathroom at the back of the house. He took off his overalls and glasses, washed his face but smeared grease on it from his hands. He filled the basin with hot water and scrubbed again with Ivory soap. It floats, he mumbled. Though Skip was in work clothes too, dirtier than his own, Ed wanted to be dressed up for his mother's passing. Passing where? He wondered if she still believed the party line, last judgement, purgatory, plenary indulgence, Jesus in the bread, everything the fat nuns taught them at Holy Angels School. He guessed he still believed it himself – it would be so much trouble to lose his faith at his age, exhausting just to think about it. He wanted to wear a tie and a brown jacket with leather patches on the elbows like Joe, but the only male clothes in this house of women would be Skip's and Skip was tall and lanky, Ed pudgy and short, so he had to stay in his blue work shirt and the dark cords he wore every day under the dungarees, the back pocket loose. He cleaned up as he could, dried on a faded pink towel, looked at his thinning hair in the mirror. He never thought himself handsome like Skip, but he borrowed a little of Skip's

Old Spice. He sat on the toilet lid and looked at the rust-stained bath tub where he'd soaked so often, where his youth drained.

He remembered the Saturday in 1926 they moved into the house. He was nineteen and already worked for the street railway, where he would stay even after the streetcars became trolley buses and then motor buses. They hired an open horse cart and drove from Cohoon Street, three trips, his father and a friend doing the heavy carrying, the horseman not lifting a finger except to smoke, and Ed inside the house shifting the furniture up the stairs into place, Skip getting in the way, not called Skip yet but little Johnny, his mother and sister Mary fixing the lunches and opening the tall bottles of Hudepohl. His mother had organized the sleeping arrangements, Ed with Skip in the front, Mary with Peggy at the back, Dad and Mom in the bed she's still in. It took most of the day but Dad went to work after, worried over the time he'd been away – he got only Sunday off.

Ed liked the new house from the start, though the street was very quiet compared to Dutchtown with its Irish bars on Madison Road and the shouting and fights in the street at night. Why did they still call it Dutchtown? O'Bryonville is its name and the Germans moved out when the Irish moved in and now the Irish will move out as the Negroes move in. Huron Avenue was like a suburb, he thought, but still near the car line and the cemetery behind the houses across the street, though you couldn't see it from this house because the land was sunken. His father was there and his mother thought she could see the tombstone from the attic window because you could see the very top of the house from his grave. So maybe he'd peer inside her bedroom and get ready her welcome.

Ed had learned electricity as an apprentice, starting at fourteen instead of high school. It was exhilarating, all that force, how you'd die touching the wrong wire, six-hundred volts DC, how it ran the trolleys just by the driver moving his lever, invisible. He'd seen four workmen killed and many injuries. It was part of the job, like the firemen or police, things open to the Irish that they were good at. He saw a boy run over on Fourth Street as he zipped across the tracks, cut in half by the sharp steel wheels, and had heard about a wino decapitated by falling down at an unfortunate moment. But mostly it was a placid job, mending frayed overhead wires, adjusting busbars, monitoring substations, testing amperage. Power in and out just like the water flow Skip worked with. Ed dreamed of capacitance, galvanometers, ohmmeters. Electricity is living, you must respect it or they'll call the priest in. At home he used a glass insulator as a paperweight for his many household bills.

Peggy arrived from work and was talking to Father Mick downstairs. Why was he still hanging around? Peggy was a red-haired flutterer, Ed thought, it was hard to know what she felt about anything, including her aunt Delia. She had lived with them on Cohoon Street, and then here on Huron until Cliff was mustered out last year. Her mother was James's sister but died young in the cholera, so Delia took over and Ed knew better than anyone how difficult his mother could be. Always dissatisfied with something, refusing to accept things as they are in her Irish voice. She still wrote out the city's name as Sinsinsi. He didn't think it was a joke.

His father had been the gentlest man. He put up with her sharp blasts of discontent, gardening and digging all his life for the rich Germans, then dead in '39 at one of the Gamble family houses where he worked. Skip sent to fetch him home when he didn't appear for supper, found him flat on the basement floor there in the big house on Madison Road built out of the profits of soap and candles for the Union Army. Probably supplied the South as well. Cincinnati, right on the border, playing both sides. At least the Gambles were Irish, so she couldn't blame his death on the krauts. She always used Ivory soap because a Gamble invented the formula. Proctor was English and though she hated the English she hated the Cincy Germans more.

He got up from the toilet seat and went back to the bedroom. Dan was still at the door looking worried. Don't be afraid, Danny, Ed said. Are you taking pictures?

No film, Dan said.

Ed gave him a burr, rubbing his head hard with his knuckles on the short haircut. Dan pulled his head away.

*

After the Japs were finished, things happened quickly and Gert wondered if the war had postponed it all. She was getting along better with Delia but when the soldiers returned and took their wives and kids to houses of their own, she was Delia's only target and well within her sights.

Then her father had a heart attack across the river, sitting one night in the unheated front parlour they used only in the summer, horsehair settee, wind-up Victrola, Drinking rum and Coca-Cola, Waiting for the Yankee dol-laar, till it wound out and the old man was still there in the morning because Granna Anna hadn't noticed. The doctor looked at the mahogany table and the upright His Master's Voice, and told them to get the family around. The old man survived but stayed slow and then Delia was sick and now candles and a cross at her bed.

Skip said, Why don't you go down? These people will want to eat. Gert wondered why she would be the one for that but no one else will so she'd get Danny to help make sandwiches. What did they have? Wonder bread and baloney. Olive loaf, sliced.

Mustard. She'd make German potato salad. Or walk to the store on Hewitt. Watermelon for the hot day. She wondered if she had the breath for it.

*

The first house in Ohio, what year was that, Delia wondered, I was so young, nine or ten and alone with Nellie because Caty got a job right away in Over-the-Rhine through our second cousin Carmel who worked next door, washerwoman and light cook, eleven dollars a month and found. They were the best jobs, washerwoman and cook, the best pay and steady, and Caty was very good at it because after Mayo mud and the ship she wanted things clean.

Nellie and me, we went to Dexter Avenue by the German cemetery. Johan Schmidt, which should be John Smith as he'd been two generations there but krauts are stubborn and don't like English names. The wife was Emma, a foreigner like us, and she was good to me as I was a child only and wasn't greedy and shared a room with Nellie and your other one who was the maid Molly Harte of fifteen years from near Sligo with a north accent and her Irish had Donegal words I didn't know. We walked to Mass at Saint Francis de Sales up the street though I thought De Sales was shops or ships.

Nellie was a good cook once she got the notion of kraut food, schnitzel and hasenpfeffer, which is jugged hare, and sliced potatoes warm in a vinegar salad with little mustard seeds and pig's trotters and knuckles that in Mayo we called crúibins and served at the Da's wake in a bucket. And the horrible sauerkraut that the smell made me gag and leave the kitchen even though it was only cabbage. Red cabbage I liked, it was sweet, and when Nellie was tired the Missus would teach me the reading for a bit in evening at the kitchen table so I'd get ahead in Das Livef.

She had funny talk because she was from the North Sea and made mistakes in English and called me Daahliaah but I didn't mind because of the flower. She helped me write a letter to the Mam that Nellie put every other month in her envelope with the remittance to Seán the Mule. On Thursday afternoons I was allowed out to play on the street with children who were mostly Irish working in the houses. Some of them were at school but it cost money. I liked the snow, angels on the ground and two snowmen facing each other in the empty street staring.

Missus and Mister had a big house of yellow brick with a furnace in the basement though the top floor was cold at night where we slept and in the summer it was hot under the roof. Us three girls did the work, clean, polish, wash, iron, shovel coal in the furnace and you'd shake a long steel handle in the floor that dropped the clinkers down the bottom grate to shovel out and carry in an old black scuttle to the bin where the Negro ashmen took them away. Nellie and Missus did the shopping. They'd take the streetcar to Jaeger's Butchers for the best bratwurst and the Findlay Market which is Race Street and sometimes I'd go but mostly I did the beds and the clothes because I was too little to scrub on the floor or carry heavy slops. But I worked hard and Nellie smiled.

We'd see Caty at Mass and sometimes she'd come to our room and we'd laugh to hear of her beau who was Brendan O'Rourke from Athlone, how they would walk out of an evening and once a week he'd buy an ice cream they'd share because of the price. Caty was very pretty, everybody said so, and carried herself like Maeve the queen. Ice cream I'd never had, and when Missus gave me a little bowl the first time I said it was too cold on my teeth and she offered to heat it up on the stove and I said yes please, but she was after joking. Nellie was not so pretty and paid no attention to the lads because of what happened on the ship and she'd always ask Caty if she was careful. Caty said she was though sometimes she still cried to think of it. I cried too though I didn't understand.

Her list might keep the snakes away, like counting sheep for sleep only backwards since sleep was not what she wanted. But she was too exhausted to go on. She understood they were in her mind, the snakes, else these people around her were blind. Mary was gone with her kraut, probably in the kitchen eating sauerkraut. Ed was kneeling, holding her sweaty hand with the rosary. His head was bowed down close to the sheet, as if he were the one who was tired. Éirigh, she tried to say, Get up, but nothing came out but sour breath she could taste in her mouth and left her with less inside. Garpháistí, she said.

Ed raised his head. She could see that his eyes were damp and his shirt smelled of burnt talcum, the perfume of streetcars. She also smelled something under it like church incense, from John's white bottle with the clipper ship like the *Germanic*. Myrrh, she thought, wise men, pagans beyond the knowing. She tried to point at the window and say Fuinneog, but she couldn't move her arm or her throat.

The scent mixed with August heat and reminded her of the day in another August they received the letter from Seán the Mule telling of the Mam's death, just two short pages in his farmer's hand. It took the usual two weeks to arrive and he'd waited days after the wake for it. She was with the Dinkelmanns then on Cleinview Avenue, already fifteen and working alone. Nellie was married to Kieran Connor and having her children fast in Dutchtown and she came about four in the afternoon with the letter in her hand and I knew right away what it was and we cried and then I asked the Missus who was Stella like the Star of the Sea for leave to go in light of the news. She said yes and was sorry and gave us some fruit to take, apples because it was almost the fall, the fall an American word that is the thing itself.

We went to Caty's house on Cinnamon Street near Pogue Avenue because it was bigger, where she lived with Tommy Keane and his mother and though they were married they'd no children. Mrs. Keane was good and made us a wake supper and called in some of the locals who brought whiskey and beer in a bucket from Donovan's saloon, though the whiskey was not Irish as it was Kentucky bourbon because Kentucky is just across the river but I found I could drink a little because it was sweeter and mixed it with lemon pop and got a headache and never again.

Nellie kept Seán's letter and we looked at it years later and laughed. In one paragraph he said Mam died and we buried her with Da on the hill away from the water with the priest and we had the wake all proper, but didn't say why she died or when, only that she'd been raving the last months about Da's bones coming out of the ground. Then he asked Nellie to tell her sisters, though he didn't bother to name us. At the end he said the pig had died as well and he was requiring it for the annual rent and would they send him a bit extra next time before Gale Day, which is what we called rent day, because he was short and needed a new pig for next year too. It wasn't funny then, though, it was heartless, I thought, but what did you expect from Seán the Mule, and now he was alone.

But soon came a letter to tell he wasn't alone because he'd married Síle McKenna from Tourmakeady just after the month's mind for Mam. They'd known each other for years, he said, but Mam didn't take to her so he waited. Heartless. She was not beautiful, he wrote, but young and strong, a great help on the farm, and he hoped for children soon. Nellie didn't keep that letter. She'd get a banker's draft to send him every other month from Barry and Co. on Third Street and we talked about stopping the remittance, now that he'd married a mule and expected little mules to follow.

3

Her eyes were almost closed and Ed wondered if what he'd heard was a word or a sigh. He pushed himself up to see that everyone else had left the room. He must have fallen asleep on his knees. He opened the front window. Is that draughty, Mom? It seemed he'd been there hours already. He sat on a small chair by the window. Between the houses across the street he could see clouds gathering over Calvary Cemetery making the afternoon dark and the air adhesive. It must be at least ninety degrees out, he thought.

There was a black electric fan on the dresser. He plugged it in, noticing the frayed cloth cord. He would have to repair that, not that she'd be needing it. He set it on slow and set the direction toward his chair. The breeze cooled him a little but his shirt stuck to his back and shoulders and he sneezed twice. Skip could sneeze five in a row without trying. Blow your nose, John, Mom would say, but he never had a hankie and she would get him two squares of toilet paper to save the Kleenex. She won't answer the phone, always says she can't hear the ring though it's like a fire alarm in the hall, but she can hear a tap dripping three rooms away. We don't live on Loch Measca, she'd say, I pay for ever drop of water. Though Skip pays now. But she won't let

Gert handle the bills, gas, light, coal, thinks she's stupid because she's German.

How she hated Gert coming into the house. She resented all of us getting married, Ed thought, but especially her last child. She still calls him her little Johnny, even though he's over six feet tall. She depended on him completely when Dad died. Skip found him in the basement of the Gamble's, came winded with the news, and she just sat at the kitchen table, a stone. Skip and Mary made all the arrangements with Finnegan's Funeral Home and De Sales and the cemetery and she went along with everything without argument, the first time ever. One thing she insisted: we couldn't hold a wake, absolutely not. She wouldn't explain why. No wake, was all she said. You wouldn't say she fell apart after that, she was far too strong and stubborn, but something was lost, like she'd forgotten how to breathe and Skip had to remind her.

Just a few months later Skip got Gert pregnant. He'd met her through cousin Peggy. They were all working girls downtown, secretaries at banks and companies, Peggy at Fashion Frocks, and met Fridays at the bar of the Gibson Hotel on Walnut, Peggy and Alma and Celeste, all a bit wild, girls let out on their own with money in their pocketbooks. Ed had nothing against girls working, but there was no one to control these girls, no husbands or brothers and their fathers weren't interested. Skip was there one night with a different girl, he always had a girl on his arm, probably a waitress, said hello to Peggy and got introduced to the club. That's what they called themselves, the club. He joined the table and in the end tried to pay everybody's bill, my brother the big spender, but he didn't have enough cash and was red-faced and they all thought it was funny, and Gert laughed the loudest and he looked at her and she looked at him and there you go. She was from across the river in Kentucky, living at home in an ancient clapboard on Watkins Street in Covington, Luganman the name is, maybe with two n's at the end, the Germans are all over Covington and Newport and Fort Mitchell. She misses two monthlies and Skip does the right thing, only he doesn't tell Mom and gets hitched with a cheap ring over there at Saint John's with German writing above the altar, married by the old kraut Father Goebbels who can barely speak English but shouts the Latin at them as if in warning.

The only place they could live was here on Huron Avenue. It was early 1940, and besides Skip and Mom it was just Peggy in the house. So he brought Gert home with the big announcement and she started raving in her Irish language, nobody could understand the words but the message was clear. Skip held his ground, she's my wife he shouted back, and Gert stayed and six months later little Dan was born in Good Samaritan Hospital on her own birthday. Mom loved Dan but never his mother, Treats Gert like dirt we used to say when we were here on Sundays and they were both out of the room.

Mom didn't like Louise either because she was a Frankel. The family had been farming in Ohio for a century but to her they were kraut dirt diggers and she hated her coming into the family as my wife, and she didn't like Mary getting together with Joe Jaeger, the Jaegers are just sauerkrauts and meat cleavers, she said, even though Joe was a doctor already. As if the Moran girls were any better, washerwomen and domestic slaves, bog-poor shanty Irish with accents so peaty you'd need what she called a loy to cut through the crust. But Gert was the final German straw and Mom wasn't going to forgive her for tricking Skip into marriage, so she thought and said more than once to Gert's face. Treats Gert like dirt.

Like when they brought Dan home from Good Sam. They'd named him Roderick James O'Daniel, Roderick after our Dad's father and James after our Dad. She accepted the James but went raving over Roderick. His name was not Roderick, it was Rody! Rody O'Daniel, she shouted, It was never Roderick, it was Rody, which is Roger in the kind of Gaelic they use in Tipperary, she said. Skip got angry too, said he'd name his son whatever he liked and his own second name was Roderick and she'd given it herself. You're not Roderick, she said, all sarcastic, looking up straight into his face, You're John Roger. Which is on the birth certificate, so Skip had misremembered and had to take it back. She hated Roderick because it was English. There'll be no Rodericks in this house, she said, and crossed her arms over her chest. If he's Roderick you can take him elsewhere and go with him, the both of ye. Including Gert in the ye.

Skip was just as stubborn and wouldn't give in until later that evening when Gert reminded him that he put the name Roderick down only because he thought it would please his mother and honour his father and help smooth things at home. And it didn't, it made it worse, so why stick with it? Skip nodded and Gert talked to the old woman and went the next day to City Hall to fix it. So Monsignor Schengber called him Daniel on Sunday morning when he poured the water on him, which made the boy cry because it was November and cold in the church. He was a pretty baby, with dark curls even then, in the starched white gown she'd bought when I was baptized, Ed thought. But they hadn't considered how the first name worked with the last because it made him Daniel O'Daniel and all the kids called him DanDan.

Ed looked up and saw him at the door. He came in very quietly, Ed thought. Dan seems the right name for the boy, gentle and a little delicate. As Rod maybe he'd be different, more manly. How old are you now, Danny?

Almost eight. Dan had to clear his throat. It sounded like he'd been crying.

Did you make your First Communion?

In May. You were here after.

Delia opened her eyes and moved her lips. Ed shut off the fan.   Do you want water, Mom?

Garpháistí, she said, and raised her index finger in a small circle.   It cost much effort.

He moved closer to the bed. What's that, Mom?

Garpháistí, Dan said.

What?

Grandchildren.

She wants her grandchildren? How do you know?

She talks to me in Irish.

You understand her?

She teaches me words. Little Dan pointed. Leaba, bed. Uisce, water.

Ed was amazed. He knew no Irish himself. Good boy, DanDan, he said, and left the room to use the phone. On the way he reached out to give another burr, but the boy pulled away. He hated burrs almost as much as he hated his name.

*

They had lost time in the storm. It was Monday of the second week and two or three days out of New York, provided the good April weather held. Delia was relieved to be in the bracing air on the deck, though it was crowded with steerage passengers and hard to get real exercise, everyone excited by the approaching arrival. Delia liked to carry the blackthorn and Nellie said she could. She'd swing it and strike the deck with it and make people jump. Nellie usually strolled with her, their faces to the sun. They keep their shawls about them and Nellie had convinced her to try out her shoes – she'd been going barefoot on the wooden decks. A promise of a new story every evening if she'd wear them. She'd exhausted the Irish tales, though Delia didn't mind hearing again about Cú Chulainn, Méadhbh, and the bull, one day in Irish, the next in English. The shoes were painful still but the stories made her endure them. Nellie borrowed Clara's book on America, which had pictures of New York, and read aloud about Washington and Jefferson and especially Andrew Jackson, a grand president whose parents were born in County Antrim, a great thing for the Irish even if they were Prods.

A group of men played cards on deck, sitting in a circle in their jackets, throwing cards down with a flourish and shouting or groaning. A tall young man usually stood above them and took a coin from each pot. Delia saw him again when Mass was organized on deck, said by a priest from Maynooth on his way to the Boston states to help the Irish there to grace. The man stood at the rear of the crowd, not answering the prayers but taking communion anyway with a little smile on his face.

The tables were down once more for meals and Delia found it easy to supply Fergus twice a day. She'd take large helpings and volunteered to clean her sisters' plates. She called his stolen berth the tree house, and pass him all the leftovers on a single plate, wash the others topside, and collect his on the way back. He cleaned it so well she didn't need to wash it further. It was dangerous so they said little. Since she had friends in the galley, she pretended she was on her way there and often did go, stopping just a few seconds to slide the food through his curtain.

Nellie suspected but said nothing, as she had plenty of worry already. Caty grew wild on board, free of home. Her brown hair was almost red, her blue eyes inviting. She liked the attention of men, and boys too. At sea they were nowhere, and the number of lone male travellers increased sexual tension. Strict segregation was enforced in the sleeping arrangements, married couples in one section, single men in another, single women in a third, but everyone met for meals and air, and in fair weather the evenings were filled with singing and dancing topside. When it came to entertainment the Irish dominated over the English and Germans. A fiddle came out, a bodhrán, a penny whistle, and always there was an older man with a naggin of whiskey in his pocket ready to sing, without accompaniment and in mournful Irish, a ballad of valiant days long ago.

Whiskey was currency on board, usually poitín from the backwoods of Monaghan, the kind of drink, her Da said, that would take your throat for a brisk walk before it shouted hello to your stomach. Anyone who'd brought a few bottles of good quality, John Jameson or Power or Paddy, and had the sense to reserve it until halfway through the voyage, was king for the rest. He could trade it with the stewards for better food, a better berth, oranges, even clean clothes, and with the other male passengers he could get whatever he wanted, if they had a thing to give.

Whiskey wouldn't buy a man a girl in bed – not an Irish girl anyway, there were rumours about London girls – but there was flirting in the evenings after the storm, ripe innuendo, and kissing in the corner as the whiskey loosened tongues and resistance. With the anticipation of landfall a deeper liberation came aboard, Ireland, family, the priests all far behind. Some lone travellers realized they could re-invent themselves in New York. The promise of America was the promise of a second birth.

It was a mirage. The Irish rarely cut the bonds of the past. It was their emotional link with the auld sod, the four green fields, the American church staffed by Irish priests and nuns, that marked them off from other settlers. The sentimental songs, Saint Patrick's Day, the Irish-American newspapers, the wearin' o' the green, the stories of the ancient warriors, the hatred of the English oppressor, made the Irish into exiles in the new world. They never lost sight of Ireland, into the third and forth generations, though they saw it in the rear-view mirror: they faced west with a green image over the shoulder. The Italians and the Germans and the Poles, they were happy escaping oppression, abandoning their languages, the Jews were in exile no matter where they were, the Chinese brought China with them. But the Irish were bilocal, dreaming of a return that rarely occurred. And when an Irishman did go back after years in America, it was taken as a sign of failure, and in his old village, the place where he'd been born, he'd be called a Yank.

But that night on the *Germanic* the future was indiscernible. All they had to believe was that life ahead could not be worse than life behind.

*

A shadow crossed the remains of her sight, not the snakes, only Ed departing. She turned her head to the left, the little she could manage, and saw Dan in the doorway with the Brownie. She'd bought it years ago and it still worked. She tried to smile at him, she wanted him to come closer and hold her hand as they often did when they'd talk in the afternoon, propped up on pillows on the bed, glancing out the window towards James's grave, but feared the smile came out as her old lady grimace. She wished her face was more pleasing but she supposed it never was. Dan came to the bed anyway. He took the cloth his Aunt Mary left and wiped her face, brushing the wispy white hair back from her eyes. Where was I, she thought, was I up to the wake for Mam in

Dutchtown? Philly Phil Dempsey got so drunk he pissed himself then tried to clean the mess on his trousers with Wiedemann beer for the fizz and crushed pretzels for the salt.

The Dinkelmann house, it was good for the domestics but hard work, they were happy people the man and wife, he was Karl I think and she was Stella I know, and five children and a mother-in-law. There was just the two of us, myself and little Annie Maher who did the cooking which I was never good at and we shared everything else. I was stronger by then, stronger than her, and I stayed there long and would've stayed longer. Their girl was the oldest and then the four sons who grew fast. Mr. Dinkelmann was a banker or a seller and they were Lutherics which is Prods in Germany but treated us fine and when little Annie took to crying for days over the loss of a brother in Kildare the Missus was gentle and sent her to the priest at De Sales who was not yet Monsignor Schengber the old kraut, and he gave her comfort.

How I loved that church, the smell of the candles and all the colours on the windows in the sun and the high carvings of the altar and the bell the altar boys rang when they entered for the Mass and the choir up high in the back, the sound like a mystery from hills afar. I'd go to confession Saturdays with nothing to say but felt good after with a few Our Fathers and Hail Marys kneeling at the marble altar rail and I'd say the dead prayer for the Mam. Then one Saturday I did have something to say and didn't know how to say it and the confession box with its dark wood spires like spears frightened me. You go in one side and kneel and the priest is in the middle and he slides the shutter open and you smell his Ivory soap mixed with the wood polish in the dark with a grill between. Ninety-nine and forty-four one-hundredth percent pure, Ivory soap. I was sure it was mortal sin but I hadn't really done it so maybe it was a venial sin, but it was hard to tell the priest because he knew me, old Father McNicholas, though he was young then. But he soon got it out of me and was gentle.

It was the Dinkelmann boy had done it, the eldest one named Gus or August who was nineteen or twenty when I was just the fifteen or sixteen. He'd said he did it with all the girls, the domestics he called us, and they liked it and he'd give them presents of little things like candied fruit and a chocolate bar and silver dimes now and then would come in handy for anyone, and little Annie had liked it and wanted more. Which I didn't credit but later she said yes she did and was proud of it because the lad was handsome and rich besides. I wondered if she thought he'd go to marry her, maybe in a fairy tale in a kraut castle but not in a kraut house on Cleinview in Sinsinsi.

The priest said it wasn't a sin if I tried to resist and I did and he knew if I complained to the Missus I'd be fired because that's what happened those days, they blamed the girl always, boys will be boys and the girl led him on. So I avoided the lad and when he'd corner me in the scullery or the linen room I'd resist to satisfy God and Father McNicholas and I made him do it so I'd not be pregnant. I kept it from Nellie so she wouldn't make me quit for then I'd get no reference but the Missus I think had suspicion and soon Gus was sent to the Prod college at Oberlin which is north of here and in the summer went to France so I was free of him except at Christmas when the heat was on him. You're not very pretty, Delia, he'd say in his panting, but I do love your big Irish ass. Which embarrassed me for the word that was in it.

*

Caty loved to dance. She was a good dancer, everybody said so,

and her face glowed with the exertion. She may had a drop taken
even though she said she hadn't. Girls didn't drink at home but
she wasn't home, that was the point. Her arms and legs seemed
rowdy, as if she wasn't in control of them, little Delia could see
that and could feel the pressure in the air, even if she couldn't
name it. She held the blackthorn tight in the crook of her arm.
Caty was doing a slip-jig in the centre of a circle of men, her
skirts raised, an old fiddler named Joe-Joe Walsh playing faster
and faster, challenging her to keep up, the audience clapping in
unison to the beat, until at last she collapsed into the arms of a
young Irishman and they slid to the deck to applause and cheers.
It was the man Delia had noticed before at cards and Mass. She
could see that he'd caught her where his hands shouldn't be.

Is that you, Mickabird, Caty said.

It is, surely, he said, Cork city accent, as he squeezed her
breasts tighter. She escaped his arms and sat with her back
against the gunwale, catching her breath. He was taller even than
her Da, solid and muscled, dark haired with pale blue eyes the
shade of beach glass. In a wool jacket and clean shirt, collar and
tie, he carried himself above his surroundings. Long feminine
eyelashes but handsome, not pretty, and commanding. Young
men sought his company and laughed at his jokes. He seemed
to get the best of the food and had his own supply of poitín. He
won at dice and cards.

Have ya got a cup of water for me?

I do, sweet Cate, he said, it's over there behind the stack wit
me drink, hid from pryin Irish eyes. He stood and pulled her up.
She straightened her skirts, dusty from the deck and salt crusted.
Those clothes never will be clean again, Delia thought, as she
watched them walk aft hand in hand, her sister still catching her
breath and laughing when the Mickabird pulled her close and

whispered in her ear.

Delia didn't know what made her follow, sisterly intuition or the excitement of spying. It was very dark, the lamplight from the dancing hidden by the smokestack which stood like an ancient megalith planted in the green sea, though the sea too was dark now, calm and black as the sky. Delia couldn't hear their words over the strident engines and drew closer. In shadow she could see Caty drinking from a tin cup and Mickabird filling it again, his left hand on her shoulder. Her shawl was on the deck and her blouse open at the top. She finished the water and handed him the cup. As he took it he pulled her to him and kissed her hard on the mouth. She seemed to yield, relaxing her back and neck, turning her head up to his. When he put his hand inside her blouse she whimpered a little, then straightened in a hurry, pulled back from the embrace and turned away.

Come now, won'tcha, Cate, , he said, his voice low, It's just a little kiss, that's all. Sure now, I mean no harm to ya.

Her voice rose in patches over the engines, like isolated phrases of music: A girl's heart . . . the waves.

Yer heart is hard, he said, but not as hard as me cock, as he pulled again at her blouse. Delia let out a small cry and he turned to her. Get away, ya little flea, he said, or I'll do ya after yer sister. He undid his trouser buttons and pulled up her skirts as she fought back. His hands were too busy below to ward off her blows to his chest. Delia ran forward and he pushed her to the deck. Caty struggled another moment before he finished his adjustments and thrust in.

Caty cried out, Get help. Delia rose and ran smack into Fergus, who'd crept up behind the dark tower of the stack, popping up like a puppet on a spring, jackeen-in-the-box. She'd fallen again after crashing into him.

Away from her, ya culchie idjit, Fergus said. He picked up Delia's blackthorn and moved in. He looked ridiculous, a skinny barefoot boy with a stick, but he stood his ground.

Who're ye callin culchie, ya snot-nosed shite? Mick turned, his erect member sticking out.

Yer a culchie gobdaw and yer gettin away from her now.

Mickabird threw back his head and laughed and Fergus saw his chance. He ran forward quickly with the blackthorn like a short lance, and drove it straight into the man's groin. Mick yelped and bent over, his hands on his crotch. Fergus then swung the knob end up into his face, cracking against his jaw. It knocked him back on his rear and Fergus hit him on the head with the knob. Mick was dazed, his penis raw and showing a bit of blood. Caty grabbed Delia, who'd seen more of a man than anyone counted on, and ran forward shouting for help.

Yer a dead man, ya Dublin fook, the Corkman said as he stood up slowly, still bent over, Ye'll not get off this boat alive, ye'll be over the side in another second. He reached out for the boy. Fergus ran off but got only a few paces before a large hand grabbed his shoulder and another took his thin arm firmly. Two sailors and an officer had come up behind him.

That fook tried to castrate me, Mickabird shouted.

Why is your business hanging out there, my man, the officer said. I'm not much pleased by attempted rape on my ship. He instructed the sailors to take them both below. He spoke with an upper-class English accent, and the two Irishmen started playing the colonized.

I did nothing, sur, Fergus cried, But save a girl from him.

Good for you, young lad, but you're the stowaway who's been hiding, so you'll ride it out in the brig too. At least you'll get fed before you're sent back. Did you think we'd not find you? There's nowhere to run on a ship.

He's a nathair and a squirmin snake, Mickabird said, he started the fight dirty like.

New York doesn't want any more rapists than it already has. You'll be sent back, too, if I have anything to say about it.

I'm not a rapist, sur, that girl was willin, so. She'd been leadin me on for a week.

We will see, the officer said.

It's God's truth only, there's many of me friends will swear.

Yes, Michael O'Reilly, I'm told your name is, especially those friends who owe you money. But it will be the girl's word that matters. And fornication is against ship's regs anyway, outside of marriage. And even then it may be suspect.

It's Micheál.

What?

Me name. It's said *Mi-haul*. In Irish, cap'n.

If you say so. The Captain, however, does not deal with the likes of you. I'm just the second mate. Do up your trousers, man.

Don't put him with me, sur, Fergus said, he'll kill me sure.

The officer waved his fingers ambiguously. Yes, yes, he said, and took the blackthorn.

*

Dan stayed with his grandmother for a moment alone. She seemed almost content, her eyes quiet. In the last months, when his child's mind began to understand she'd come from another place, somehow he saw that her difference was not alien but congenial. The moist, flaky skin of her hand did not bother him: grannies came with characteristics, a droopy chest or a light grey moustache. If she yelled at him or his mother, that was part of the deal, as Skip put it, the deal they had on Huron Avenue.

He heard them coming up the stairs again. They probably had

beer below or coffee, two drinks he hated. Coffee had the smell of burning, mixed with soap and walnut shells and dishwater, and beer reminded him of the stale urine of the Dutchtown bars Dad took him to on Saturdays. You're too sensitive, Danny, Peggy would say, If the smell bothers you, don't smell it.

Gran moved a little in the bed and groaned. Her face was set between a weak smile and customary discomfort. Dan leaned close to arrange the pillows, which were damp and had her smell. She whispered something like Snakes and closed her eyes.

Then they all came back, uncles and aunts and his Dad, and Peggy whispered that Gert had to go to Covington because her father was sick. Uncle Cliff was driving her so Skip could stay here with his mother. Dan didn't know what to make of it, his German grandfather and his Irish grandmother both sick. Hail Mary, Hairy Mary. He picked up the camera from the bed and went up to the attic to think. It was quiet there and they wouldn't find him.

*

The night was women's business.

Nellie spoke brutally to Caty even when the ship's nurse was present, blaming her sister's lack of concern for her reputation and the family name. The nurse had a cursory look, found no cuts or bruises, and spent little time examining her nether regions. She hated the fetid air of the steerage compartments and left as soon as possible. She offered the use of sickbay for the night but Nellie wanted to hold down rumours.

Then the married women poked and prodded, asked questions the poor girl barely understood. They brought a basin of warm water and carbolic soap to wash out any blood. Or semen, God forbid. Clara, though she was not yet married and supposedly untutored, brought herself into the discussion. She asked Caty the same question again and again, stroking her face with a cool cloth, Did he do it to you, my love? The truth was Caty wasn't sure. She felt violated, that's all she knew. Irish girls did not wear underpants or bloomers, only strapped themselves in cloths for the monthlies, but if he'd entered her it was for a brief moment only before Fergus appeared.

At last they arrived at a consensus: though her gate may have been unlatched it had not been opened. There were no scars and very little blood, and they advised her to mention the attack never, especially in America where a courting man might think her soiled. Caty herself seemed in shock and half asleep, which was a blessing; the fewer details she understood, the better. That was the opinion of the emergency committee on virginal status.

Delia understood even less but the fear that had gripped her from the start of the journey settled into a vague sense of loss. She remembered the doll drowned in Queenstown Harbour. Busy with activity or cuddled with her sisters in the berth she'd barely noticed its absence but now she was inconsolable; she'd not have it ever again, the one thing her Mam had made especially for her. At home she'd hold it tight in bed, give it a kiss before sleep, wake up still clutching it in the crook of her arm. Noreen, she called it, after one of her aunts from Tourmakeady, and when she couldn't sleep she'd sing it a lullaby in a whisper.

In the morning after she cried in Nellie's arms, Noreen, she said, Bheag Noreen, over and over. Nellie said they'd find a new doll, a good American doll with real arms and legs and a proper face with eyes, but Delia didn't want a new doll, she wanted her old life and the fire and the Mam singing again. When she'd cried herself out and washed her face and drank a little cold tea left from breakfast and was walking the deck again with Nellie, her thoughts jumped from the doll to Fergus. We must help him,

Nellie, she said, he saved Caty and he didn't even know her.

Nellie was sympathetic but didn't see what they could do. He's a stowaway, Bridgie, she said, the ship people can't allow that, else more would be bold.

There was a fierceness in her little sister that Nellie hadn't seen before. But he doesn't want to go back to Dublin, Delia said, and we're so close now. We should go to yer man and ask.

What man is that?

The man with the gold on his white cap, who told the sailors to take them away. He has your blackthorn too.

Nellie didn't know how to find the man. She wasn't inclined to go out of her way for a ragged buachaill even if he had helped Caty but she didn't want to bring Delia to tears again. They were within a day of docking and needed to be a proper family for the authorities, dressed well, looking healthy and happy. Ship's officers did not usually appear in the steerage areas, but later that morning Delia saw one of the sailors who'd been with the man with the gold on his cap and he agreed to pass along the request. Not long after the second officer sent word to meet him at the ladder to the second-class decks. A chain blocked the way from below and the officer stood the other side of it, three steps above the two Moran girls. It was a dull day, with light rain blowing over the ship in gusts. Nellie pulled her shawl tight.

We want to thank you for our sister, sir, Nellie said.

Is she well now?

She is. It was good of you to help. The man nodded and looked at the sea. We wonder, sir, if you still have my blackthorn stick. I'd like to keep it, if I can. It's from our brother.

Yes, of course, I'll bring it.

What will happen to the lad, sir, the one who saved Caty?

Fergus, Delia added.

Is that his name? He wouldn't give it me. Not that it matters, he'll be going back when we turn around. In view of his courage I won't prosecute him on return. It's theft, you know, to stow away, and the company cannot tolerate it. People like yourselves pay good money. His kind think they can just take it.

Could you not, sir, Delia asked, Could you not forgive him this once only, for Caty's sake. We'd be forever grateful.

It is not up to me, lassie, it's company policy. He has free passage back to Queenstown. Or he can disembark at Liverpool if he's so keen on emigrating. Is that all?

Thank you, sir, Nellie said. Come on, Bridgie, you've tried.

The officer started to turn away but Delia wasn't giving up. What if someone paid his passage for him?

And who would do that?

Not us, Nellie said, we've no money.

But we do have it, you've got it right there. Delia poked the waistband where the sovereigns were hidden.

We need that, you know we do.

The officer seemed amused by this family drama, and was impressed by Delia's pluck. Well, would you pay or not, he said, I've never seen anyone do it before.

How much would it be, Delia asked.

I can speak to the Purser, if you wish.

Let him do it, so, Nellie, please?

Nellie sighed and nodded.

Meet me here at two o'clock, he said, when the ship's bell strikes four times. Don't be late – I won't tarry. He moved up the ladder.

Caty was still half-conscious, as if she'd slept too long, and greeted Delia's plan with no enthusiasm. Nellie was adamant, set against giving up any of their money. She pointed out that none of them had a firm job in Cincinnati. They owed their cousins in Lawrence eighteen pounds for the passage and outfitting – what they had should be saved or used for that, as it would take years to pay it all back. Delia had no counter except an absolute conviction they were obliged to Fergus. It's what our Da would want, she said, and you know it's right and proper. In the end Caty agreed, won over by Delia's determination, so Nellie was outvoted.

True to his word, the officer met them at the ladder as the ship's bell struck. He passed the blackthorn to Nellie. The Purser was surprised at your offer. Under the circumstance he said he'd let the lad go for child's fare, two and a half guineas.

So much, sir? We have so little.

It's what you paid for your little sister there, isn't it? It's half price, even though he is older.

Nellie, please, said Delia.

It's too much, Bridgie.

But we owe it to Fergus, we do.

The officer was touched. Give me two pounds, Miss Moran, he said, and I will make it right with the Purser. Do not tell anyone, or I will be reported to White Star and could not help the boy.

Please, please, Nellie.

Nellie gave in. In fact she had already given in, because she'd removed the two sovereigns sewn into her waistband and put them in the little leather purse around her neck. She was not happy, and was ashamed to be standing below this Englishman on the ladder, bargaining the price of a boy she didn't know. She handed over the coins, the gold shining in the dull white sun. Here you are, sir, she said, but it's *MORE-in*, not *Mur-ANNE*."

As you wish, he said, but why are you people so particular

67

about pronunciation?

You'll let Fergus go, sure now, sir, Delia asked. You'll let him land in the New York.

Dear ladies, he said, you have my word as a gentleman. He went briskly up the ladder, jingling the coins lightly in his hand.

*

Be merciful, we beseech Thee, O Lord, to the soul of Thy handmaid Bridget: that she may deserve to attain to eternal rest.

*

She was about to shout at the snakes when the room filled and frightened them away. They're gathering like in a movie, she thought. She'd not seen many movies though you could have a matinee for a dime when she was with the Dinkelmanns and one bit for the best seats. But it wasn't possible to stay in that house much longer. Gus got married and moved away but the next brother was hoping to take his place. Russell he was and only sixteen. Did he think it his duty to keep the maids happy? Perhaps the two boys discussed it. It didn't keep me happy and I stopped him easy by saying Does your mother know what you're trying on? Because I talk to her every day about the house. By then I was twenty-three and stronger in myself than him, a skinny lad with a high voice and pimply face who wore a striped blazer for the school and home only Sundays.

They went to the big Lutheric church Over-the-Rhine and had a big dinner with a joint after and we'd get the leftovers which was plenty. Sometimes a capon or guinea hens and a big goose at Christmas and roast potatoes and sprouts and grunkohl which is only green cabbage. When they had that horrible sauerkraut I'd get sick and ask for the day off to lie down so they stopped and I think the Mister had it for lunch at Wielert's Garden where the waiters spoke only German because I could smell it on his breath when he said hello. Annie would make a fruit pie or they'd bring in a thick cake from the kraut bakeries Over-the-Rhine where Wielert's was before it closed during the first big war and the krauts had to hide themselves and some changed their name from the shame but the Dinkelmanns didn't. And they changed the roads too, German Street to English Street and Bremen where the Jaeger Butchers was then was Republic.

Then Annie was gone, just not there a Tuesday and they never told me why until years later I saw her in Dutchtown when she looked lined in the face. She said she'd got married and her husband died in the war but I think she had no husband and was pregnant by the lad Gus and the baby died or she did away with it which happened in those days more than people knew. Behind the shebeen in the alley off the Madison Road where an old gypsy woman did you for a dollar and three quarters and you might live to tell the priest.

4

Standing at the doorway again, Dan could see her on the bed and also in the mirror above the fireplace. And he could see just a bit of himself as well, short pants, holding the Brownie like an idiot at a wake.

Delia could see the mirror too, the light bouncing off it. Before she married she'd often looked at herself in the hallway mirror at the Dinkelmann's. To her the mirror seemed illuminated from within so that the reflection was not a copy but the original. It was her face that was the reflection, without identity. It adjusted itself to fit the mirror's frame, as it adjusted to fit the frame of her life. A life of transfer from There to Here. The names weren't important, it was the transfer that mattered to the mirror each morning as she passed it on the way to hanging out the kraut laundry. Where is the There now, she wondered, knowing already it was lost along the way.

That's what had marked her face, she thought, when she allowed herself to look at the mirror for more than a glance. She had been told she had sharp features with dark eyes that seemed to absorb light rather than reflect it, and a reverse smile, thin lips turning down at the edges no matter what she was feeling. She remembered they had not a single mirror in the house in Mayo.

Her sisters would look at themselves in the little window glass at night, turning their faces to the side and front again, the lamp light behind them. Her mother would shout, Whyre yees lookin out the windy, is someone comin?

Delia, your eyes are marble, people said, black as washed coal. Maybe she was one of those black Irish, the descendants of the Armada that wrecked off the coast long ago and the Spanish soldiers and sailors swam ashore to fertilize the virgins of Munster and Connacht. But her pale skin belied that. She was not from the Viking days either, those red-haired raids around Dublin that left freckles on the native skin like Peggy's. When young, her hair was blacker than her eyes. She thought she had the true Celt in her, the pure Gael's blood, coming from – where was it the Gaels came from or were they always there? She thought still in her mother tongue. She spoke English but disliked its Germanic harshness and precision, so ugly compared to her native metaphors and ambiguities. Irish was the language for deferral, for never saying no to a thing but not saying yes either. Like a boy come courtin, her mother warned in her own parody of English, you walk out wit him but if he'd not got anytin from ye he'd come back still lookin.

She had been too young for courting in Mayo but in Sinsinsi she was dusting and ironing and folding and laying fires and that for the Schmidt family right off at age ten in a big house, not a Big House as in Ireland that belonged to the quality but big still for ordinary folk and those krauts were ordinary. Because if you didn't work you eat naught and who would send the remittance? And when she was stronger, washerwoman and general housework. No brother to protect her, just her older sisters, so she adopted the Mayo ways, what she remembered of them. When she met a young man, it was always after church or a tradesman in the course of her chores in the house or in the road or at the Fifth Street market, she'd cast her eyes down, turn her head slightly away and keep her mouth as neutral as it allowed, half-listening to his blather with the side of her face that made her eyelashes longer.

It was blither and blarney, most of it, though it was pleasing. How're ye, young Delia, or A fine day for the early spring, sweet Delia, I'll carry your basket through the market, and the now-and-then American fellow, born here like the natives but still poor with an Irish father and mother, but his talk would not be the same as hers. Such a fellow was more at home and would be bold and ask straight out where she lived and could he walk out with her next evening. To that she'd raise her eyes to look at him, just for a second, to see what he was in himself, how young or old, and then she'd turn and go on with her work if she had work or walk on if she was shopping for the Missus, and he'd try his only Irish which might be Cad is ainm duit, colleen dubh? or maybe A chailín mo chroí, but that's brash and she'd not answer.

She was no beauty, especially compared to those German girls you'd see near Grandin Avenue or at the Findlay Market, but she knew she wasn't ugly. She had an ambiguous face, like the Irish language, and she was young and strong and her voice held the music of the old land and some men and a few lads thought that enough. Her legs were not thin, no. Back home they'd joke that Mayo women had a dispensation from the Pope to wear their legs upside down. She was a farm girl bred, culchie to the core, her hips wide enough for the purpose God intended, and she'd find a man because there were many about and most wanted to make something of themselves and they couldn't do it without a bit of a house and a woman to keep it and have their children. She'd breed, that's what the Irish did.

Why did we breed so when the krauts didn't? The priests said God wanted more souls but some krauts were Catholics too and the Irish wouldn't listen to the priests if they didn't want the children. Hibernia, land of breeders. So many born, even during the Hunger, then sent away. It didn't make sense, she thought, the births. No wonder the No Nothings and krauts thought the Irish were beasts, all that fucking.

America was still biting its way across Indian land when she came, but how could that matter to her? Being poor was a habit but being full in the stomach a new pleasure and not cold in winter. So when James came calling one Sunday she thought, him as well as another.

He was the son of Rody O'Daniel or ó Dónall from County Tipperary. Rody a famine emigrant who came by sail to New York, worked as and when, went on the road digging ditches by the seasons then drove the mules on the Miami and Erie Canal and when that stopped because of the railroad he was in Sinsinsi and met a Joanna Fitzgerald, origins unknown but culchie for sure. He worked as a labouring man in town when he could and when he couldn't she brought home laundry. He thought he lived like the Earl of Munster until he suffered the apoplexy and got paralyzed and when I met him, Delia thought, he could barely talk and on one side of the mouth only. They were on Pogue Avenue and James lived there with his sisters and laboured like his father till he got the gardening work which he liked because it was outdoors for rich krauts like the Schmidlapps on Grandin Road looking over the river and they wouldn't be standing behind your every backswing like a No Nothing foreman on the canal.

James didn't speak Irish, born in America, except for a few words from his father, and would never learn. So she decided she would live her life where she was and not where she came from, and would forget the old ways and raise what children God gave.

I saved the pay and we was married in ought-six, she remembered, when I was thirty or near it and I put down twenty-five on the paper because there was none to say different. Then I became O'Daniel and I put down Delia and stopped using Bridget because Delia was what I was by then. Even Caty changed to saying Delia but Nellie still called me Bridgie. I left the Dinkelmanns and we moved to a house on Cohoon Street in Dutchtown because James was also thrifty and we could pay the rent. Which was a long narrow red house with a side yard and a tiny garden at back with the privy and we had but the one room though it was large and the use of the kitchen but they had a big coal-fire furnace that warmed you all over.

I'd go to the Dinkelmanns for the day on the streetcar till Edward our son came then Mary the daughter and we got a second room for the children and then John the other son and we moved down the street where we took the whole small house because we had Peggy also. Her mother was James's sister and died of the typhoid and I raised her like my own and she was with us on Huron too until she married her kraut, and beyant because they sent him to the French people in the war but he came back and took her away at last.

And I said no more children, I'll not be like the Irish in that, and showed James how to do it like the boy Dinkelmann but he said the priests didn't agree and kept his distance for a while until later. We bought the house on Huron with money I'd saved from steady work and James paid the bank with his wage. And Nellie too, she got a house and was married and had babies and we were like the others who'd travelled and never went back.

From Ireland you travel once, you don't again, and though Ireland became free and called Éire it was still poor as a rotten potato and they was fighting each other for years.

Seán the Mule wanted the remittance but we were married, Caty too, and stopped sending and the letters that came were few and then they stopped and the wife wrote us she was a widow and could we help a little as he'd sent us here to live in wealth after all. Because Seán died of the TB, is what she wrote, but how did he get it out in the bogs of Mayo, it being a Dublin and Cork city sickness? She was wrong, he hadn't paid the passage and we paid back the cousins who'd sent that money long before except for one who said he didn't need it and that was kind. I wrote the widow, who had been little Síle McKenna from Tourmakeady of my own age, we did not live in wealth and what was lost was lost, and she never wrote back.

You have children and the children have children and that's what you leave, solid flesh, not the memory of the turf fire and a rush light in the dark.

*

O God, we humbly entreat Thee on behalf of the soul of Thy handmaid Bridget, that Thou wouldst not deliver her into the hands of the enemy nor forget her forever, but command her to be taken up by the holy Angels, and to be borne to our home in paradise.

*

The ship arrived in New York harbour at night in spring fog. They passed the stone pedestal in the water for the Statue of Liberty, which would be set there later in that year of 1886, and anchored in the basin until morning. The final two days went so quickly that Delia didn't think again of Fergus until they were in the receiving hall at Castle Garden, a huge open space where luggage was collected, chests inspected, sea chests and human chests, and the travellers divided into sheep and goats, the Last Judgement. The Moran girls caught the anxiety in the hall but they had no reason to worry. They were young, healthy, and energetic, admitted without hesitation to a country ever more anxious for labourers, servants, piston and gears inside the machine of America.

The passengers from the *Germanic* rapidly mixed with those disembarked from other ships. Everyone looked different on land to Delia, whose legs were still rolling from the weeks at sea. She staggered as they sought the Irish Emigration Society and were advised to move on to Cincinnati immediately and not stay in New York even for the night. They had time for a few wonders of the city before departure at four o'clock, after a lunch not scented with salt water.

But Fergus was nowhere to be seen. Nellie guarded the chest while Delia and Caty looked for him in the grand hall and the smaller rooms. They checked the hospital and restaurant and the immigration desks. As they were returning to Nellie, they heard a cry across the room: There ya are, ya lyin bitch. It was Mickabird crossing quickly to Caty. She thought he would hit her, and Delia raised the blackthorn, but there were immigration police about and he restrained himself. His face was red. He was dirty from the brig, needed a shave, and smelled. Ya cost me a small fortune, ya fookin cunt!

Delia was too frightened to say anything. Caty stood in front of her, facing down his anger. What are you doing here, Mick, Caty said. They said you'd be sent back.

It cost me five bloody quid to get free. The price of the ticket over again. People were staring and he lowered his voice. That fookin officer is as bent as the sailors who steal food to sell below.

You bribed him?

He set the price hisself. He wanted guineas, the greedy bugger. A gentleman deals only in guineas, the fooker said, but I jerked him down. He let me out to collect what I was owed from the card game and watched me the whole time. Mick spat on the floor, close to Caty's foot. I was goin to use that money for startin in New York. Now I'm short, cause of you.

The Captain should stop that.

Ya think they tell the Captain what happens below? He's too busy dining with the first-class toffs. The officers have their own game goin.

He was about to say more when Delia conquered her fear and stepped out. Where's Fergus himself?

What'd ya want him for, the Dub slummer. He's sent back for stowin away, now sure. I punched him dead in the face. I hope I broke his nose, the crazy shite.

But we paid the officer –

Mick laughed. Did he get money from youse as well? The shifty bastard. He poked Caty with this finger, pressing her shoulder blade. Serves ya right, ya snipin tease, he said. How much he get off youse?

Caty tightened her shawl. Come, Bridgie, she said, and they turned and walked away, back to Nellie.

Mick shouted after them. You'll soon find out what you've come to with no money in yer pocket. I'm coming after ya, I hope to see youse all die in a ditch, ya fookin bog trotters!

Caty said not to tell Nellie. Don't lie, she said, just say we didn't find him.

Delia was holding her hand tightly and struggling to keep up, thinking of Mick's threat. Will he do that, you think, come after us?

Caty smiled. He doesn't know where we're going.

Delia still looked worried. She was tired from the excitement of the last days and slept all the way to Cincinnati, twenty hours on the train. The time went by like the spring fog, though it wasn't spring on the banks of the Ohio but sticky summer. Even on the warmest days on Loch Measca, in the hottest of summers, the air was cool. Here, when the summer arrived full grown in July that first year, and the temperature was ninety and the humidity above that, she found breathing difficult, sleeping impossible, and work in kitchen or scullery exhausting beyond anything she'd experienced on the farm. Her native moderation gave way to this place of extremity, thunderstorms and tornadoes, electrical storms that burnt the air and filled the head with static.

Cousin Imelda met them at the station with a dray cart and took them within an hour to Caty's job in a big house on Upland Place. Caty hugged her sisters and cried and they went on to the Schmidts on Dexter Avenue. The open dray, pulled by a grey mare of uncertain age, wove through the confused traffic of handcarts and hackneys, horse-drawn trolleys and pedestrians and pigs. Cincinnati was known as Porkopolis and pigs were driven through the streets on the way to slaughter houses and packing houses and river barges. They ran muddy through the footpaths, butting against a person's legs, sometimes run over by a brewer's dray, pedestrians and drovers shouting at each other.

Delia was too young to have imagined a city of so many people. And the boats and barges on the river, docking at the Public Landing, loading and unloading the brick warehouses on Front Street, commerce of coal and grain, salt pork and beer. Once established with the Schmidts with Nellie, though, the sense of awe settled into relief. They had made the journey, they were safe, she was ready. Even later, when she'd adjusted to the heat and snow, when she could find her way by horse car as far as the Fifth Street Market on Tuesdays, she kept under the breastbone a breathlessness over the steep freedom of it, the exhilaration of promise.

In the next few years she grew taller, stronger, more aware of her surroundings and class, but still she hardly knew what desire was or could mean. She had so much she'd not had before, good food, soft bed, friends, no farm slog. She had her dreams fulfilled before she knew they were dreams. She was no longer judged by critical eyes – her Mam, Séan the Mule, the priest, the village biddies ready to tattle and condemn. The work with the Schmidts was hard, its own type of drudgery, her pay was low, her room shared and cramped, plenty of people were ready to find fault. NINA was written on shop windows: No Irish Need Apply. But none of that stopped her future. If that was to be shattered by years of disappointment, it remained engraved in her mind, a moment of expectant peace.

*

She held Dan's hand and whispered. Ed asked what she'd said but Dan didn't know. Then Mary came to the bed, herself filled with memories of houses. But no matter which house, it was dominated by her mother's peasant sensibility, as Doc Joe called it, the certitude that disaster would overtake them at any moment if she ever let go her hold on the life of the place. Mary wouldn't put it as abstractly as Joe, my husband the doctor philosopher, she thought, aware of how his own losses pushed him to reflection, she making the best of what he had left which wasn't a lot what with the whiskey and the few fees. And her mother lying there, still looking like she resented something, her life, her children, the idea of being, who knows. The priests had nothing to say about that, they just assumed what is and what was, that's all God-given, but that didn't explain it and if she were going to get philosophical she would want to know how that state, of simply being here, her mother in that bed, she kneeling beside it, not on some star or not at all, Gert's candles and cross, the breeze through the open window to Huron Avenue, how could all that come about, in all the random effects and possibilities of the universe, and meet in this place?

Death comes with philosophy attached, Mary thought, in its wake or before it, but saw no answers or even precise questions, only the light fading, of the day and her mother's eyes, though that was corny to say but there it was, you could see it go bit by bit. And when she died – Joe said she was going to die today or tomorrow – there would be the tedium of the body taken down the stairs on a stretcher and the dreary funeral home with the mortician with the oily face and choosing the expensive casket and the newspaper notice and little holy cards with her name and a picture of the Sacred Heart or something soppy like the Christ child pointing to his breast with *Jesus Mary Joseph* on the printing, indulgence seven years each time, and the laying out and the whispers of the mourners and the removal and the Mass at De Sales in black vestments and the cemetery and coming back to this house for coffee and cookies, the American style of wake.

Dies irae, dies illa,

Solvet sæclum in favilla,

Teste David cum Sybilla.

And her leg, would they bury her amputated leg with her? Mary wondered if the ghost of her leg stayed attached for these last days in her bed. Ghost blood on the sheets. She saw all that horror movie in advance and that was something to resent, she thought, how those ritual things became details for the survivors to cope with rather than . . . she wasn't sure what she'd rather. Except skipped over, just eliminated, and she left kneeling alone at the grave, her father's and mother's grave, in the warm rain with a black umbrella and a bunch of marigolds or pansies on the mound of bare earth, something without a smell that wouldn't last but a day or a night in this steamy weather, and she could then let go of the old lady at last, her sorrow her relief from the clutch of the hand on her shoulder and the lie of what we say and the regret at what's unsaid and the disappointment instilled early that would never go away.

Was her mother ever happy? Mary knew that she'd dismiss the question, as if Mayo people didn't think it important. Mary remembered Thanksgiving a few years ago, it must have been 1944 because Joe wasn't home, but the rest of the family was at table, eleven or twelve in the house, and the youngest was Danny who'd just turned four. She asked him to say grace and he began, Hairy Mary, full of grace. Everybody laughed and he turned red but Delia was serious sitting next to him and whispered a prompt and she looked down the table and nobody dared laugh again. And there was the food, because we pooled our ration books and got everything, no turkey but a big chicken from the cellar she'd killed herself with the hatchet and roasted with marge and herbs from the Victory Garden and bread stuffing, and she smiled and even drank a glass of sherry wine.

We don't know how old she is, Mary realized, to put down on the death certificate. She was used to filling those out, acting as Joe's secretary, amazing how many people die every day and she never thought about one of those deaths as anything but a clerical chore and now her mother, to be here then not here, and a little piece of paper, a half-sheet form, to say there once was a woman named Delia Moran O'Daniel. Or Bridget. She didn't know which name to put down either.

*

In sixty years what struck with Delia was travel. People her age said how horses to cars changed the world, but to Delia travel was a delight from the start, no matter how. On the second day of the new world she took the horsecar down Gilbert Avenue with the maid Molly, learning the route to the markets and downtown shops, rolling along in the tracks in the road with a dappled mare pulling the streetcar. Soon she was able to do errands for the Missus on her own and loved the independence. For a country girl it was a revelation, the city's stories lying in wait on each journey, the people mounting and dismounting the cars, each one a character, dressed up or down, shaved or bearded, veiled hat or shawl. Even after Findlay Market became routine, or the German baker on Race Street or Jaeger's butcher shop, she continued to revel in the solid brick houses of Over-the-Rhine, the massiveness of Music Hall for the German singfest, the Lutheric church, and the great open space and market stalls of Fountain Square with its funny statues spewing water all the day and night from their hands.

When the horse cars on Gilbert were replaced by cable cars she was frightened. It was unnatural, she thought, like a ship without sails, even though she knew the *Germanic* had steam engines as well as sails. Before she would mount one Missus had to explain how they worked, with a cable running in a groove between the tracks all the way from a central station, always turning so the driver could grip it with a thing to pull the car along. How the cable moved Missus couldn't say. Then came the electric cars, two overhead wires, so fast she felt the wind on her face and smelled the spent electricity in the air. That would be Ed's job and she felt she owned it.

And the inclines to Price Hill and Mount Adams and other hills too steep for street cars. They say Sinsinsi is built on seven hills like Rome, she thought, but you can just look around and see more than seven. At Mount Auburn they drove the streetcar right on to the incline platform and set it back in tracks at the top to go off again, and you never once stepped down. The cars looked like they were ascending by magic, sticking out from the hillside as if floating up on rising water or falling. At the summit from Lookout House, a view of the river curving along, the city seemed to be floating on the water in the sun, Kentucky a dream on the other side. The sun shines bright on my old Kentucky home, she'd hear Gert sing later, and you could ride across the Suspension Bridge still for a nickel. Weep no more, my ladies.

She wouldn't weep, that's sure, and she knew she had little reason even when James died on the Gambles' basement floor, for he was a good man and didn't run with whores or drink like your regular Irish, a beer now and then at O'Leary's bar after Sunday Mass, just a shebeen on Woodburn Road so she wouldn't go in herself though he said they didn't sell whiskey and some would tell the old stories she loved. Weeping was for the weak ones, she thought, and she'd not be one of them and when life turned sour in her sixties she'd hold up her face to the sky and the God who might be in it and vow she would stick it out.

James stopped by Labour Day of aught six. She came to the front porch to, he looking refined in his best suit and a flat cloth cap of grey and blue Donegal tweed. When he removed it his hair shone dark and shiny from brushing, undisturbed in the windless weather. His eyes, pale blue like the sky, looked away from her when he spoke, and that was not encouraging. How are you this day, Delia, he said.

I am well, James, thank you. Are you well in yourself?

I am, I am.

Then the pause. A domestic could not bring a gentleman caller to her room and Missus did not like her sitting on the porch, especially on a fine day when the neighbours were about. Walking was what was left to them, and they strolled to the bottom of Cleinview where a bit of the river could be seen beyond the big house at the end. He kicked a stone with his brown boot, scarred but highly polished, dusty from the footpath though he'd only walked the mile from Dutchtown. He cleared his throat twice and she looked at him from the side, a handsome man, more handsome than she had a right to expect, normally secure in himself but uncomfortable standing there, feeling the scrutiny of the world on his face. Did you want to say something, James, she asked.

He got it out in a rush. He said he wanted to marry but couldn't afford accommodation for them and have children too and didn't see how he could manage it in the next few years and he could not ask her to wait forever. She was near thirty and near weeping; time slipped in one direction only. Instead of tears she took a breath and proposed they ride the streetcars, so they stepped to Madison Road and caught a car downtown with the holiday crowd. She had taken the blackthorn for luck and James carried it. They walked along Third Street and stopped for coffee and a bun at Heister's, though she had tea which she found too weak, two sugars, and they talked about what they wanted and what they could get. They were Irish servants, she a culchie with a strong back and no schooling and he but a labouring man. They rode another car to the Eighth Avenue incline and went up to Price Hill for a grand view of the sunset, the river always moving west only, onwards to the Mississippi and New Orleans where, James said, the Irish built the town out of a swamp wetter than the bogs of Mayo and heavy with a fog of mosquitoes as well.

They were quiet on the streetcar to the incline, listening to the clatter of steel on the rails, turning a song of its own in loud language, the brake's screech like a peacock's cry. They dismounted at the top but he had no more money for a table at the Price Hill House so she spread on the bit of grass the little blanket she'd brought in her market basket and watched the light drop off the Kentucky hills. She decided to make a stand, her heart speaking at last.

James, she said, for us it's now for we'd not be younger the next year and for having babies a woman grows old quick, so.

She told him of her savings and how they could use that to find their own room in Dutchtown and hope for a house if the babies came in any number. He was surprised at what she'd saved and asked how and she said, For I was always the frugal one.

Father O'Meara married them that November in Holy Angels. They had a photograph taken at the Young and Carl studio in full dress with borrowed gloves and their witnesses, and she would always claim they'd started a life because of a day on the streetcars.

She especially loved to ride with Ed, who knew every driver by name. They were always polite to her and even though she should have put the fare in the box, as his mother they waved her by and that made her proud. If pressed she would admit that all her children had done well, Johnny could fix toilets and lay pipe, Mary had her kraut doctor, but Ed – Ed could ride all the Sinsinsi streetcars for free.

She thought of the day on Cohoon Street when her nephew

from Churchfield arrived without notice and had to be taken in. Liam Moran, he was, Seán the Mule's second son, running away from certain death because he'd offended somebody in the new Irish government with his drunken talk. It took a while to get the story from him, and she never believed it entirely, but she'd have no drunks in the house, even if he did sleep on the floor, and after a few weeks or so out he went to find his way in Dutchtown on his own. I won't open the door to him again, she said, but he came more than once to Huron Avenue anyway and James was soft-hearted and let him in and they sang songs of the old country.

Caty died first in '34 of the apoplexy, then Nellie in the '37 flood of pneumonia, then James in '39, and I held the house up in the war with the coming and going, this Delia could say. It was the house that kept us, all the houses, they stay when we go and hold the memory for us but are silent. She knew also that this house on Huron Avenue was her legacy and memorial. Not the little stone on the grave across the street but these walls.

One day her hands seemed detached from her. She held them up to look, outstretched palms, fingers crooked, refusing her orders, mutiny on board, shaking at the wrists and the second joints. Whose hands are these? Where was the middle of my life? Because it seemed she'd skipped from a girl to this bed without an in-between. Her right leg hurt, breathing was difficult, panic breathing, noisy gasps. Only Gert was home, not feeling well herself, but she wouldn't rely on Gert. So she sat down on the edge of her tightly made bed, James's side empty for eight years now. She'd be joining him, if you believed in that. She said a Hail Mary on instinct, like taking your hand out of the fire. She saw her knarry white feet sticking out at the bottom of her housecoat like two fish flopping on the shore, blue veins pale with watery blood, bunions and ugly yellow toenails, the right foot swollen. She thought she glimpsed something coming out of the fireplace, though John had put a board there, a green scaly flash on the wall. She was a country girl, a realistic woman, and she knew what was coming. There was no sense arguing with it, it would be like discussing a point of religion with a tiger. She'd seen the tigers in the Sinsinsi zoo and was taken by their beauty, so pitiless and full of rectitude.

An old tune came to her, some sentimental thing from the last century she heard Liam sing. How did it go? She comes to me, something something. He had a good tenor voice, an Irish voice, reedy and soft, even if he was a wastrel.

She comes to me in a voice I remember,

She sings to me a song from before.

It put her in mind of Fergus from the ship, and she wondered what became of him, sent back to start over again. How people disappear from your life. James was not romantic, no. But Fergus, dirty and rough as he was, streets of Dublin scum, he was a hero. Did she love him, in the way of a young girl?

She fades away as a flame becomes ember,

Then she is gone and I see her no more.

Backwards the mind travels, she thought, no matter what we want, and she was on the green hill where her Da was buried under the pile of stones, looking at the loch and the farmhouse below, holding Noreen, her lost ragdoll, and as she stood up from the bed, dizzy so she had to steady herself on the little table, she turned back to the window and like Lot's nameless wife became a pillar of salt.

*

The list was complete and they were all there now, her children and grandchildren and Peggy and wives and husbands and she could go. Everyone but Gert, which she didn't mind, and Cliff back with the news that Gert's father had died. Nobody knew what to do so they stood around looking at her in the bed then looking away, and she was not in a state to explain. Doc Joe appeared beside Mary and looked in the old lady's eyes, briefly flashing his penlight, and pulled back at what he saw, her alertness and anger. She struggled to move and Mary understood she wanted to be raised up. She set the pillows and with Joe gently slid her head on them so the scene was a church painting of the deathbed except there were no angels hovering, only the snakes in the old lady's head.

She had prepared a speech over the days since her return from the hospital and was to give it now, an address to her descendants about the Ireland buried in her heart. It was a fine speech, worthy of her countrymen, filled with ancient stories and Irish words and dealt also with her own history, her hidden history of leaving and arriving, maintaining and preserving, the houses and their people, of the secrets of the passage and her bitter love for them all, and would end with what now could be said, the ship's officer and Mickabird and Fergus the Gaelic hero, Seán the Mule and her lost brother Willie, her Da and the Mam and their bones on the hill and the depth of Loch Measca in moonlight which like the banshee called her name.

*

Her voice opened at last. Séamus, she said, Máire Áine. Micheál. Dónall. She pointed to her grandchildren and spoke softly in her south Mayo accent: Shamus, Moira Oinya, Mihaul, Donnel.

What's she saying, Ed said.

She had sunk back on the pillow and looked at the ceiling. Snakes there. Look away.

She's hallucinating, Joe said.

It's just our Irish names, Dan said. He moved closer to the bed and took her hand. It felt cold and sweaty at once.

May the angels lead you into paradise, and carry you to the holy city of Jerusalem.

She found at the bottom of her breath a final impulse and raised her head. Slán agaibh, she said, Filligí ar Éirinn.

She sank down again, her eyes open and moving like fire. She hadn't taught Dan those words and he didn't understand. He watched her, the moment between living and dying, he saw her leave. How does that happen, he wondered, a person is here and then not here. He wished he'd had film in the camera so he could study the picture later.

*

Doc Joe saw she'd stopped breathing, though her eyes were still wide open with a stare he'd not seen before, in Italy or at home. A liveliness in those eyes, he thought, or maybe it was just the reflection of the light from the window. He sought her heart with his stethoscope to make sure. All the family standing around, waiting for him to say something. Mary crossed herself and a child cried softly. It seemed for a moment that no one in the room was breathing. As for Delia, the ground owned her now and the ground would take her. With his thumb and forefinger Joe closed her eyes and looked back at the scene as if he were not part of it, the objective physician dealing with life and death without emotion. What a crock of shit that is, he thought. He wouldn't do anything so dramatic as cover her face – let them look at her a while.

He turned to her and did the same, but couldn't stop a smile forming at the corners of his mouth as he thought of the Requiem Mass at De Sales in a few days, which was bound to be said by the old kraut Monsignor Schengber. He could already hear it:

Requiem æternam dona ei, Domine. The funeral arrangements made him smile more. He had a deal with the Nurre Brothers mortuary near his office and would have Mary call them now. The old woman on the bed would think it the final insult, to be buried not by the Finnegan boys but by another set of krauts from Over-the-Rhine.

*

Dan was still holding her hand. He had felt her grip tighten, then loosen. He watched his Uncle Joe close her eyes. Skip put his own hand on his son's shoulder. Let her go now, Danny, he said, let her go.

PART TWO

A DOCUMENTARY LIFE

1945–1972

5

Notes for documentaries, film clips of lost time. The first memory I can date: my father sitting at the Philco. The speaker was behind a cloth screen that bubbled with bass notes you could see. I was in the basement, fooling around with an old iron thing, some forgotten machine part, that felt sweaty with rust. Gran was doing the laundry, working the crank on the wringer with grunts and curses in Irish, when Dad called me up. My hands were black from coal dust. Gran told me to wash them so I used the laundry sink with soap, standing on a little step, and didn't dry.

The Philco was a mahogany radio console with an oval top, the knobs and yellow dial recessed and illuminated. A tall Hudepohl bottle sweated on a coaster, the bottle the same rust colour as the iron part in the basement, a Lucky still smouldering in the ashtray next to it. I lay on the bare floor in front of the speaker, chin on my hands. What the words meant wasn't clear, a solemn nothing. Dad leaned forward into the sound, the voice of the president, the new president, he said, with a higher pitched voice than the old one who'd died last month, and I could tell Dad was excited because his own deep voice was thick, like when he was angry.

The war is over in Europe, he said, now we have to finish off the Japs.

I wondered about the We. It didn't include him, though some of my uncles were there, in France or Belgium or maybe even Germany by then. And he was healthy. They said it was because he'd worked a year in a defence plant in Cleveland and maybe didn't tell them when he stopped. He was a plumber but he did something there with planes, or was it bombs? Something in the air anyway. Is there plumbing in the air?

Remember this day, Danny, he said, raising the bottle in a toast to the airwaves, This will be the most important day of your life. I asked why. Because the war has ended, isn't that enough?

But what about the Japs, I asked, and he told me to go outside and celebrate.

Why was he not at work? It was a Tuesday. Maybe they knew the war was ending and everybody got the day off. I hadn't started school yet, what was I, four? Four and a half. I often reflected on this later, Dad and the war, and memory can't fill the blanks.

I went outside, solitary by circumstance and by nature. If I had a BB gun I'd shoot it in the air like Roy Rogers in *The Cowboy and the Senorita*, last Saturday at the Woodburn movies. I asked for a BB gun for Christmas but didn't get it. I knew people threw shredded paper things, weddings at church or at New Year's. We had a little hand bell in the kitchen junk drawer inscribed Ring out the old, Ring in the new, wartime tin, Gibson Hotel it said on the other side, 1943. I still have it, the clapper rusted away.

I rang it then, making a little tinny sound, and pulled up blades of grass from the front lawn and tossed them in the air and shouted Hooray and Yippee. Gone, that boy. I imagine my fingernails still dirty from the coal; I see myself trying to clean them by scraping along the grass. It was a chilly morning for May and dull, that I remember for sure, and there was no one out, no kids or parents, not even Corny Lynch, who often slept on his porch down the street when he came home drunk at three in the morning. His wife locked him out. Tuffy would stand on the sidewalk in the morning and bark at his snoring.

Tommy Hertz hadn't appeared. I knocked on his door but no one answered, so I picked more grass and tossed it up harder, the breeze catching it before it fell to the sidewalk. It would make a good scene, the end of the war, time emptying itself on an ordinary day. I'd want to shoot it from a window in the house, his mother looking down on him, a skinny boy celebrating what he didn't understand. He tosses the grass but it refuses to fly up. The sky is grey. The tone is grey. The camera slowly pulls up and back on an insignificant street named Huron Avenue, though in Cincinnati it usually came out as Urine Av.

*

Memory plays tricks but remains hard work. What do you get for the labour? Not clarity but a kind of fog, a gauze curtain hiding other gauze curtains. You brush one aside only to meet another, and another, layers of vapour. To make these notes for a film of a life I have to let memory steep like the tea Delia made until dark and bitter. What's sure is that the house had two floors, plus a basement and attic, in their original state from the turn of the century. My bedroom was on the second floor, though my billet changed with the troops on station. Cousin Mike was there while his father was away, Doc Joe, an army surgeon in Italy in a brown uniform. We were the same age but Mike was bigger. Once when we were dressed for the snow he shoved me off the basement landing and I fell to the cement floor below, a good ten feet. I cracked my head and was unconscious for a few minutes, and Mom scolded Mike, though she never scolded very loud. But I got up and went outside where Mike rubbed snow in my face for getting him in dutch. But you did it, I said, you pushed me down, as he pushed me down again and forced snow in my mouth, making a kind of cackle in his throat. Then we went sledding on the little slope of Urine Av.

The attic was also unfinished, one long space under the steep slanting roof, a window at front over the street and another at back over the yard. Its door was locked but the key was in a giant seashell somebody brought back from Florida, set outside in the hallway. I went up there most days, even in the cold, pulled the long string on the bare bulb and sat on a steamer chest filled with clothes in mothballs. Other junk was there too, in ancient cardboard boxes covered with dust, their top flaps cross-folded, papers and photos way back to Gran in Ireland. I'd rummage in them all, filled with dust inside and a smell of old paper and the slimy touch of old photographs, like snails had crawled through the years. I had trouble refolding the top flaps of the boxes in that complex way, in and over, in and over, down.

It was quiet in the attic even when the house was full. The boxes promised things secret, unknowable. A tintype of Gran as a child – you could tell it was her from the downturned mouth – with two women, her sisters maybe, who were dead before I was born. Standing on a dock in front of a ship, dressed in an old-fashioned way with shawls and hats and long pleated skirts, holding large carpetbags with wooden handles. Arrived in America. And three old copper coins, verdigris coming off them on my fingers, an old queen's head on one side, Latin on the other. At the bottom of the Irish box, a small yellowed envelope with tiny cross inside, on a chain the size of a baby's ankle. It looked so delicate, so thin, it might crumble. I was afraid to ask Gran about it for fear she'd shout to stay out of her attic. I own this house, you live here because I let you.

But Mom was lovely. Her real name was Gertrude so she was Gert, which sounded harsh, not like her at all. She once won a bathing beauty contest, no, came second, and was beautiful in the photo. She had a lovely smile and was kind. Sometimes she coughed and always had a hankie she kept down in between, she said, tucked just inside the middle of her shirt. While we were finishing off the Japs she took me downtown on the streetcars, only one transfer. I loved the bell on the car and you'd come in the front and go out the back. She let me put the nickel in the fare box. It fell down through chutes like slides in the playground inside the glass so the driver could count it, then he'd press a lever and it dropped out of sight. You had to ask for the transfer, a thin slip of paper he would tear off a pad clamped to the box. It had printing that gave the time and you'd have to use it before an hour but coming back you had to pay another nickel.

Mom wore white gloves and a hat like the other ladies downtown. There weren't many men because of the war, just some bums and a few in the stores with thick glasses or limps, otherwise it was women in flower dresses. We went to Pogue's, and McAlpine's, and Mabley and Carew in the Carew Tower, the tallest building in town with a fancy lobby of marble. All the department stores had counters of candy and roasting nuts which I loved to smell. She bought me salted cashews in a little paper bag but they made me thirsty. She didn't buy much else because money was short, she just wanted to be out of the house for a while, she said. She got a pair of nylons because they had them again but you had to give in a coupon and she asked me not to tell.

We went to the Ace Café for lunch. A long counter with red stools that swivelled. It was a hot day so the big fans were going. We shared a club sandwich because it had three layers of toast and it came cut up into sections with toothpicks stuck in them. Pepsi Cola hits the spot, Twelve full ounces that's a lot. Mom said since the war they didn't put much chicken and bacon in it and more lettuce, but it was my favourite anyway, I think because of the mayonnaise we didn't have at home. I was sleepy on the way back and leaned against her on the seat holding the little bag of nuts and smelled the Mom smell. When we got home she looked tired and said she would lie down for a while before she made dinner. I went to the attic and hid the nuts on the top of an open beam by the window for later, a secret place Mike wouldn't find. I sat on the trunk and closed my eyes and memorized the trip, the downtown stale air and metal and soot, and went over every streetcar and street and store once and then again, and kept it close beside me.

Twice as much, for a nickel too, Pepsi Cola is the drink for you.

Dad was the Irish side. I knew that Gran came from Ireland a long time ago. She still talked like it and taught me words in that language. Everybody called Dad Skip except Gran. She said Johnny, and sometimes Buachaill, which is lad. I asked Dad about the name Skip and he said something about another man called O'Daniel who had a limp, but that didn't make sense to me because Dad didn't have a limp.

Gran didn't talk much about Ireland. I would ask where is it and how old was she. I was older than you, she'd say, But too young and we came and here I am. That's how she talked, sharp and quick, though she was patient with me when we sat in her room and she told stories, what she called the old tales, of Fergus and the Red Branch warriors and bones rattling on the hill. She'd heard them from her father. Who was a great one for the tales, she said, but he drank the poitín by the bucket as if he were at his own wake. I asked how to spell that. It's said *pocheen*, she said, how do I know to spell it?

She looked at the picture of her husband on the dresser, my Irish grandfather. He left me to cut the turf and lay the fire alone, that's how she talked, and then she'd say something like Riamh nuair a fuair sé bás roimh that I thought meant He never died before and laugh at herself.

I watched a thunderstorm one summer afternoon from the narrow attic window, thunder breaking through the roof and flashes against the dark sky. The street filled up with rushing water from curb to curb, too much for the drains so it was coming out the gratings instead of going in. I ran downstairs, took off my shoes and rolled up my pants and joined Tommy Hertz wading through the stream. We were on a tropical island trying to keep a boat afloat when I slipped and fell. What if I went down the sewer, I thought, I'd wind up in the Ohio River and I'd swim to a barge and we'd go on to Louisville and Cairo – I knew it's pronounced Kayro – where the Ohio joins the Mississippi and like Huck Finn float to Memphis and Natchez and Baton Rouge and New Orleans and maybe Mexico. Then I thought of the turds in the sewers that must go into the river and didn't want to go after all.

*

A photograph of my mother, smiling in a Cincinnati Reds' windbreaker with leather sleeves. She's on the back steps, petting Tuffy. Did I take the picture with the Brownie box camera? The print has scalloped edges. I can't remember the moment but I can imagine the scene, a cold fall day, I'm raking the leaves in the backyard, and in a minute she's going to get up, a little breathless, and help me pile them for burning. Nostalgia is a drug: just say No.

*

But say Yes to one glimpse of her life. Mom was German. Since the war people were careful to add, But not *from* Germany. Her father and mother were German, not from Germany, with a German name, Luganman, a funny word, I thought, but Germans liked those kinds of words. Schnauzer was another, the kind of dog Tuffy was. Her parents didn't speak German to each other, though they used some words and lived across the river where there were a lot of Germans even though we had a war with them, which was confusing. Sometimes we went to the German church in Covington where the priest had a war-movie accent and there was a painting of a white-bearded God the Father on the ceiling with the words Gott im Himmel. That grandmother I called Granna Anna. She was stooped over but sang me a German song.

> Ist das nicht ein Schnitzelbank?
> Oh, du schöne.

That *sch* sound again. She made warm potato salad that I loved for the vinegar and onion.

My grandfather had big eyebrows. They lived on Watkins Street in Covington in a narrow clapboard house from the 1870s. That's when he was born as well, so in my memory he was always old. The house was heated by a big-bellied coal stove in the kitchen, and their bedroom was up a steep flight of steps. I slipped on them once and cut my lip and never went up again. The front room was an old-fashioned parlour, reserved for guests, a fireplace but never a fire and no guests. In summer the rough horsehair sofa prickled my back but I liked the room because of a mahogany Victrola, credenza style, Andrews Sisters, Roll Out the Barrel, One Meat Ball. It rose almost as high as me. I could just manage to wind the crank, though not all the way, standing on an upholstered footstool, setting the big needle on the record until Grandpa caught me scratching Glenn Miller's The Nearness of You, vocal by Ray Eberle.

Kids don't think of how grownups make a living, so it was years before I learned how snobbish and lazy Grandpa was. His father had been an immigrant from Oldenburg who managed to raise five children by odd jobs and connections with the German community in Cincinnati. Grandpa, whose name was Johann Luganmann, though he went by John and dropped the final N in the last name, wormed his way onto the water board and the racing commission, first in Ohio, then in Kentucky when he married and moved to Covington. Something happened and he lost standing. He was a tall, irascible man with a large head and hands, a long nose with dark hairs poking out, and frightened the chickens in the coop just by staring at them. He remained out of work because he refused to touch manual labour or commerce, though that didn't stop him from living off Granna's earnings as a grocery clerk down the street.

She was a slave to him. Though she moaned about it along with her other complaints – bad leg, lumbago, and bunions (she said *ba-NI-ions*) – she always did his bidding, some Old World attitude bleeding through the Americanized genes. If the salt was missing from the dinner table, he would tap his forefinger on the wood surface, slowly and maddeningly, about one tap a second, tap, tap, tap, but wouldn't look at her or say a word. Her duty was to scan the setting and correct it, then he'd stop tapping. When he wanted more coffee he'd move his cup slightly off the circular ring of the saucer. If she didn't notice he'd move the cup again, making a faint clack on the china. If that failed, he tapped.

He hated paying for cigars; he thought his wife's employment at the store should entitle him to free smokes, but Granny applied her pitiful discount to food. Occasionally he'd send me with a quarter: Two La Coronas, and a nickel back, he'd say. In my mouth it came out Two wakaweewees and a wikee back, and Grandpa kept the wikee.

We had a tug of war over the backyard hose. It was coiled on a turning reel and I loved to pull it out and wind it up again, like the Victrola. But Grandpa wanted a tidy reel and began to turn the handle while I held on to the end of the hose, an eighty-four-year-old man against a seven-year-old skinny lad. Mom was afraid of him but her older sister Dot shouted at her father to let the boy play. I can still see the fury on Grandpa's mouth and in his watery blue eyes, enormous under bushy black-and-grey brows.

He'd be gone much of the day, wasting time in the old city hall in downtown Covington, or he'd take the trolley car across the suspension bridge to Cincy and walk to the Over-the-Rhine district where he was born and where his German buddies lived, the few still alive. Maybe he was looking for some soft job or a handout, thinking of the days when your slice of graft depended not on ability but where you stood at the feeding trough. Usually all he'd bring back was a slice of pickle loaf or a small piece of what came out as *schwartenmagen* in the Cincy accent, a kind of head cheese, given to him by a friendly butcher at Findlay Market, and present it to Granny as the golden fleece. If he had an extra quarter, some mettwurst or Glier's goetta or the blood sausage he called Johnny in the Bag. When he'd stayed on the Kentucky side and went to Newport, where the whorehouses and gambling dens were, he'd come home with nothing.

*

But he told stories on summer evenings. They would come at night in the backyard of the Sangers' house next door. Most Saturdays Dad would drive us from Cincy to Covington in a black Chevy coupe with a cramped back seat, and we'd stay till Sunday evening. When the weather was warm we'd all have a shared dinner with the Sangers outside. An Ohio Valley feast, jello salad, warm potato salad, tomatoes with sliced raw onion in white vinegar and sugar, pickled pigs' feet, wieners, bratwurst, baked beans, corn on the cob, sandwiches of limburger cheese and onion that made me throw up, pickled watermelon rind, thick German cakes and homemade ice cream. Their yard was mostly dirt but extended far back to a large wooden table with coloured light bulbs stretched above it. Beer from the bottle, Hudepohl, sometimes the kids would sneak a taste. Leonard Sanger, who had a good baritone, sang comic songs, dressed in suspenders and a white shirt.

> Every day by our back door
> People gather by the score.
> We have a concert each afternoon
> Played by a Dutch band all out of tune.

His wife Emma liked to dance with a glass of beer balanced on her head, singing Roll Out the Barrel, never spilling a drop. In winter she'd pump it out on the pianola, the beer glass still in place.

Grandpa disliked Hudepohl; he would drink only Wiedemann's from Newport or Heidelberg from Covington. He was canny about this – by refusing Hudepohl he escaped contribution to the beer money. Instead he'd send me to the saloon on the corner with a chipped enamel bucket and a half-dollar to get Heidelberg on tap. I'd bring it back in an old wooden wagon with one slat missing. It would last him the night, scooping it from the bucket at his feet into a glass with Granny's soup ladle, and if it didn't last he'd claim I'd spilled it walking home.

He was quiet during dinner until the beer got him. With so many people around, cousins, the Sanger children and grandchildren, you wouldn't much notice him sitting solemnly in a collarless white shirt, black trousers with suspenders, an old jacket, worn black brogues highly polished. He waited for the right moment, usually as the women cleared the table.

Where he got the stories is a mystery. He'd follow local politics in the *Enquirer* or the *Covington News* but never read a book or a magazine. They might have been handed down by his parents or perhaps he listened as a boy to folk tales in German brought from the forests and meadows of Oldenburg or Schleswig-Holstein. They might even have been Scandinavian because when his father left the old country, before Germany was unified, Oldenburg was ruled by a Danish grand duke. It's possible he made them up.

Now this is a true story, he would begin, and it happened to me a long time ago when I was little. He would gather all the children apart from the big table, in the half-light, the coloured bulbs dancing in the breeze, making his eyes shine like the lighting bugs. His voice like a priest's.

*

Now this is a true story.

Is it, Grandpa?

None of your backchat. It was long before your fathers were born, or your mothers, a different century, but happened right there across the river. He would lay his big hands in front of him, palms up, a magician showing he'd nothing to hide, then turn them over like a blessing. His voice would take on a new quality, the hardness gone, a storyteller's voice, artless and full of art.

In those days, he said, there were only horses and mules on the streets of Cincinnata, no cars, no trolleys. Y'd be careful crossing the road else y'd step in horseshit.

The kids giggled, he stared them down.

I was on my way to school. I never finished cause I was sent to work in a pickle factory at age twelve. He smelled his hands as if pickle juice still clinged to them. But on this day, he said, I was hurrying so's not to be late cause I liked school. Did you know what they used to call Cincinnata? Porkopolis. Hundreds and hundreds of pigs running around, more than the horses. Farmers would bring them from all over and drive them through the streets to the river boats, going to S'Louie or N'Orleans. Or they'd take them straight to the slaughter houses and turn them into your bacon and ham.

They'd kill them, somebody asked.

Did you have a bratwurst tonight? That's a pig done up small. This day I'm telling about, a pig come right up to me, looking up with its little eyes, and says, I'm lost.

Pigs can't talk, Joey said.

Who's telling the story?

You are, Grandpa.

This pig wasn't very old, not big, about the right size for a boy my age, had pink around its eyes and nose and some dark spots on its short coat. Had no tail – sometimes they cropped them, don't know why.

Was it cute, Dottie Sue asked.

Pigs are ugly, Grandpa said, never liked them. But this one, well, he was interesting, cause he could talk and he could think too. Next thing he says, Can you help me? Like Joey, I say You're not supposed to talk, are you? And he says, No, but I'm lost so's it seemed important. Where're y'going, I ask, and he says, I'm trying to keep from getting killed like the rest of them. I have to get off the street.

How'd you know it was a boy pig, Dottie Sue said.

I looked. Well, I say, I'm going to school. Don't think they kill pigs there. Okay, he says, I'm coming.

Like Mary had a little lamb, Mary Ann said.

I broke me off a switch from a tree and scooted him along, trying to look normal like those pig herds all over town, and when we got to the schoolhouse I didn't know what to do with him. Then I remembered it was show-and-tell day.

We have those at Saint John's, one of the Sangers said. I showed my granddad's shocker thing where you turn the handle and you give shocks to people.

I decided I'd show off this pig and that would explain why he was with me. Talked it over quick-like and he agreed.

What grade were you in, I asked.

Didn't have grades in that school. I was about your age.

I'm second grade.

Let's say I was too. Now the pig caused a ruckus but I whispered to him to sit under my desk in the back and he did, nice and quiet. Our first lesson was arithmetic. I was good at numbers but pig was better and he gave me the answers faster than I could figure. The schoolmarm was old Mrs. Fleishenkopf – we called her Meathead cause that's what it means – and she was half blind with glasses this thick so's didn't notice. Dave Metzger sat next to me, sharing the same desk, and he got the answers along with me, which was cheating.

But you were cheating too.

He was my pig.

What was his name?

John-Boy, I'm getting to that and I don't like so many interruptions. Spelling was next. Turned out the pig was poor at that, couldn't write at all. Why's that, I asked him. Look, he said, no hands. When it was time to show and tell I took him to the front and addressed the class. There was giggling but I explained this was no regular pig cause he could talk. Mrs. Meathead squinted at him – she might have thought it was my little sister. I began a conversation, asked him where he come from, where he's going. You know what happened? Pig refused to utter a word. I whispered to him that he had to say something, else I'd look a fool, reminded him I was helping him escape, but he was stubborn and just stood there like, well, a hog on a log. I asked Dave Metzger to support me, as he'd heard the pig work the arithmetic, but he was afraid he'd be flunked for cheating and refused. He's just a stupid pig, some boy shouted out, just bacon. Johann's Bacon, another boy said. At that the pig snorted – Grandpa made a loud snorting noise, which scared me – and the pig looked hard at the boy who named him and snorted again and looked like he was going to charge the fella. Now a pig can do some damage, even a little one, can drive you right against the wall and push you down and tramp on you, knock you out and eat you, and these boys were close enough to the farm to know that. So this lad, name of Roy Schaff, this Roy looked frightened of a sudden.

Old Meathead woke up and said to take the pig home, I was done for the day, though it weren't yet noon. So I gathered up my satchel and my pig switch and got out of there, everybody laughing at us, shouting Johann's Bacon. I can hear it still, rough cackles, children are nasty, Johann's Bacon, Johann's Bacon. Out on the street I asked the pig, Why'd y'do that to me? Now I'm a laughing stock. Pig says, If I talked they'd put me in the zoo or the circus, and that would be worse than dying. He had a point. They'd just opened the Cincinnata zoo and the circus was around all the time.

I never seen no pig in the zoo, Dottie Sue said.

I say to the pig, Look here, I helped y'out, y'should return the favour. Now what do I do with ya? You can take me home, pig says, put me in your yard, you'll have me to talk to when you're bored. I don't know how pig knew I got bored, it was painful for me when I'd nothing to do, but it didn't matter. We don't have a yard, I say, we live in three rooms on Vine Street above my uncle's butcher shop. Pig says, No butchers!

Now in those days everything was close in Over-the-Rhine, the school, the markets, the church, and lots of older people spoke German. Pig spoke German too, cause when some old fella bumped into him, pig said Vorsicht, Dummkopf! The man turned and looked at me and I thought I was in the privy sure cause it was old Herr Truthahn who knew my Pa, but pig gave a loud grunt and we moved fast around the corner. Well, pig, I say, that's the second time y'caused me trouble this morning and I'm about done with ya. I'm sorry, I apologize, he says. Take me to the edge of the city and I'll find my way to a farm. They might eat ya at a farm, I say, and he answers, Not when the children get to know me.

I'd nothing else to do so we headed north, got him as far as Burnet's Woods and Mount Storm, which is a long walk, and on the way he told me how he came to talk. It seemed that the lady of a farm down here in Kentucky, name of Frau Zuchter, wanted a baby bad but couldn't get one, as sometimes happens.

Like our Aunt Peg, Joey says.

So what happened, pig tells me, is that he was the runt of the litter and she took him and cuddled him in her bed in a blanket and gave him milk from a bottle, pretending he was a human boy and he was suckling at her breast. And she did suckle him, he said, though her milk tasted funny. She talked to him so much, in German and English, that he soon learned how to speak and could sing nursery rhymes and that made her happy. Since she did the farm accounts, he also learned numbers. Now her husband, the farmer, Wilhelm Zuchter by name, this was late winter, early spring, he was away by Lo'ville visiting his mother for a month cause she was near to dying, he come back and shouted bad words at this situation, that it was unnatural, he'd get the priest and the sheriff and the judge, divorce her on the spot, unless she give up that false child.

That was a terrible time for me, pig says, and I was scared awful, thought he'd kill me in bed with a long knife. The woman, she began to cry and blubber about how lonely she was isolated on the farm and how she wanted a baby bad and he couldn't give her one, so much that his heart softened and he let us be. But the next morning when the woman was washing clothes the farmer took me, pig says, and tied my brothers and sisters in a horse cart and sold us all to an Irish pork merchant who drove us by foot along with fifty or sixty others all the way from Erlanger across the bridge to Cincinnata where I escaped and found you this morning.

What happened to your brothers and sisters, I asked. I tried to warn them, pig says, but they wouldn't listen. Well, I say, they couldn't talk like you. Stupid pigs, he says. At that he offered his trotter to shake and thanked me. What's your name, I asked. I would like to think of you as something other than Johann's Bacon. Pig will do, he said, and I saw a tear in his eye as he turned and walked on. That's the last I saw of him. Did he find a farm and live a long life? Did he find children to play with?

Was he run over by a plough in a field or shot by a hunter? Don't know, though I never met another pig that could talk.

*

Len Sanger was giving a reprise:

>Some are thin and some are fat,
>Each one wears a soldier hat,
>Ready they stand, awaiting command
>From the leader of the German band.

The stories always ended the same way. One of the kids would say, Was that really a true story, Grandpa? And he'd say, It was, and it wasn't. In graduate school I learned that was the opening formula for Arabic folk tales, It Was, and It Was Not, like Once Upon a Time. Where did Grandpa learn that? Whatever the explanation, the next day he'd be as grumpy as ever and we'd have another fight over the hose reel or the Victrola.

It wasn't until I started making films, when I had to think about plots, that I wondered how Grandpa had collected his tales. By then most of the people who might know were dead. I asked my cousins but none of them remembered the stories. Dottie Sue said she would surely remember a talking pig. You must have made that one up yourself, she said.

>Schmidt makes such a hit,
>His cornet solo goes so high.
>Schmalz may have his faults,
>His trombone pokes in Heiny's eye.

Aunt Dot lived to be older than Grandpa. After Thanksgiving dinner in the 1980s, a few years before she died, she spoke about her father in a different way. Her working life was spent as the secretary to a psychiatrist at the University of Cincinnati, and though she hadn't gone to college she read a lot and was intelligent in a hard-headed way. She wasn't sympathetic; she still hated her father's harsh manner and stubbornness. She claimed it had ruined her mother's health. But at the distance she tried to understand him.

There had been a scandal back in his father's day. This Arnold Luganmann, who left Oldenburg for Cincinnati in the 1850s, had married twice. The first wife, Alma Rinder, had journeyed with her parents from Hessian farmlands and became the mother of three Luganmann children, including Johann. She almost died giving birth to him and something happened to her mind that caused her to think baby Grandpa was a pig.

We laughed at this but Dot knew it was serious. Alma would be in bed nursing him, she said, and would suddenly shout, Ein Schwein in meinem Bett! Her husband would come running to find little Johann frightened and howling. This happened over a series of weeks and eventually he had to take the boy away from his mother, fearing she might slaughter and smoke him. Soon after Alma disappeared and was never seen again. Some of the neighbours in the tenement apartments suspected Arnold had done away with her, one way or another. Her father, old Herr Rinder, asked the police to investigate, but nothing came of it and after a year Arnold married again, this time to a German-American girl named Gretchen Hammel, who had worked as a laundrymaid in the house. She was younger than Alma and gave him two more children; she was probably already pregnant when they were married. Dot actually remembered her. We always called her Grossmutter, she said, and thought she was our grandmother. Alma, her real grandmother, was never mentioned. I asked how she learned about Alma and she said there had always been rumours. They were confirmed by an old friend of her father's, who told her the story at Grandpa's funeral in 1948. She mentioned it to her mother, who insisted she forget it.

Jake is such a fake,

He plays the piccolo with one hand.

Did Arnold kill Alma or drive her off to wander the muddy roads of Ohio? Or put her in some fledgling madhouse, no questions asked? Maybe Dot inherited Grandpa's skill and was weaving a yarn for me to remember her by. When I came back for her funeral, I did some research in the Hamilton County records, looking at the years around Johann's birth in March 1875. I found Alma Maria Luganmann in the 1870 census, seventeen years old, living with her husband Arnold, age thirty-two, and a male infant, at an address on Bremen Street, Over-the-Rhine. There is no mention of her in the next census of 1880. Gretchen is there, however, as the wife of Arnold, with four children, same address. There is no death record for Alma. I struggled through the surviving local newspapers in German for March, April, and May of 1875 and found nothing.

But Heinz shines like the fifty-seven kinds,

He's the leader of the German band.

A few years later a friend who is a local historian sent me back to the records, this time for 1917, at the time the US entered the First World War. I searched across the river in Covington, where Grandpa was already living on Watkins Street. He was chairman of the water board for Kenton County, riding high on the mule of Kentucky bureaucracy, then suddenly was removed. The *Covington News* carried a story in May that year about a large number of men of German birth or German descent who had been detained as potential subversives. There was a lot of chauvinistic hysteria in the region. Any German speaker was suspect, German teachers were dismissed, roads in Over-the-Rhine were renamed, Bremen Street became Republic Street, and some people anglicized their surnames as well. Maybe

Grandpa was one of those arrested. His career in politics was stymied in any case. After the war he managed to fill in here and there in Covington city offices, but by 1922, when he was still under fifty, he'd been sidelined and became the grouchy old man I knew after the next German war.

Two versions of abandonment. Do they explain a life?

I found something else, a copy of Len Sanger's song. It's called The Leader of the German Band, published in 1905, words by Edward Madden, music by Theodore Morse. Before the First World War, when the Germans who dominated Cincinnati had pride in their heritage, Over-the-Rhine was a centre of cultural life. The streets were filled with the German language. If you go to Findlay Market on Race Street today, you can still see shops and houses with German phrases carved into stone doorways. The district is entirely African American now, and people say it's not safe, but Over-the-Rhine is a glorious monument to an immigrant's way of life. Beautiful brick houses. Cincinnati Music Hall was built over the pauper's cemetery around the time Grandpa was born, designed for the German Saengerfest, a wonderful, naïve building, Venetian gothic, like a castle from a bad horror flick. It's still there, but Grandpa's world was gone long before he died.

6

After we finished off the Japs, we made the attic the headquarters for an army club. I was captain because it was my attic, Tommy was lieutenant, and Charlie Wilson the sergeant who drilled the recruits in the backyard, though there were never more than two recruits, always little ones. We had a couple of soft khaki hats, Overseas Caps the uncles called them, with a peaked crown along the top that you could dent into a rakish shape, and we pinned some patches and stripes to our shirts and a couple of medals out of one the cardboard boxes, American Expeditionary Force and a Purple Heart from Tommy's dead uncle. We stretched a walkie-talkie from the rear window all the way down, two tin cans with a string. Ear to can, then mouth to can, but you had to say Over and Charlie usually forgot so we'd end up shouting orders through the window.

I'd go down once a day to inspect the troops in the backyard. I'd seen General Patton do it in the newsreels, carrying a swagger stick. I carried Gran's old blackthorn, and beat it against my left hand.

We had passwords with a system of codes drawn up on a sheet of paper. Quasimodo for Tuesdays with odd dates, Blisterburn for Saturday mornings, Canman for Sunday afternoons, Ed

Sullivan's Toast of the Town for after school. Tommy had made it up and set it down in neat printing, but the recruits couldn't get the idea and nobody could remember the right word without the sheet, which ruined the point. Still, if somebody knocked on the attic door or came to the backyard the lieutenant or the sergeant would say Halt! Who goes there? Even if it was Aunt Dot, who never played along and just hung up the laundry right in the middle of the parade ground, warning us not to march under the sheets or she'd show us what military discipline was really like. She'd lost her husband in the war, so we obeyed.

The backyard was my job, trying to push the stiff lawn mower which squeaked, picking up Tuffy's poop along the way with a stick, Tuffy following behind and pooping more. The four or five backyards on our side of Urine Av were open to one another, separated by rolling terraces of grass, the land sloping down to our house at the bottom. Dad had fenced the yard for the dog so you couldn't run up and down the terraces anymore. Another backyard met at an angle a little higher up, its house on Graydon Avenue, where the burned man lived. He'd been damaged in a fire somewhere, people said, his face and hands and arms scaly and discoloured, pale red and pale white, scar flesh stretched across his cheek bones, eye sockets tight. Ching Chong, Tommy called him, but you could tell Tommy was afraid of him. He was probably in his twenties, though it was hard to tell from his face, and I didn't dare ask. He often came to the corner of the fence between the properties. He talked without reservation: he was an adult but damaged, friendly and disabled, like a child set off from the world.

What are you doing there? I hadn't seen him at the fence and jumped a little. I had heard his name was Mark or Martin but didn't know if he should call him that or Mister. I was raised to be polite to my elders, but I was confused so didn't name him at all. There were bushes and one tall tree near the corner on the other side, the yard a little wild, and the burned man always appeared without warning, pulling back a branch. Shazam, he was there like Captain Marvel.

I had a hammer and nails and some old boards from the basement, half rotten, and a crate from Red Button Radishes, the vegetable man. I'm making a house for Tuffy, I said. It was a project I woke up with and started right after Shredded Wheat. N-A, B-I, S-C-O, Nabisco is the name to know. Gran was in bed sick. They said she was dying and it bothered me that they said it so calmly. I didn't know what I'd do without our Irish lessons. I drove a nail into two boards set at an angle. I hit it too hard and the wood split.

You haven't got the right lumber for that, he said.

The nail was long and went into the soft ground underneath. I nailed another to form a triangle for the entrance. Then another triangle for the back. Then a longer board at the peak to connect them upright. I started to pull the slats off the crate, light like balsa wood for model airplanes, and tried to nail them on the frame.

You want waterproof sides and a roof, he said, and tar paper. I didn't know what tar paper was but wouldn't say it. I thought your dog slept inside, he said.

This is for when he's outside.

He'll get cut on those nails sticking out. You got to saw them off with a hacksaw.

There was a rusty one hanging with the discarded tools in the basement, dating back to my dead Irish grandfather. All those tools had greasy coal dust on them. Dad had plumbing tools in a metal chest, too heavy for me to lift.

I could see that the nails were too thick so I went through the basement door and found some carpet tacks on the shelves, in a little paper box. There was also a box of old bullets but no gun. I could have used some help but the burned man wouldn't come over the fence. I asked him once and he just shook his head slightly. Don't your parents let you out?

I don't have any parents.

I knew that wasn't possible.

For a breakfast you can't beat, Eat Nabisco shredded wheat.

*

Uncle Cliff was married to Dad's cousin Peggy. He'd been beat up in the war in France and drove a laundry truck. On his rounds one day he found an old crystal radio. He helped me attach an antenna wire and we fastened it to a water pipe for the ground. The cat's whisker was broken but in our basement we found a strand of thin wire to replace it. I loved that crystal set. It didn't need electricity and you listened through an earphone. It can't be detected. I could get the Reds' games, Waite Hoyt giving the play-by-play, The Lone Ranger, Straight Arrow, all in secret.

*

A documentary is a fiction made out of truth. I'd shoot this one in harsh tones, colour stock but muted, a little grainy, handheld camera, short jerky takes, rapid cutting, *cinéma vérité*. It would look like life, I know how to do that, but it would be through the boy's eyes, as if he didn't know he was its subject.

When I was ten years old Saturday outings with my father were to the saloons in his old neighbourhood. We'd drive to the hardware store on Madison Road for some small tool or part, or visit one of Dad's friends who was shut-in; those were the reasons for the trip as far as my mother was concerned. She was often in bed. About eleven o'clock we'd get to the bars. The district was officially O'Bryonville and had been Irish a long time, but people still called it Dutchtown after the earlier batch of immigrants. My Irish grandmother had lived there much of her life, working as a maid for prosperous German families in the big houses on Grandin Road. Dad grew up on Cohoon Street, in a tenement house around the corner from the bars, and I guess he still felt at home there. More than Urine Av in Walnut Hills, even though his parents were in Calvary Cemetery across the street. I used to jump the wall to say hello.

There were three saloons in a staggered row: Paddy's, O'Toole's, and Donovan's. They all seemed the same to me, brass foot railings never polished, bare scuffed floorboards, a row of bottles, a smell of stale beer mixed with piss and disinfectant. Brass spittoons on the floor. Chewing tobacco must have passed out of style because I never saw anyone spit in them; they held a scum of water with disintegrating cigar butts. The faces were familiar no matter which bar we were in.

Dad was tall, handsome in the rugged way that appeals to men, and was always noticed when he entered a room. He still had his hair in those days, thinning but slicked back, dark, parted at the left, and on Sundays wore a brown fedora to church in a confident Bogart manner. He was at ease in company, admired for his stories. He was Skip to everybody and everybody bought him drinks, and he bought more than he received.

He would start with a joke. How's an Irish wake different from an Irish wedding?

I don't know, Skip, how's it different?

One less drunk.

Little Skip, they called me, those Saturday men. I'd say I had a proud Irish name, that it was Daniel, Dónall in the Irish language, named after Daniel O'Connell, the Liberator. And who's he when he's at home, somebody would ask. The main street in Dublin is named after him, I'd say. I knew because my grandmother told me. I had a smart lip and it made the barroom laugh. But they still called me Little Skip.

We were in Paddy's a cold Saturday about noon. The owner was called Art – there never had been a Paddy. He was a burly man from County Mayo who said he knew my people from the old country. He always put a maraschino cherry in my Coke. I'd pour it myself, slowly, watching the bubbles and the dark foam get as close to the rim as possible yet remain safely inside the glass. Sometimes he gave me a second cherry and a bowl of pretzels; for Little Skip, he'd say, in memory of lovely Delia Moran. That was my Gran's name before she married and became O'Daniel, though I didn't see how she could have been lovely. My father had moved off with his beer to trade lies with cronies. Somebody bought him a glass of whisky, always Irish, Jameson by preference.

Did you hear about old Séamus Murphy? He opened the paper and was surprised to see his own death notice, in by mistake. So he rang up his friend Mick.

What'd he say, Skip?

He said, Mick, did you see me death notice this morning? Mick says, I did, Séamus, I did! Where're ya callin' from?

I sat on a bar stool near the door, reading the comic book he'd just bought me, the Classics Illustrated *Odyssey*, fifteen cents, entranced by the pictures of Ulysses tied to the mast of his ship, tormented by the Sirens, while the crew moved below him with rags jammed in their ears. The Sirens were wispy female heads on top of smoky bodies, rising from an island like the wind.

When I looked up it was only half-twelve, as my Gran used to say, and Dad was at the door. Be right back, Danny boy, he said, but he wasn't. I had a second Coke and a second cherry, Ulysses got home, and I'd been given some nickels by an old guy to play the jukebox. I'd gone through Glenn Miller's Tuxedo Junction, Sarah Vaughan's Black Coffee, and two songs by Bing before he was back. Some of the Saturday men sang along with When Irish Eyes Are Smiling. I was thinking of the Sirens, how music could be painful, when he returned with smiling eyes. Ready, Dan, he asked, as if I'd been holding him up.

How was it, Art said. Dad gave him a warning look, but everybody was laughing, so Dad laughed too and bought a round for the house. In the car I asked him why he'd been so long but he shrugged me off. He seemed a little tipsy or a little angry, they were much the same with him, and drove home fast. I looked out the window at the dirty snow stacked along the curb.

My mother was out of bed, though not downstairs. I went up to tell her about the morning, her way of connecting with the world. She was coughing less and quizzed me about Dad, but I knew what betrayal meant and ignored his long absence from Paddy's. I suppose most children find themselves now and then caught between two loyalties, though I wasn't used to it. I showed her the pictures of Ulysses and the Sirens. He's suffering for the crew, Mom said, like Christ suffering for our sins. I hadn't thought of that, but with his arms outstretched Ulysses did look like he was pinned to the cross. We looked at other pictures, a gruesome set of the Cyclops. Nemo, Ulysses tells the Cyclops, My name is Nemo, No Man, before he pokes out that single eye with a sharpened pole. Later, when his brothers ask the blinded giant who did this to you, he answers, No Man did it. I thought that was clever and so did Mom, but she started to cough and I helped her to bed.

Aunt Dot came in. She was Mom's sister, living with us

since her husband had been killed in France, and she acted as Mom's nurse. I was told to go outside until suppertime. There was enough new snow to sled down our hill.

Next Saturday we made a quick visit to Donovan's and went home before I'd finished my Coke. Dad was upstairs fixing a leak in the bathtub. Dot was making me a bologna sandwich in the kitchen when I heard him go out the front door. I looked up. He has some business, she said, spreading mustard on white bread. Mom was asleep, last week's snow had melted, and Tommy across the street wasn't home. I listened to the crystal set, Straight Arrow followed by the Lone Ranger. Dad was late getting back and I heard Mom complaining to Aunt Dot. You know how he is, Gert, she said, you knew before you married him. I put my ear against the door and heard Mom crying.

Christmas came and went. Toys, I imagine, still wartime manufacture, a sweater, a windup tin tractor with a cardboard farmer in the seat. Midnight Mass without Mom. She was at the table for the turkey, but left without eating. I remember that the Christmas tree kept falling over, top-heavy in its stand. In frustration Dad nailed it to the floor.

*

January, back to fifth grade, sloshing home in overshoes with metal clips, ice down my socks, dragging a stick in the wet snow. Cincinnati can be awful in winter. I had a fight with Pat Moyle over Santa Claus. I admitted that only babies believed in the Easter Bunny, but Santa Claus was different. You must be a baby then, Pat said; if he's real, how come my parents are always broke after Christmas? That logic was too much for me so I took a swing at him and we hit the ground wrestling. He rubbed snow in my eyes and I got teary. Baby, he said, when we stood up. That did it; I pushed him to the ground again, leapt on top of him and hit him with a rock. It cut his forehead, which got me in trouble at home and at school. Called before the principal, Sister Dorothea, for defending Santa Claus, fighting for a disappearing world.

Saturdays, back to Paddy's and sometimes Donovan's. I asked why we didn't go to O'Toole's anymore. The owner's a jerk, Dad said, the first time I heard him admit he didn't like someone. What's wrong with him, I asked. To me he seemed the same as the other barkeeps. He don't know shit from Shinola, Dad said. I knew what Shinola was, because I had to polish my shoes with it every Sunday before church, but couldn't figure out how it could be confused with a word I wasn't supposed to say.

A few weeks later he did another disappearing trick from Paddy's. I didn't mind at first, caught between Captain Marvel's latest adventure, ten cents of my own allowance, and an old guy who was retelling the Irish Civil War. This was a relative of Gran's named Liam Moran, who was usually there, looking unkempt and smelling of old sweat in his Donegal tweeds. He referred again and again to Dev and the Big Fella. I deduced they were on opposite sides, and that the Big Fella had been shot, maybe on Dev's orders. A tragic land, a tragic land, he said, but his tale was so convoluted I couldn't follow it. Now I figure those barroom men were all drunk, even at noon, but then it was just Saturday behaviour.

The clock at Paddy's was set fast to sweep out the drunks at the end of the night, but I knew to subtract seventeen minutes. I'd been waiting for Dad for two hours. I excused myself to go to the men's room and went through the stacked beer barrels out the back door without my coat. There was a late January thaw and the sun felt a little warm. I'd been secretly listening to the Shadow at night on the crystal set, though it was against the rules because it gave me nightmares. In my charcoal wool sweater I imagined myself invisible like him. I scurried down the alley, past the back of O'Toole's and the coffee shop and the drugstore, and opened the rear door to Donovan's.

There was a dark, narrow corridor giving off to the toilets and a storeroom before opening to the barroom itself. I crept forward and stood in the shadow while my eyes adjusted. I saw Dad in a corner booth with a redheaded lady. They were sitting on the same side, with glasses of beer in front of them, half-obscured from the rest of the bar. He had his arm around her shoulders and she had her palm pressed flat against his chest. They looked like they were about to dance sitting down. Whatever it meant, I knew it was wrong. I pulled back into the gloom just as Dad laughed at something the lady said and looked toward me. His face froze and he started to get up but I scurried out the door, back to my barstool at Paddy's.

The old Irish guy was still rambling on, to the barkeep or to nobody. Dad was there in five minutes, tapped me on the shoulder and jerked his head toward the front door. When he was silent I knew he was angry. He drove home slowly, his fists hard on the steering wheel, veins standing out on his hands and neck. He didn't look at all handsome; even his hair seemed thinner. He lit a Lucky Strike, took a long drag, blew the smoke out. Finally he said, What were you doing, spying on me?

I wanted to see where you were, I said. You were gone a long time.

What did you see?

Nothing.

Are you sure? His voice was thick.

I saw you in a booth.

Did you see anything else? I said no. I could tell he didn't believe me, but he didn't press it. Spying on people, he said, that's cowardly. Men don't do that, spy on other men. We turned the corner to our street. Tommy was playing with a couple of boys, hide-and-seek or kick-the-can, and I desperately wanted to be with them. Dad parked in front of our house. The engine was off but his hands were still tight on the wheel and he was looking straight ahead out the windshield, down to the corner of Bonaparte Avenue. Even worse is telling tales on people, he said. Do you understand?

I was scared. He had never hit me but I knew he could flare up suddenly. I'd seen him turn on my mother more than once. I swallowed and said I did, I did understand. Good, he said, with a little smile. He didn't look at me.

Cleaning my brown brogues the next morning, I got polish on my hands and realized it wasn't so easy to tell Shinola from shit.

*

At the nine o'clock Sunday Mass the school children sat in the front with their classes, parents in the back. I was between Tommy and Pat and the service moped on, endless. Meeting Dad on the steps after, I said I'd walk home with Tommy. No, you won't, he said, You'll come in the car. Tommy backed off quickly – his father used to smack him, sometimes with a fist to the side of the head, so he knew the warning signs. Dad didn't hit me; instead we repeated the tense drive home. You were fooling around with your friends all through Mass, he said. Punching and whispering. That's disrespectful, that's a mortal sin, worse than if you weren't there at all. I felt like saying something smart, like you ought to know about mortal sins, but I wasn't suicidal. You're back to the noon Mass to make up for it. And you better pay attention.

Mom was sympathetic but said we have to follow his rules. I'd go with you if I could, she said. She couldn't get to Mass any more but Father Mick came once a week to give her communion, which she called a great comfort. I took my time getting home after the noon Mass, stopped to look at the posters at the Woodburn Avenue movie theatre, all love stories, rang Pat Moyle's doorbell, no answer. Dad quizzed me at dinner about the sermon, just to check I'd paid attention. It was about lust, I said, one of the seven deadly sins. I barely understood what lust was, but he said nothing more.

I wasn't invited to go along the next few Saturdays. Dad gave some excuse, but it was clear I'd become a burden or a danger. He stayed out later each time. The house was tense and Mom often had tears in her eyes. She looked pale but resigned to whatever was happening to her. Doc Joe made three or four visits and shook his head each time. It's way beyond me, Skip, he said, and sent her back to the hospital.

I didn't know how serious it was – I suppose they were protecting me, or assumed a small boy wouldn't understand. She'd had TB for two years, and spent much of the time in Dunham Hospital, which was the Cincinnati sanatorium. This was before streptomycin was available and they treated her by collapsing half of the infected lung. To do this the surgeons had to remove seven ribs in a series of three cruel operations. It worked and she was sent home, but she was weakened by the surgeries, found it difficult to walk or stand, and eventually the infection returned.

We'd all been exposed. Dad burned her mattress in the backyard in the snow while I watched from the clubhouse attic window. He poured gasoline on it and tossed a match. Whomp. He jumped back. At first the flames rose high, then the stuffing smouldered a long time, black smoke in front of the window. For months after you could see a rectangle of charred grass.

I wasn't allowed to visit her in the hospital out of fear of contagion but Dad went to Dunham every Sunday for an hour and I'd send a card or a letter with him. I wrote a story about a boy whose mother is lost in the forest, held by a witch with a magic spell, until he's brave enough to walk through the dark trees to rescue her. He defeats the witch with a glowing rod, uranium rays coming off it like in Captain Marvel. I added some childish sketches of the forest with wolves and a bear and Mom inside a circle of flames. Dad said it made her cry and told me not to send any more of that nonsense.

His Saturday routine continued, despite my mother's illness. I went along one more time to Paddy's, comic book in hand.

Dad was in form. Pat was dying, he said, and called his friend Fintan to his bed.

What'd he say, Skip?

Pat said, Fintan, I don't mind goin' but be-jaisus I'm going to miss the whisky. Do ya think, on the anniversary of me death, you'd come out to the cemetery and pour a bottle of Jameson over me grave? Fintan considers a minute and says, Do ya mind if it goes through me kidneys first?

We took a break and I drove with Dad to Dayton to visit a friend of his who was in the Soldiers' Home. Looking through the attic boxes years later, I found a postcard of the place addressed to Mom at Dunham, two-cent stamp: Hi Darling, Having a nice time in Dayton. Ate our supper on these grounds very nice. Saw Mr. O', poor devil is in bad shape. Well Baby we are starting for home now. Bye, Love, Skip. And one from me: Dear Mom, I enjoyed our trip. I hope you can get up soon, Dan.

The next time Dad asked me to go to Dutchtown I claimed

I had to write my letter to Mom. Late that evening, after I'd gone to bed, I heard Dot talking to him in the kitchen in a quiet voice. I stood at the top of the stairs, out of sight, and could hear only bursts of phrases but it was enough to gather that she was scolding him. He was angry. I heard a chair scrape harshly on the linoleum and scurried back to bed.

*

Maybe it was listening to the Shadow again. Maybe it was Straight Arrow – he was a Comanche raised as a white man who returned to his true identity when needed to right wrongs. Maybe I'd just got a taste for spying. I rode my bike to Dutchtown in the March wind, pulled my black watch cap low on my forehead, and searched until I found our Chevy, parked on Cohoon Street in front of the house Dad grew up in. I hid my bike in the bushes a block farther on. It was a black Schwinn Cruiser, scratched up; he would recognize it right away. I thought I might stake out the car, then try to follow him, but the wind was so cold I walked to Madison Road instead.

I'd learned not to use the rear doors. I kept low in front of the buildings, hoping nobody would recognize me. I wasn't sure what I could do, a ten-year-old with a runny nose. You couldn't see into the saloons because the front windows had been painted on the inside. If I went in any of them I'd be recognized right away. Here's Little Skip, they'd shout, and I couldn't think of a credible explanation. I could wait outside until someone left and ask if Big Skip was there. I could hide in a doorway until Dad came out and follow him. These were unappealing. As I was tossing the options around, I saw him through the glass of the brightly lit coffee shop next to O'Toole's. He was sitting at the counter, talking to a waitress in a white apron. I stood back but had a good view over his shoulder and recognized her as the redhead from Donovan's.

He was holding her hand, leaning in, explaining something. She was looking down, a small hankie in her other hand. Now and then she dabbed at the edges of her eyes, the way women do. Then she withdrew her hand and turned away, took out a compact and repaired her face. Dad stayed on the stool a moment, finished his coffee, and got up quickly. He said something more but she didn't turn. I scarpered away as he made for the door, back to my bike in the bushes, and pedalled home furiously, out of breath.

I was allowed to visit Dunham two months after Mom was sent there. Because the risk of infection was especially high for children, I was on the other side of a large glass window set in the wall, like a police interrogation room. She was propped up in an isolation bed, pale, with flushed cheeks. A nurse stood behind her. Mom waved to me and smiled, mouthed some words. I could see there were tears in her eyes. I was terrified and frozen in place. I doubt if I even smiled. She blew a kiss, then her hand dropped like an iron pipe and she lay back on the pillow. As the nurse wheeled her away she tried to turn her head for a last look, but the angle prevented it.

The next Saturday I found Dad in the attic, rummaging through old boxes. I'd never seen him there before and I felt like he was violating my clubhouse. I stood on the stairs, only my head showing. He didn't notice me spying. He found what he was looking for, a small picture in a frame, and stared at it a long time. I stamped on the steps and pretended I was just coming up. He was surprised to see me, then asked if I'd help him put the boxes back on the shelf. He set down the picture, which was of Mom in a bathing suit, looking young and beautiful on the shore of a small lake. He didn't go to Dutchtown that day.

*

The funeral was across the river in Covington, where she was born and where her mother still lived. The viewing was at Middendorf's Funeral Parlour, filled with relatives and friends with names like Dahlhoff and Funke and Dinkelmann, people I knew from family visits. Everybody from Dad's squad was there as well, Irish on one side, Germans on the other. Dad and I knelt at the coffin together before the crowd arrived. They'd wound black rosary beads around her hands. She looked the same to me, pale and thin, except for the red lipstick. I said to Dad that she never wore red lipstick, but I don't think he heard me. He kissed her forehead. I wouldn't.

The next hour was misery. Everyone wanted to say a few words to me, the same words, we'll miss her, you must be a man now, and I wanted to escape. The air was heavy with the perfume of aunts. I stood there in my new dark suit, sweating in the June humidity and the overkill of flowers, white flowers for death, desperately wanting it all to stop, for time to go back to where it was before. Just when I couldn't take another minute, she was there, the redhead. I hadn't seen her enter, but there she was, wearing high heels and a red dress. I think it was red, but that could be memory playing tricks. She looked out of place and staggered a little when she entered, as if she weren't used to the heels. Dad was standing next to his mother-in-law; the funeral parlour went quiet.

She looked at the coffin, her red lips slightly parted; she seemed confused, as if she were surprised to find a dead body in it. Then she turned to Dad. Well, Skip, she said softly, Well, Skip, well, Skip.

Aunt Dot said, You've no business here.

Fuck you, the redhead said. I'd never heard that word spoken by anyone except bad boys showing off. It sounded like a silenced bullet. Someone moved in front of the coffin, protecting the corpse from the intruder. Well, Skip, she said again, Well, Skip. Her record was stuck.

Uncle Doc Joe started toward her but Dad put up his hand. Gail, I told you – he said, and got no further.

Well, Skip, she said again. He was frozen in place, his hand still outstretched, like the picture of Lot's wife in the bible. The woman turned to me, breaking the spell. I see Little Skip there, and there's Big Skip here. She pointed at us in turn. Little Skip knows all about us, don't you, little spy. What's your real name, Little Skip?

I guess she was drunk because she slurred her words: Little Skip came out Little Shit. Maybe she meant it that way. In the room it felt like death had conquered.

Go on, little shpy, tell us your proud Irish name.

With all my heart I wanted to say, My name is Nemo, I am no man. But I was too frightened to speak.

Joe took her arm and moved her along gently. On the way out she said, Well, Skip?

I don't remember the rest. I suppose we drove home and I cried myself to sleep. If so, I doubt anyone noticed. I was a little thing inside the big thing, and the Requiem Mass and burial were still to get through the next day. I didn't go because I woke up sick, vomiting, coughing, fever of 104. Dot stayed home, cooling me with a wet cloth. Doc Joe came around noon and sent me to the hospital, afraid I might have contracted TB. Siren, chest x-ray, middle of the night, completely lost, Dad holding my hand, saying soothing words. When I recovered two days later, he was still there and his beard was dark. He hugged me and his whiskers scratched my cheek. Whatever I'd had, it wasn't TB, though there was a mark on my lung where I'd been infected. It's there still.

He took me home and we reached an accord of sorts. There was little to do that summer. It was hot and humid, a number of days over a hundred, but all the public swimming pools were closed because of polio. I continued to blame him for Mom's death, thinking it was the business with the redhead that caused it. Children have a great sense of fairness about themselves but don't apply it to parents. At least I didn't, even though he probably never saw her again. Gail, I mean.

I hate that name.

He kept the blackthorn in the umbrella stand by the front door. No shenanigans from you, he used to say, Or I'll crack it on your head the way my mother did to me. I think he was joking.

Aunt Dot moved out and Granna Anna came to look after me until I left Cincinnati for college. Dad helped financially but never seemed to understand what I was doing – I had to explain it each time I returned. Once he asked me to write Anthropologist on a slip of paper so he could remember the word; on my next visit it was stuck on the fridge with a magnet in the shape of a chili pepper.

So, Danny, he said, What did the anthropologist say to Saint Peter when he got to heaven?

I don't know, Skip, what'd he say?

He said, Can I make a few notes on the culture here? I still have an article to write.

It seemed he knew more about my work than I thought.

Before I started making documentaries in South America I wrote a book on marriage rites in the central Andes; I did the field research by spying on tribal practices in Ecuador and Peru. I gave Dad a copy and he kept it on display on the living room mantel. I doubt he got further than the title and the dedication, In

Memory of My Mother, Gertrude Luganman. Was he hurt that I used her birth name and didn't include him? There was a time when I hoped he was.

Remember, I didn't know shit from Shinola.

7

Short subjects, scraps of celluloid:

After Mom died, Aunt Dot took me to a matinee once a year. She made it an event, downtown on the streetcar, lunch, ice cream, Milk Duds. She liked musicals. *Song of the South*, Uncle Remus by Disney, Zip-a-Dee-Doo-Dah. *Fantasia*, Mickey Mouse, the Sorcerer's Apprentice. *Easter Parade*, You'll find that you're / in the rotogravure. But it was the Lyric Theatre that impressed me, a vaudeville house converted to a cinema. Red velvet, plush cushions, a thousand seats. I wanted to be part of it. I had no idea how that could be; the world it represented was not my world. Of course it wasn't anybody's world, it was a screen world, a make-believe world, where darkness gave meaning to directed light. I suppose I half understood that was its appeal. Then one year the Lyric closed and we went to the Paramount for *Singing in the Rain*. I was bored by the movie and the décor of the building made it worse.

Most Friday evenings I'd walk with a couple of friends to the local theatre on Woodburn Avenue, which showed second-runs in double features. They printed a little flier for the next week's program, a single sheet folded, with poster images and short descriptions. We wanted westerns and war movies. I remember

Criss Cross, a film noir with Burt Lancaster and sexy Yvonne De Carlo. *It blasts the screen with fury! When a double crosser crosses a double crosser, it's a criss cross!* I couldn't follow the plot. Bobby Behrens, who used to drink ink in school when he was thirsty, and at home loved to down a shot glass of vinegar, hated love scenes. Whenever there was kissing he'd get on his knees on the floor between the aisles and eat all the dropped popcorn.

I saw Marylyn Monroe there for the first time. Can't remember the film – it might have been *Niagara*. Her skirt rose up slowly. Gimme some of that, Bobby said, and didn't go down for popcorn. He'd changed. I heard later he'd become a priest.

*

The Friars Club was founded by the Franciscans in the nineteenth century in Over-the-Rhine as an after-school activity for children of poor German immigrants. Later it moved to West McMillan Street in Clifton and we'd go there because it had a big indoor swimming pool. The pool was boys only and by tradition everybody went naked. Nobody seemed to think that was strange. It was like jumping into a swimming hole in the woods.

One Saturday I was drying off in the locker room with Tommy and Pat when a slightly older boy named Alan came through complaining that he'd lost his watch. An attendant was with him, a man in his forties, probably a volunteer. He was dressed but Alan wasn't, looking around in the lockers and on the floor. Alan had a huge boner; it looked gigantic, standing up at a forty-five degree angle, rigid as a water spout on Fountain Square. We all stared at it in amazement. He seemed completely unconcerned, and the attendant, plainly embarrassed, tried not to notice. It was the kind of erection that boys dream of having.

Somebody called out, Hey, Al, what you got there?

Al glanced down at himself and said, Oh, that. My mother says it just proves you're strong. He smiled; he was completely unfazed by what he was carrying.

What you going to do with that, Al, another boy said., Put it in your locker for later? We laughed then, breaking the tension, but most of us followed Al with our eyes as he moved off in search of his watch. I looked down at myself, and got dressed quickly.

*

The burned man's name turned out to be Marcus and he didn't like to be called Mark. He did like to play Scrabble and we became friends over that. He still wouldn't come out of his house and yard, so that winter he invited me in. He lived with an old aunt who supposedly took care of him, though in fact he took care of her. She had many ailments and was often in bed. They had the groceries delivered from the store on Hewitt Avenue; Marcus made their meals and often took hers up to her room. She was fond of Campbell's cream of tomato soup. Sometimes I stayed for lunch, crumbling saltines into the bowl as Marcus did, using one hand. Mmm Mmm good, that's what Campbell soups are. He was excellent at Scrabble, fast and accurate. I never successfully challenged a word, though he used long ones I didn't know, fifty points. I had almost failed spelling in third grade and didn't get much better. Perhaps I'm a little dyslexic, though nobody knew about that then. My letter tiles remained locked in themselves, refusing to form words longer than four letters. I can't do acrostics or anagrams and don't see the point of crosswords.

It had always been hard to look at his damaged face: *face*, he showed me, is an easy *café*. Over the fence that separated our backyards, half hidden in the branches, it was possible to pretend to look at him, but at the kitchen table was difficult (*lucid tiff*, he once spelled out). I usually studied my tiles rather than his café, but I remember it clearly. His eyebrows were gone, his skin pasty white and mottled red like the tomato soup with cracker crumbs. His mouth and chin were desperately scarred, his left hand was missing the little finger, the skin stretched tight over the back, his right in a white cotton glove like the ones my mother wore downtown. He always dressed in a long-sleeved shirt, buttoned at the cuffs and neck. What damage (*mad age*) it hid was left to my imagination.

But he was a gentle soul. He spent most of the day reading. He had an early hi-fi set with an automatic record changer going continuously, making comments about the recordings, my introduction to classical music. He was especially fond of early nineteenth century opera, Donizetti, Bellini, the young Verdi – he said Verdi went wrong after *Ernani*. I know what you're thinking, the music, the Maria Callas records, but he never touched me. He was too self-conscious of his appearance; he just wanted a friend. Gradually, over Sunday afternoons, he told me his story. It came out in pieces and I don't remember every detail. It went something like this.

Eight years before, when he was eighteen, he was in his last year at Walnut Hills High, a rigorous college prep school. He was considered handsome and was popular with girls. He lived with his parents nearby, somewhere off Gilbert Avenue. One day in April a letter came from Harvard accepting him on an academic scholarship. His father had just been discharged from the army – Marcus always called him the Sergeant – and was overjoyed to see his son advance in life. His mother, a small and feisty woman from Akron, was less so; he was her only child, her comfort while her husband was in Britain and France in the war, and she wanted to keep the boy near. What's wrong with UC, she asked, referring to the University of Cincinnati, not California. There was an argument, which turned into harsh accusations on both sides. Money was short, the Sergeant was still battle-weary and hadn't found a job, the house needed repairs. For his part, the Sergeant reproached his wife with infidelity, a common worry of soldiers abroad, of course, but Marcus hinted it might have been true.

He pleaded with his parents to stop fighting but they were in high dudgeon and he was ignored. He shut himself in his room upstairs. The argument got more and more heated: two unhappy people trading abuse that he could hear through his door, insults he can never forget. For the fight to get so heated so quickly, things must have been simmering for some time. Suddenly all went quiet. He thought he heard the Sergeant stomping down the basement steps, another pause, then a gunshot, the loudest sound he'd ever heard, he said. He rushed downstairs to see his mother on the kitchen floor, while his father stood with a Luger P08, a war souvenir, pointed at his own temple. Sorry, son, the Sergeant said, I hope you enjoy Harvard. Now get out of the house. He pulled the trigger and fell to the floor.

Marcus bent down to his mother, who was still breathing, despite the hole in her face. He rushed to the telephone in the entrance hall, then noticed smoke coming up through the bare floorboards. He opened the basement door and flames rushed into the kitchen. His father had apparently set a fire on the wooden steps with gasoline. Marcus picked up his mother – she weighed less than a hundred pounds – and carried her to the backyard. He then went back for his father and started to pull him free, but was overcome by the smoke and fumes and collapsed. Firemen arrived within minutes, called by a neighbour, broke down the front door, and pulled Marcus to safety. But he had been burned over eighty percent of his body. The house was destroyed, his father consumed in the flames, his mother dead on the grass.

Marcus recovered, if that's the word, and his spinster aunt took him in. He couldn't stand to be stared at, to be pitied as a freak, so he didn't go out. This is my life, he said, what you see. He felt responsible for the tragedy. The causes went deeper, he knew that, into the war and the character of his mother, but he was what he called the Proximate Cause, a phrase I never forgot – I remember it as *Primate Ox Sauce*. The secret parts of him, the parts only The Shadow knows, wouldn't let go of the horror. Guilt is superglue on your fingers.

I no longer felt sorry for myself. I still replayed the sight of Mom through the glass wall at Dunham Hospital when I stood frozen, unable to wave back as she was wheeled away to her death. I detested myself for not caring enough, not loving enough. But Marcus showed me something else. I'd been told all my childhood that God has a plan, secret and unknowable, but what God takes a kid's mother away? *Span the Ship*, Marcus spelled in Scrabble tiles, and left me to figure it out.

*

Ted Kluszewski was on deck, biceps on display. His huge arms and shoulders were hampered by the sleeves of the Reds' uniform shirts, so he cut them off. The front office objected but Klu said change his uniform or change his swing. Dad and I were with one of his fellow plumbers, Flick somebody, who came from Tennessee and sounded like it. Gus Bell struck out and Flick said, It's up to the Klu, which was blazingly obvious since it was the end of the ninth with two outs, but the way he dragged out *Kluuewe*, trailing off at the end, halfway between a cheer and a plea, made it sound optimistic. The Reds were six three behind the Dodgers, still in Brooklyn then. It wasn't looking good for the home team, but Johnny Temple had beat out a throw to first, Roy McMillan had walked, Klu stepped to the plate, and Dad gave my arm an excited bump: Here we go.

The game of baseball was designed for the movies.

I was only halfway at the ballpark. I'd eaten one of the hotdogs they sold at Crosley Field; Dad said I'd get sick and I did, two innings after I ate it, right on schedule with the last time, bright yellow mustard and dull green relish on my shoes. I was a slow learner. But my mind was elsewhere mostly because he'd sprung a surprise that morning. It was my mother's birthday – she'd been dead for two years – and we crossed the river to Covington to visit the cemetery. Standing there, windy day in late April, Mr. Mighthave came jumping up from the grave wearing the suit and tie of Mr. Never. I was thinking about the length of eternity, how it goes on and on, which is a head banger even without the nun talk at school, when out of nowhere Dad said we were moving to California. He said it so gently he might have been talking to Mom. I asked him to repeat it, and he did, the same words, my soft-spoken fate.

When, I said.

After school lets out.

This was the second-to-last thing I expected, right after Marilyn Monroe taking off her bra for me. He'd never mentioned it before. To me California was a concept, not a state. You mean it, just you and me?

Yep, you and me.

I don't want to go. It came out whiney and embarrassed me.

You'll like it. Beaches.

My friends are here.

You'll make new ones.

What about Granna Anna?

She'll stay in the house.

But she's old.

Your aunt Dot is moving back in. He had it all planned and I was a little kid without a vote. I was already twelve and a half and thought I deserved better.

Why didn't you tell me before, I said, still whiney.

You weren't ready.

It went back to last summer, when he had a visit from an old friend who now lived in southern California. Her name was Gloria Otten, though Dad knew her as one of the Price family from Dutchtown. He'd gone to school with her older brother and used to spend time at their house. She was a tomboy and joined in their war games; Dad said she liked to play the Indians and whoop. She came east to visit her relatives every other year and would stop by our house. When my mother was in the sanatorium she visited her as well, since they liked each other and could laugh at Dad together. Gloria saw how unhappy Dad was after Mom died, which didn't take much sight. Why don't you move, she said. California is booming, a man with skills could get a steady job in housing construction, and with Gert gone you have no reason to stay. Her husband was a bigwig doctor and they'd just moved into a house they designed, plenty of room, a view of the sea. Come on out, Skip, stay with us, look things over, that was her message in our living room. She was tall and graceful; it was hard to picture her around Dad, who drank beer and had workman's hands. I liked to feel the comfort of his calluses, though we didn't shake very often. She had a deep voice and had lost her Cincinnati accent. We have horses, she said.

Dad never did a thing by halves so chose to make a complete break. What about Tuffy, I said, still standing by the grave. Granna Anna didn't like dogs.

He'll come along.

But he gets sick in the car. Dad admitted that was true, so Tuffy flew.

We gave a ride to Walt Schmidt and his wife as far as St. Louis. He was a vague relative of my mother's and I got relegated to the back seat with Martha, who talked about communists. Washington was rife with reds – for a while I thought she meant the Cincy ball club. Even J. Edgar was suspect, mostly because he wasn't married. The day before we left I said goodbye to Janet, my sort-of girlfriend. She had noticeable breasts and I thought she was pretty, though she also had bug eyes which tended to distract you. We met in the schoolyard in the shadow of the big Saint Francis de Sales church. She looked distant already. I joined her on a bench, gazing across the yard to Purcell High School, where I'd expected to go in another year. As farewell I tried a real kiss but she moved her head and it wound up on her chin, a little slobber attached. She got up and said, Don't be disgusting, Danny.

I watched her walk down Hackberry Street. In the car Martha mentioned Alger Hiss and, my mind still on Janet, I heard Alger Kiss, which confused me about communists for some time.

*

Don Newcombe caught Klu looking. Steee-rike One, the umpire said. Klu stared straight ahead, unfazed, ready for the next pitch. Geez and Christmas crackers, Flick said. We didn't go to the ballpark very often. I found that without Waite Hoyt calling the plays on my crystal set I had to supply my own reactions, and I was so mixed up I didn't know what to think or feel. Most fans were on their feet.

*

After we dropped off the Schmidts in St. Louis, I remembered that the Cardinals were based there, the westernmost club in the majors. I was leaving baseball behind, as well as Janet. We took a northern route because people said it was cooler, and Dad was afraid the old Chevy would break down in the desert. It was blazing hot anyway, the middle of the country empty of interest, and cars didn't have a/c in those days. We stopped at motels without swimming pools and ate at roadhouses where there was a beer sign in the window. Skip and Dan's road movie. I sent Janet a postcard of the Garden of the Gods in Colorado Springs. Dad wouldn't detour to see the sights; I got the card at a gas station.

I'd never been outside the Cincy region and now I was standing in June snow at the Continental Divide, breathing thin air at the summit of some pass through the Rockies. But we weren't on vacation, we were travelling. We met the coast at Monterrey, stopped on a bluff, novices staring at the sea. Nothing beyond the water but the curve of the earth. I knew there were places out there, Pearl Harbor and Tokyo Bay, names from the war. I wasn't going to them. This would be my life now, this blue edge.

Santa Barbara was a sleepy little town where gas stations looked like haciendas, kept that way by wealthy conservatives who ran the place. Dr. Otten greeted us in front of a house painted barn red with white trim, set by itself on an impressive rise. A discreet sign read Welcome to Esperanza. Call me Bill, he said. We haven't met, Skip, but I've heard a lot, etcetera. Hey, young man, he said to me, are you Little Skip? I thought it was blazingly obvious who I was, since we'd arrived in the same car, which now looked old and out of place.

He likes to be called Danny, Dad said.

Then Danny it is.

Gloria was right, there was a view of the sea. She was in the big kitchen baking a devil's food cake. Did she know it was my favourite? She offered coffee, Dad asked for beer, I was given a Pepsi in a glass with ice and told the children were out riding. Children? I looked at Dad. He hadn't said anything about children.

How old are they now, Gloria, he said.

Little Bill is eight, she said. Big Bill corrected her. Nine, then, she said, looking at him. Cathy is thirteen. Billy was born here, Cathy was three when we moved.

Two, actually, Bill said.

Two and three-quarters, she said.

Bill's voice sounded familiar, but I couldn't place why. We were standing by a brick fireplace in the kitchen. I'd brought in Straight Arrow's latest adventure; I was too old for him but I kept up out of sentiment. Is that a comic book, Danny, Bill said.

Straight Arrow, I said.

I don't allow comic books in this house. I think they destroy the reading habits of the young and provoke violent thoughts. They're Un-American, etcetera.

Straight Arrow's an Indian who does good for America.

Nevertheless.

Dad said we'd get the luggage. Seems like he's got a straight arrow up his ass, he said as he opened the trunk. We were taking out the two bags we needed when we heard the horses returning. The corral was below the driveway on sloping ground, obscured from the house. The girl was in front, light brown hair, riding a horse that looked too big for her. The boy followed on a smaller one. They dismounted and unhitched the saddles. She looked up for a moment and smiled. I hid the comic book in the trunk.

For dinner we were served something they called tamales, made by the maid. She'd appeared while I was alone at the kitchen table, an exotic looking woman in a flared skirt. I was writing in my travel notebook, keeping track of where we'd been. She spoke Spanish to me as she put a big dish in the oven. In broken English she said she was Maria. I said I was Danny, and when she left she said, Adios, Danielito. I liked that – it sounded like a name from Straight Arrow. I'd never had the combination of tastes before, Mexican spices and sauce and wrappings. Little Billy told me at length not to eat the corn husks and gave me a lecture on Mexican food, enchiladas, tacos, refritos, jalapeño peppers, his father looking on in admiration, until Gloria told him to can it. Dad pushed his tamales around and ate the cornbread, which they called something else. There was a big salad, and then the devil's food cake. It wasn't as good as my mother's.

Cathy took me to see the horses. It was getting dark and chilly. The sea air brought in fog at night, she said, which seemed strange to me, used to sitting out late in the summer in the backyard at home. Do you ride, she asked.

Only my bike, but it's in Cincinnati.

Mother took us to Cincinnati once, to show us her old house and meet the cousins. It seemed all right, but I'm glad we moved. Then we went to Tennessee to visit my father's people.

That was why Big Bill's voice sounded familiar – he had the same accent as Flick.

*

Flick said, That's bad. Klu had taken a huge swing at a fast ball and missed completely. Dad said, He'd have knocked that out of

143

the park if he'd connected. Steee-rike two, went the ump. I felt sick and thought I'd throw up again.

*

Cathy was still talking. Gramps is a Baptist preacher down there in Tennessee. He's got some strict ideas. She looked pretty standing there, brushing the big horse, a bit of light left in the sky over the ocean and a bare bulb lit in the stall. She was a few months older but had just finished the seventh grade like me. Tomorrow I'll show you how to ride, she said, if you want. How long are you staying with us?

Until Dad finds us a place, I guess. He says we're not going back.

Does he have a job?

Not yet.

What happened to your mother?

She had TB.

Hold this, she said, and handed me the wire brush. She gave the horse a carrot and patted him gently on the neck. Then I noticed that he had a boner of giant proportions, longer than my arm. I'd never seen a horse's erection before and it embarrassed me, but Cathy took it in stride. Now, now, Rusty, settle down, she said. He's after the mare. She pointed to the other horse, then closed the stall and put out the light.

What about the other one, I said, don't you brush it?

She's my brother's. She's a good animal, but he's a brat.

I followed her to the house. She had an unusual way of walking up the hill, swaying like a girl but with long strides like a boy. I had my own room with its own bathroom and decided to take a shower before bed. At home we had only an old tub with claw feet that probably had been there when Gran moved in. I stood in the tiled stall under a stream of water and got a little boner myself. One of the horses whinnied.

Over the next two weeks Cathy and I became friends. We found we both liked to read adventure novels, and she had a shelf of stories about old California that appealed to me. She showed me how to ride, first on the smaller horse, who was called Belle, then on Rusty. Cathy stayed with me on the bridle trails, which wandered into the hills and down to the sea. We went swimming, and she taught me to body surf. The salt water stung my eyes. We brought lunch in the saddlebags and stayed out until dinnertime. Little Billy was upset because we'd commandeered Belle but his father was working most of the time, saving lives, getting home late, and his mother said that guests come first.

Cathy was tanned deep brown. She looked small and young in her bathing suit, though I must have looked even younger, skinny and pale. I tripped over my own feet and on Rusty I always felt uneasy. I could swim but not nearly as well as she could. There was a small cave carved out of the soft sandstone at the base of the cliff at the beach, and we'd retreat in it and imagine staying there, cooking over a fire, sleeping on the sand with a horse blanket. I didn't think of her as a girl. I mean I wasn't attracted to her like Janet, but now and then the image of Rusty's boner would flit into my mind.

I found a photo from that month in one of the attic boxes. I'm standing in front of Esperanza, holding a BB gun in shooting position. The day is foggy; you can see a small lake in the middle ground below the house. A tree has been recently planted, still supported by guy wires. I look as young as the tree. Written on the back in Dad's hand: Dan at last has BB gun, Gloria's house, Calif.

One foggy Saturday Billy went out on Belle early and we stayed at home, reading on the carpet in her room. I left to get a pillow from my bed and when I returned she was in her bathroom with the door open, changing her shirt. From behind I saw the tan line across her small back and her small white breasts reflected in the mirror. She caught my eye in the mirror, turned around, held her shirt in front of her chest, and stared at me. I looked away and she said nothing when she came out wearing a red cowboy shirt.

*

Klu rubbed his hands in the dirt, watched a pitch come in high and away, fouled one behind Roy Campanella, the Dodgers' catcher, took one low and inside, then hit a fast ball into foul territory toward me. I had my glove ready but it drifted to the left out of reach. Dad steadied me on the bench so I could see over the heads of the men in front of me, who were all standing now. The count was two and two.

*

That evening after dinner Cathy and I were sitting on a couch in the little den watching TV. I wish I could say what was on – it would make the scene more vivid. At a dramatic moment in the show she grabbed my hand and without thinking I turned and kissed her, on the lips, not the chin. She put her arms around my neck and held the kiss. The Alger Kiss. I slid my hand under her cowboy shirt, the pearl snap-buttons popped open, no bra. Was that getting to first base or second? I'd hadn't been there before. Billy might have been waiting, I don't know, but the brat burst in the room as if expecting to find something. Ha! he said, and ran to his mother. The Doc had again not made it home. Billy was so excited he said, Cath is making out with Den in the Dan.

Dad was talking to Gloria at the kitchen table and told me later that she laughed and said, Good for her, but the little shit wasn't going to let such an opportunity pass. His grandfather the preacher used to ring from Tennessee every Saturday evening. The boy intercepted the phone, and soon Big Bill got a call that took him out of the operating room.

I have to hear this from my father, he said to his wife.

You'd have heard it faster if you'd been here, Gloria said.

He'd sent Cathy to her room, punishment to follow. I was standing at the kitchen door, in the dock.

This wouldn't happen if you watched her. You invite these people into our home and what do they do? You never learn – you can't trust everybody. Look at this little whippersnapper, seducing your daughter under your nose.

They're just kids, Bill, Gloria said, Kids fool around.

Not in my house they don't, not with my daughter.

Little Bill said, He had his hand on her thingies, you know, up here.

Go to your room, Gloria said.

Stay here, Billy, his father said. You give her too much freedom. She runs loose all day, horses, tennis, surfing, etcetera. No wonder she's wild.

She's not wild, she's just a young teenager.

The most dangerous time.

Dad had been silent but to me the signs from him were blazingly obvious. He stood up from the table. Danny, he said, his voice clouded, Get your stuff.

No, you're not going, Skip, I won't have you run out because of this. It's a silly thing, it's not important, Bill will apologize, won't you, Bill? And we'll sit down and discuss it calmly. Here, we'll all have a beer. She went to the fridge. Bill looked both angry and deflated, which is quite a trick, but I knew Dad wouldn't give in now no matter what happened. I figured he'd made up his mind at These People, and Whippersnapper confirmed it. I went upstairs to pack and saw that Cathy's door was closed. I could hear her crying but I didn't knock, coward that I was. Dad threw his clothes in a bag and we were out the door, Gloria following. Skip, I want you to stay.

It's no good, Gloria, it won't work.

At least stay the night. It's late. Where will you go?

There are lots of motels in Santa Barbara. It's a tourist town.

And that's where we went. I remember the place still: La Hacienda Motel. It looked like a gas station.

*

Klu hit a fastball so hard he cracked the bat. The ball went long, heading toward the 380-foot marker, just off the sun deck. Carl Furillo and Duke Snider were converging in the outfield. From my angle it was headed out of the park.

*

Wrapped up in myself I hadn't paid much attention to Dad. He'd been using the mornings to look for a house with Gloria's help, then trying to get established in the local building trade. He'd been a plumber for years for the Cincy school district and it must have been demeaning to beg. He had a couple of promises from contractors but nothing permanent, and houses in Santa Barbara turned out to be too expensive for us to buy. He hadn't done his math homework.

Nevertheless, as big Bill would say, we moved into a rented apartment on the east side of town and Dad began to work within a month of our arrival in California. We didn't see the Ottens. I thought of calling Cathy but didn't know what to say. Whenever I picked up the phone I saw her face as the brat burst into the den, and felt guilty.

It was a lonely summer for me because there was no chance to make friends before school started. The great moment was collecting Tuffy at the little Santa Barbara airport. He arrived in a cage and was still groggy from a sedative. I was so happy to have him back that I forgot he was a dog. Dad got me a used bike and Tuffy and I spent the rest of the summer exploring the town and the beaches, eating at lunch stands. We agreed that tacos were better than hotdogs.

I discovered there was a back entrance to the development around Esperanza, a shorter route than the one we used to take in the car, up a steep hill from a remote beach. We made it there one afternoon, though Tuffy was panting all the way in his black curly coat. I hid behind the stable. Rusty was gone so I figured Cathy was too. I had a glimpse of Maria going into the garage. Then Belle got disturbed, probably by Tuffy's smell, and whinnied louder and louder, so I left without seeing any of the family.

Life had no centre, I didn't belong to anything. Janet answered a letter I wrote her; news about Cincinnati and school friends, nothing personal, not even I miss you. I meant to reply but didn't get around to it.

In September I started eighth grade at Our Lady of Guadalupe school, named after an apparition of the Virgin we didn't know about in Cincinnati. About half the students were from Mexican families but the nuns were familiar to me, Irish faces of zealous dissatisfaction. The school building was L-shaped, one-story classrooms with an outside corridor enclosing a paved yard. It looked like La Hacienda Motel. But the boys accepted me right away – people in California were already used to new arrivals. One very cool guy named Max Ramirez gave me useful sartorial advice. Hey, man, he said, Don't wear your pants so high, you look like a *pendejo* from back east. At recess they played a game called tether ball. We'd never heard of that in Cincinnati either, and I couldn't get the hang of it.

Things didn't go well for Dad. He missed his cronies in Dutchtown, and he thought the tract houses he was working on were poorly built, put up by developers out to make a quick buck. In a letter Granna Anna complained about Aunt Dot getting in her way, and on the phone Dot complained that Granna was getting more cranky. By December it was all over. Dad bought a better car, a used Pontiac Chieftain, blue and white. Cleaning out the trunk of the old Chevy for trade-in, I found the Straight Arrow comic book I'd hidden there our first night with the Ottens. That seemed an eon ago, a different boy. I threw it away. We drove back in time for Christmas, this time on Route 66. We ran the song backwards, San Bernardino, Barstow, Kingman, don't forget Winona. No kicks. It was cold in the desert and we didn't stop to look. Tuffy flew.

Can six months ruin a person for life? I never was at home anywhere again. Janet had taken up with Andy, a kid I never liked, and she thought I was a failure. I felt like one too, back from the Golden State without the gold. Klu's batting average declined and just before the season opened the Reds traded him to our hated rivals, the Pittsburgh Pirates. Dad returned to work with the school district and I went to Purcell High, but all I wanted was to get back to California. It wasn't Cathy who pulled me – I'd almost forgotten her in the rush of adolescence. It wasn't the weather or surfing or any of that Beach Boys crap. It was the vagueness of the place I missed, the soft edges, the forgiving landscape, the disconnectedness. The perpetual promise of a future better than the one you'll get. I was hardly the first deluded wanderer. I wanted to be done with the past, the visits to my mother's grave, my backpack heavy with history.

*

Dad couldn't afford to send me to college in California, so I worked hard at Ohio State. Tuffy got old and died, and I cried like I did for my mother. Eight years after we left Santa Barbara I had a graduate teaching assistantship at Berkeley in anthropology. The subject suited me: we're spies, anthropologists, outsiders looking in. By then there were five major league teams in California, and Kluszewski ended his career playing for one of them.

That January in Berkeley, in one of those coincidences fiction avoids and life arranges, I ran into little Billy Otten in front of Sproul Hall. He was wearing a jacket and tie and recognized me despite my beard and long hair. He asked me to call him William. He was in his last year of pre-med, expecting to follow in his father's footsteps. He told me – he didn't disguise the glee – that Cathy was married to a successful lawyer, had two kids, and was living in the Bay Area. I feigned indifference, but a week later a note came from her, addressed to me at the anthropology department. She asked to meet in San Francisco and I went along one afternoon to the Buena Vista Café, at the end of the cable car line, where they claim to have invented Irish coffee.

She was elegant like her mother, a major league beauty. Dark green skirt and brown jacket, pearl earrings. Shoulder-length brown hair with careful highlights, diamond on one hand, gold band on the other. You look like a Beatnik, she said, and laughed. We passed an hour in what's called catching up. I pretended interest in her children, who were three and one, a girl and a boy; she pretended interest in my studies. Marriage rites in the Andes, she said. When will you go?

Next year, if we get the grant.

Exciting.

I nodded, and the conversation came to an end. I offered to

pay for the drinks. I invited you, she said. The check in her hand, she looked straight at me, brown eyes flashing. That summer you came to our house – do you think Skip and my mother were fucking?

The word from her took me aback, and so did the idea. I had been so innocent it had never occurred to me, despite Dad's fling with Gail the redhead. Gloria was a mother and I suppose I saw her in light of my own mother, as sainted as the Virgin of Guadalupe. I don't know, I said, Do you?

Well, when you look at it logically, I think yes. She was having trouble with my father, and left him the next year. She married another doctor and moved to LA. Why did your Dad come to California, if it wasn't for her?

I still don't know. Did he really want to make a new start, just the two of us? Get away like me from the memory of my mother? Would that explain leaving everything he knew behind, including his brother and sister?

You look pale, she said. By the way, you weren't the first boy they caught me with. In fact, I got pregnant in high school and was sent away in shame, back to my grandfather in Tennessee, where I was required to do penance.

What happened to the baby?

It died, she said, and touched my hand with her finger tips, a delicate flit, and was gone.

*

The ball seemed to drift forever. The crowd had gone silent; even Flick was quiet. The Dodgers watched it fly. I imagined Waite Hoyt on the radio saying, It's going, it's going . . . Our three runners crossed home plate. Klu rounded third and turned to watch the ball; it's definitely a home run, he thought, you could see it on his face. At the last second Duke Snider rose in

the outfield next to the wall, glove extended, an impossible leap.
In my memory the Duke's up there still, soaring on the breeze.
The camera holds him aloft, a forever freeze frame.

8

The spring after we'd returned to Cincinnati, when I was thirteen and finishing the eighth grade at Saint Francis de Sales, Monsignor J. Henry Schengber, the long-serving pastor, marked his sixtieth year as a priest. The parish organized a grand celebration for him that included an operetta about an Ireland of leprechauns and poor cottages. The point was lost on me, and I suspect on him as well, an immigrant from Hanover whose idea of Ireland had been formed in America by other immigrants. Janet played an Irish colleen, Pat Moyle was a herald, and I was chosen to open the evening with a speech. It had been written by Sister Dorothea, beginning a long tradition for me of using other peoples' lines. I led out a group of first and second graders; though I can't remember what I said, we did a call-and-response gig, a litany of praise for the old kraut. Though he lived another ten years, he was already frail when at the end of the evening he expressed thanks in Teutonic English.

He reminded us of the story of Big Joe, the nickname of the bell hanging in the gothic steeple high above the church. Donated by a parishioner named Joseph T. Buddeke, it was cast in Cincinnati in 1895, the largest swinging bell ever manufactured in the US. Fourteen horses hauled it up Gilbert

Avenue to the church, a load of 35,000 pounds. The clapper alone was about the weight of four men. The bell was rung for the first time the following January and broke all the windows in the neighbourhood. Pieces of stone and masonry fell from the steeple and surrounding buildings. It had to be immobilized and Big Joe has never swung again. A foot hammer was installed that tapped the rim for the Angelus three times a day, deep bass notes that frightened me every lunchtime but broke no more windows.

Sometimes, Monsignor Schengber said, things intended for one purpose have to be adapted to another. So it was with him, becoming a priest in another century in a Germany that no longer exists, and devoting his life to a place not his own. So it might be for you as well, he said to the school children. The world is always changing. We must adjust to the new place as we find it, not try to remake it in a familiar image, because God made it as it is and on earth we are all his immigrants. Sometimes we are immobilized like Big Joe and have to change our voice to a lesser note. We have been sent away to be tested in a foreign land before we can return home. He meant home to Gott im Himmel, but I began to wonder about Urine Av, how it didn't feel like home since Mom died, and after California. Aside from Himmel, where would home be? And, if we're all immigrants anyway, did it matter?

*

Purcell High came at last. I was liberated from the nuns only to be confined by the Brothers of Mary. They were serious, the Marists; we called them the Marxist Brothers, though they were never communist and rarely funny. It was all-male, sweaty and pimpled. In winter afternoons with the windows closed the classrooms smelled of dirty socks. The curriculum suited me, Latin and science and the expectation I'd be the first in the extended family to go to college. Once there was even a lecture about social anthropology, though it came with a warning about the higher truth of the bible and church teaching. I still went to confession and communion at De Sales, without much to confess. I bloomed late. I didn't have a girlfriend and I hardly understood masturbation until Pat Moyle explained the higher truth of soap.

School passed quickly. I thought of the summer two years before, our aborted California migration, Cathy's tanned skin, the sense of unlimited potential. In Cincinnati, humid and confined, I sat in my room on Urine Av sorting through old comic books, Marvels, Straight Arrows, Lone Rangers. They'd be worth thousands now, but then were useless pulp. They went to the rag and bone man, who came by the house in a horse cart that June for the last time; one of them gave up, the horse or the man. Tommy Hertz across the street went to a different high school, a different road to auto mechanics, and we lost interest in each other. I cleaned out the remnants of our soldiers' club as well, and lingered over his carefully printed system of daily codes and passwords. Astorhouse, Blisterburn, Canman.

The annual plumbers' picnic occurred on a Sunday in July. After Mom died, Dad took it for granted I'd go with him. It was harder each year to pretend I wanted to be there. I was serious about the softball game but the plumbers, usually drunk before the food and worse after, thought it was a joke and stumbled their way around the bases regardless of being tagged out. That year we were at an ancient campground on the Little Miami River, on a point of land before it flowed into the Ohio. The game was always Irish against Germans but the micks rarely won because they were drunker than the krauts, which I found embarrassing in a hazy ancestral way. Afterwards Dad pitched horseshoes for money, a dime a point, leaners counting two. He said he'd stake me but I knew I'd lose all the money so I went off by myself and sat on a little rise under a willow, tossing stones into the water below, desperate for a different life.

I had my new camera with me, a twin-lens reflex Dad had found in a used camera shop on Vine downtown and gave me for my birthday. It was a Yashica Model A, a Japanese copy of a classic Rolleiflex, sturdily made, 120 film, designed for portraits but excellent for landscapes. There was a scratch on the viewing lens but the shooting lens was perfect. I'd already finished the roll and was idly looking through the viewfinder at the fading light on the river, holding the camera at my chest, thinking of Gran's old Brownie you held the same way, looking down into the image. I still had the Brownie, and sometimes preferred it.

I saw movement below and a girl came up from the river. I thought I recognized her; she saw me and waved. She had a beach towel around her shoulders over a two-piece swimsuit, not a bikini, but it didn't hide her features. Her dirty-blonde hair was wet and frizzy from rubbing. I remembered her as she got closer, Helen something, a German name, two years ahead of me. She went to Saint Mary High, our sister school, and I'd met her at what in those days was called a mixer, well-chaperoned by the Marxist Brothers. They used rulers to check if we got too close to the girls on the dance floor. The official distance was eight inches; they probably figured that the average erection was well short of that. But they tended to stick a foot-long wooden ruler in at sternum level, which will move you back in a hurry.

Hello, DanDan, she said. I was astonished she knew my name, since we'd talked only for a few minutes at the mixer, You here with your father, like me? She sat next to me on a fallen log, long legs, narrow waist, sexy moves, not at all like a

Catholic school girl – the first lesson the nuns taught them was how to press their knees together. I said I didn't know her father was a plumber.

They know each other, our dads, she said. I saw them talking when I sneaked a glass of beer.

Beautiful and risky: my lucky day. You know my Dad, I asked.

Everybody knows Skip, he's the funniest plumber in Cincy, according to my dad. Funny ha-ha, not funny strange. Though maybe also a little strange.

I felt tongue-tied next to her. I managed to say, You've been swimming in the river?

Aren't you brilliant, she said, shaking her wet hair at me. I had too many beers. The water clears the head.

How many did you have? I'd had none.

Plenty enough, she said, and looked at me sideways, sizing me up. You like Purcell?

I like it okay, I said, A lot better than De Sales.

George Hendrick, you know him? He said you're smart.

George was a star on the basketball team and it surprised me that he knew who I was. I said, Do you go out with him?

He's a prick, she said. She gave a long yawn and closed her eyes. She smelled of the river, green weeds, slightly stale. Under that, unmistakable girl smell. She opened her eyes and caught me looking at her. She smiled, a little ironically, and it forced me to look away. George told me you'd been to California.

We were in Santa Barbara for six months. It didn't work out for Dad.

Santa Barbara?

It's in the southern part.

Did you like it?

Sun, mountains, the beach. People are, I don't know . . . freer.

My Mom went there for a vacation, Helen said, Just before she died.

When was that?

Last year.

My Mom died when I was ten, I said.

Sometimes I miss her so much I cry, she said. We were quiet for a moment. Loss is separate.

She stood up suddenly, shaking off memories. I'm going back in the water – there's a little pool over there, behind a rock. Join me?

No suit, I said.

Doesn't matter – it's tucked under the hill. Come on. She took my hand and pulled me. We got to the edge, about four feet above the pool. She dropped her towel jumped in. Take off your clothes, she said, treading water. I hesitated. Aside from my mother, no girl had ever seen me naked. Except my cousin Dottie Sue, when we played doctor, age seven, and I'd shown her only the vital bits.

Come on, come on, Helen said. I set down the camera, turned my back and undressed quickly, tripping a bit as I pulled down my jeans. I heard her giggle. Converse sneakers, white socks, off, off. I leapt in, holding my balls. Fair's fair, she said, and took off her top. She tossed it at me. I was no expert, but her breasts looked magnificent. They floated on the surface of the water. My feet were easily touching the bottom; I could feel the silt squish between my toes. She lay on her back, arms moving just enough to stay afloat. There was a little light left in the sky, reflected on the slow-moving water.

You dropped this, I said, holding up her top. In my priapic state I could feel the current caressing my penis as I waded toward her. It might not be as big as Alan's at the Friars Club but right then my whole body was cock. The image of getting caught with Cathy at Esperanza flicked into my head.

Hello again, DanDan, she said. I kissed her, tasted beer in her mouth. Was she still drunk? Who cared? Here it was at last, the longed-for moment, the body finally getting what it considered its due. Just a minute, she said. She slid off the bottom of her swimsuit, then scissored her legs around my waist and put her arms around my neck. I'd always worried about the details of sex – like most boys in those days, what I knew came from dirty talk. It turned out I didn't need much instruction.

Here we go, I thought. Just then I heard a stone being kicked and a shout in the trees. I saw the beam of a flashlight falter, then right itself.

Danny! Danny!

It's my father, I said, and in panic dropped her top in the water, where the current took it. I don't know where the rest of her suit was; it wasn't in her hands, because one was holding on to my shoulder and the other was doing something to me that was entirely new. But she stopped suddenly and dropped her feet to the mud.

Danny, where the hell are you? It's time to go.

Don't let him see me, Helen said, He'll tell my father and I'll be in trouble again.

She swam away quickly and tried to hide under the overhanging rock. Before she got there the flashlight hit her in the face. Then it hit me.

Oh, sweet Jesus, forgive us our sins, Dad said, standing right above us, swinging the light back and forth like a Nazi interrogator. Adam and Eve in the blessed garden, he said. It's Father Mick for you in the morning, son. And you, young lady, don't I know you?

Please, Mr. O'Daniel, we weren't doing anything. Dan just wanted to swim and he, well, he sort of made me, take off my clothes, I mean. I started to object but she went on, If you'd just toss me that towel, please, I'll get out of your way.

What's your name, young lady?

Please, Mr. O'Daniel, sir, don't tell my father, he'll beat me.

She had no shame. Dad's flashlight lingered on her chest and she didn't try to hide her boobs.

Ah, what the hell, he said, It's the picnic. Come on out. He tossed her the towel. She managed to wrap herself in it and moved demurely out of the water and up the incline. I suppose she found her clothes and found her father, the innocent lamb back to the fold.

You going to make a habit of getting caught? That's what Dad said in car on the way home, laughing.

I didn't think it was funny. Years later, making love to my wife, I always half-expected someone to burst in the door holding a flashlight.

She's a pretty one, though, he said, old Charley Leibold's girl.

You know who she is?

Sure, I've watched her grow up, every year at the picnic.

I asked if he was going to tell her father. Of course not, he said. Relax, boy, relax. You'll get there. I wasn't sure what he meant, especially as he made me go to Father Mick on Monday. Finally I had something to confess, though I wasn't sure how to explain it: almost a mortal sin, *peccatum interruptum*? Is that the right declension? I wanted to ask the Marxist Brother who taught Latin, but thought better of it. Father Mick went easy on me, just five Our Fathers and five Hairy Marys, with an injunction to avoid the occasion of sin. That part was easy as well; Helen Leibold came to no more Purcell mixers and I never saw her again.

*

There had been a lot of funerals. Because my German granny still lived with us, we had to go to Covington for all the deaths on her side – Zimmers and Metzgers and a big family named Goebbels, who had a boy called Joseph, though they let him drop that in 1943. They used his second name afterwards, which was Adolf, and thought it an improvement. I'm pretty sure the priest who married my parents in Saint John's Church in Covington, when Mom was already pregnant with me, was named Father Goebbels and came from the same clan.

An entire generation of these relatives seemed to die at once and Middendorf's Funeral Parlour, where Mom had been laid out, already painful for me, soon became intolerable. The smell is still in my nostrils. If anyone is listening, please cremate me and scatter the ashes in the Ohio River, don't lay me out among lilies and gardenias. Dad sensed my aversion and I was excused at some point from Kentucky death rites.

So the next funeral I attended was for his brother, my Uncle Ed, who died suddenly in his fifties. He wasn't killed by the electricity he worked with, unless you consider a heart attack an electrical malfunction. He failed to come home one Thursday and his wife Louise was in a panic. Unlike Dad, Ed drank sparingly and would never stop in the bars after work. He was found about eleven in the evening in the car barn, in an out-of-service Gilbert Avenue trolley, sitting near the entrance in a passenger seat, taking his last free ride. My cousins Mary Ann and Jim loved their father, a quiet man who rarely disciplined them. They were still in shock three days later at the rosary at Finnegan's Funeral Home on Madison Road, just down the street from De Sales church.

I had an intestinal dislike of Finnegan's, an intimidating stone mansion with a blank façade. The year before the California trip I was walking home after confession, wondering if I should get the bus, which stopped across the street from Finnegan's. When I reached in my pocket I found I'd lost the dime I'd been given for the fare. But the bus was approaching and the missing dime went out of my head. I rushed across the busy road and was hit by a car. I woke up on my back in the middle of Woodburn Avenue surrounded by people staring down at me as in a film, their eyes and noses out of proportion, waiting to see if I was dead. It can't be true, I said, and repeated it. More than once. It can't be true, I've found out, usually means it is.

As if from a distance a lady's voice announced that one of the Finnegan brothers had phoned for an ambulance; even in a semi-conscious state I felt the irony. The driver kept saying he never saw me. He popped out of nowhere, he said, Nowhere. I felt the need to be truthful – I'd just been to confession – and admitted it was my fault because I hadn't looked. Did you hear that, the man said, He didn't look. He said he didn't look.

I may have passed out again because I don't remember the ambulance ride or the exam at the hospital. Luckily Dad was home when they called the house; he happened to be working nearby and stopped in for a cup of coffee. I had our home phone number in my wallet, which I kept in the left hip pocket of my pants. Hankie in the right one, coins right front, keys left front. Everything fell out when the car hit me.

Dad collected me and put me in my own bed. I'd cracked my head on the car's hood or the asphalt, the same way I had when Mike pushed me off the basement landing, but the X-rays were inconclusive. It might knock some sense into him, Granna Anna said, though her tone suggested otherwise. Thereafter I walked home from school another way, down by the tennis club, and if I had to pass Finnegan's I didn't look.

*

Here I was, though, a few years later, driving with Dad in the California Pontiac up to that fearful house. A Finnegan met us at the door, with a smarmy face and Digger O'Dell voice. One of the Dutchtown wags said that poor Uncle Ed looked quite sick in the coffin: it's clear he'll never recover, he said. Tears abounded, but it was an Irish wake and I heard stifled laughter in the corners from the Dutchtown boys who'd grown up with Ed and Skip, telling funereal jokes they'd told before. It's a cliché but true: death brings out the best in the Irish. We're genetically inclined to expect it, then we put it in its place. To prove the point, after the visitation and the endless tedium of the rosary, led by Father Mick, the real wake was held at Donovan's saloon, where I'd seen Dad with that redheaded Gail five or six years before.

I was in my last semester at Purcell High. I wasn't good at sports. In my second year I'd tried out for football to please Dad but the competition was fierce. Roger Staubach, who became a great quarterback for Navy and then the Dallas Cowboys, was one of my classmates. At my try-out for the team as an end I had the honour of dropping one of his passes. I was good at talking, though, and public speaking came naturally. I was a bullshit artist. I won a few speech contests with some red-baiting sermons that had been ghost written by one of the Marxist Brothers; it seemed I believed that a return to an old-fashioned morality would convert Russia, end the Cold War, and bring peace on earth.

My new-found sophistication, combined with the memory of Gail, made me ill at ease with the old men who frequented Donovan's. I was sitting in a booth with my cousins, trying to cheer up Mary Ann, who burst into tears every time someone offered condolence. She was older than me and had been given a beer, though I could tell she'd rather have my Coke. I went to the toilet, down that dim corridor where I'd acted the part of The Shadow, and peed next to an Irish guy I vaguely recognized. I stood behind him as he rinsed his fingers at the only sink, a miserable fixture half off the wall, and realized it was Art McIntyre, the owner of Paddy's down the street, who always put a cherry in my Coke in the old days. Little Skip, he said, You're almost as tall as your Da. He made room for me at the sink, and handed me a towel stained by many hands. There's someone I want you to meet, he said.

The man was sitting at the bar alone, hunched over a newspaper in the poor light, a glass of something next to it, untouched. He looked familiar but I couldn't place him until Art introduced us. It was Liam Moran, Gran's nephew, the man who told me a drunken version of the Irish Civil War when Mom was ill. He looked older than Dad, had a kindly face and, to use one of Gran's expressions, eyes that spoke more than his mouth did. Good to see you, he said, Good to see you. Come on, sit down, come on, sit down. Dad used to make fun of him for his habit of repeating; he nicknamed him Come On Sit Down.

Mabel Donovan was behind the bar, called into service for busy nights like this, and Liam pointed to her and waved to us. Have a drink, have a drink, he said. She poured me a Coke and one for Art. And yourself, Liam, she said, Another seltzer to go with the one you're not drinking? Apparently I was between the only two Irishmen in Dutchtown who didn't take alcohol at a wake. Liam was smoking a hand-rolled cigarette, and kept it going until a remnant. His fingers were stained yellow. He deftly rolled another immediately and lit it with a wooden match.

I already had a few faded snapshots of his back story, little ideas for a movie, half-heard at home: how he had appeared without notice one evening on Delia's doorstep on Cohoon Street, fresh off the boat, expecting to be taken in, and soon made a fool of himself in the Dutchtown bars begging drinks, bragging of his exploits in the fight for independence. Later I learned that he'd fought against the British, rose through the ranks on the pro-Treaty side in the Civil War, but afterwards became a lazy drunk in Dublin and an embarrassment to the new state, which he loudly criticized for its priest-ridden ideology. It got so bad that around 1925 a fellow ex-warrior took him aside and made it clear that were he to continue his harangues against the Irish Free State government, one fine morning he'd go for a swim in the Liffey with a hole in his head and no questions asked in the Dáil. He took the hint.

Now, apparently, he'd cleaned himself up. He was wearing a dark suit and tie, his hair was silver and neatly combed, his eyes were clear. I glanced at his newspaper: it was in another language. What's that you're reading, Uncle Liam, I asked.

Good lad, good lad, he said, I like the uncle, I see Delia raised you proper. But did she not teach you your native language, did she not?

She taught me words of Irish and some stories, but not to read it.

She wasn't so good at the reading herself, she wasn't. But reading's easy, if you know the words. A few tricky spellings, that's all, that's all.

You sound just like my Gran.

We grew up in the same house, though I was born much later. I'm her elder brother's son. There's Morans there for hundreds of years, some there still.

Churchfield, I said, Outside Tourmakeady. He had a fountain pen in his pocket and wrote it in Irish at the top of the newspaper: *Tuar Mhic Éadaigh.*

Loch Measca, I said.

We ambushed the Black and Tans there in twenty-one, a great day, a great day. Pen still in hand, he was lost in the past and I thought he'd continue the war story. But he shook his head, dismissing it. Arthur here, he said instead, He's from nearby, otherside the loch.

Ballinrobe, Art said. I was fifteen, no work to be had. A cousin brought me here, and I met Delia and James her husband the second day. They were still living around the corner. He pointed with his chin. She was a fine lady, yer one.

She was, she was, Liam said.

I'd heard the grownups claim she was not so pleased to have to support him, and said I remembered her as grumpy and unhappy. I was thinking of my mother: treats Gert like dirt.

Maybe she was, Liam said, Maybe she was after her James died. Who wasn't in those days? We left all we knew for the sake of something we didn't know at all. I'm not sure the trade was ever equal. Was it for you, Arthur?

It was as it was.

Did you know my father, Liam asked.

I saw him, Art said, The one they called Seán the Mule. He won a mule in a bet that turned out sick and died.

He was a hard man, me Da. Sent Delia and her sisters to America so he'd have the farm to hisself. And the baby brother too, Willie, he was called, pushed off to Liverpool and lost.

Who has the farm now? I said.

My elder brother got it, he said, Seán he's called too.

Two old guys reminiscing about the old country with unpolluted heads, that was new to me. It's up to your generation, Liam said, You've never known the bog, nor your father, or what we fought for. Was it worth it, Arthur? All those boyos in the dirt, the reprisals, a killing for a killing. What did we get for it?

We got a country for it, Art said.

So we could go on with the killing, and the winners set up like gods. De Valera thinking himself the Father of the Country, all by himself, and letting the bishops have their way. Civil servants eating the fat the priesteens leave on their plates.

He finished the cigarette and drank his seltzer in one go, his hand shaking slightly. He looked me in the eye. I hear you're going to Columbus in September, he said.

I was off to Ohio State in a few months to study anthropology, and asked how he knew. I keep up, I keep up, he said.

That's good, Little Skip, Art said, Don't let those krauts take advantage, so.

I'll give you this paper, Dónall, you can study your language. I get it sent every week. He handed it to me and I stared at the title of the article he'd been reading, Filligí ar Éirinn. It seemed familiar when I tried to sound it out; I thought it was what Gran had whispered to us on her deathbed, and asked its meaning. It's a tourist column, in all the time, he said. Go to Ireland, that's all it says, go to Ireland.

Is that what she wanted for her grandchildren, a return?

*

I hoped to talk to him longer but he left – someone was waiting, he said. He wasn't at the funeral the next day, though the church was packed and I might have missed him. Monsignor Schengber celebrated the Mass at De Sales, a very familiar sight. I sang in the choir when I was at school there, no jeans, tie required. The students attended Mass every morning before classes began, and it was usually a memorial Requiem Mass for some departed soul. A source of income for the parish but a morose way for children to begin the day:

Dies irae, dies illa,

Solvet sæclum in favilla.

Doomsday. The Last Judgement. I can still sing it. Death played out in front of that implacable white marble altar with its gothic spires like ice picks threatening the roof. O day of wrath and doom impending. My successors in the children's choir sang Ed to his eternal rest. Funny, isn't it, that the main hope for the dead is not joy with God but rest?

The burial was not in the cemetery across from Urine Av but at Saint Joseph's in Price Hill, a long, silent drive with Dad and Aunt Peggy on a miserable winter day. May the angels lead thee into paradise. Ed was planted next to his grandfather, that mysterious immigrant from Tipperary. It was the first time I'd seen his stone: *Rody O'Daniel, d. 1892*. Nothing more, no birth date or place, not even Rest in Peace. An almost blank memorial for a man who was a blank. Later I tried to find something about him, anything, but it was hopeless – unlike Delia's, Rody's thread had been cut. No frayed edges, nothing to untie or untangle. And his wife, Johanna Fitzgerald, lost in time as well. She was not even buried with him.

Peggy went with Ed's family back to their house and Dad I rode home alone. As we drove over the Western Hills Viaduct, I stared down at the railroad tracks massed below, all empty of trains. The world seemed abandoned. Dad started to say something twice and stopped. It was the only time I saw him cry.

*

Come On Sit Down wants to see you, Skip said. His wife called last week. He's fading fast. Better go quick, better go quick.

It was six years later and I was home for a week in June after my second year in grad school at Berkeley. It turned out Uncle Liam was younger than he looked; he'd been fifteen when he ambushed the Black and Tans in Tourmakeady in 1921. He had quietly married a young widow from Over-the-Rhine about the time of Uncle Ed's funeral – quietly because she wasn't Irish and because he'd been in her bed before she was a widow. He lived a comfortable life with her in his remaining years. Despite giving up drink in middle age, the damage to his liver caught up with him at fifty-eight.

He was in Good Sam Hospital, where I was born, and he looked wrinkled and diminished, propped up on three pillows, green-yellow skin, patches of white whiskers left on his face, like a child's painting of a sick man. His wife Gretta was in the room, an attractive plump woman with gold hair and gold jewellery. She left as soon as she introduced herself. Ten minutes, Liam, she said.

Come on, sit down, he said, come on, sit down, as if mocking himself. His voice was weak and I had to pull a chair close. I've got something for you, Dónall. It's there in the locker next me. In the drawer was a large manila envelope. Open it, he said, open it, put it here. I took out a large handbill, folded once, and laid it flat on the bed tray between us. It was headed *POBLACHT NA H EIREANN*. The rest was in English, starting with a second heading in large type: *The Provisional Government of the Irish Republic to the People of Ireland.* It was poorly printed on cheap paper, a bit crinkled. Irish history, Liam said, touching the paper, They printed it in secret and Patrick Pearse read it out at the start of the Easter Rising. Stuck them up all over Dublin that day, hundreds of them, and the British army tore them down as soon as they found them. Most are lost.

I'd known the story since I was ten when he first told it to me. April 1916, a sudden uprising by the Irish Republican Brotherhood. No one had suspected it. After six days of hard fighting and many casualties, Pearse ordered a surrender. By then martial law had been declared by the British Lord Lieutenant, who had that power because of the First World War. The Rising was considered treason during wartime and dealt with under military law. The leaders were immediately court-martialled and fifteen of them were executed over the next week in Kilmainham Gaol, including Pearse and the six others who signed the proclamation. One of the signatories, James Connolly, had been badly wounded in the fighting. He was so close to death that he couldn't stand to face the firing squad, so he was shot strapped to a chair. The British response turned a fairly small event into a great one. Most Irish people were not in favour of the Rising, or failed to understand it, but after the hurried executions opinion changed. It was clear the colonial power didn't know what it was doing, much less what it had unleashed.

I wasn't there, of course, Liam said, I was eleven, in the wild bogs of Mayo.

I asked how he got the copy. When I got to Dublin after independence, he said, A few were still floating around, kept for sentimental reasons, I suppose. Nobody thought about them. I was in the pub one night, just before I left the country, and an auld fella from Inchicore gave me this one. He thought it was unfair I'd been ordered out of Ireland and told me to keep it safe for the future. I want you to have it, Liam said to me, I want you to have it. If I wait till I'm dead they'll throw it out.

He lay back, exhausted, just as Gretta returned. She scooted me out before I had a chance to offer my thanks. I put the paper in my room on Urine Av and didn't think about it again. The next day I left for the summer for a project in the Andes with my graduate supervisor. Liam died in July. When I got home again in September, Dad said that Gretta, a widow for a second time, had brought a small parcel wrapped in butcher paper that her husband had left for me. *To my nephew Dónall*, he'd written on the front.

I cut the string and unwrapped it. It didn't seem like much, a few yellowed newspaper clippings dating from 1918 to 1921, mostly reports from the *Cork Examiner* about the war of independence, carefully composed to avoid confrontation with the British. Some old photos of Liam, including one of him with a squad of young men variously armed, all in ragged woollen civvies. He's holding an Enfield rifle at port arms, a shadow across his face so the expression is unreadable. I studied another photo, dated 1922 during the Civil War, a small, faded portrait of him alone, standing in front of a studio backdrop of Dublin Castle in an Irish Free State army uniform, arms confidently crossed. Considering the time and the subject, it seemed odd that he was smiling. He was seventeen.

Old coins lay in a small brown envelope: a Victorian silver threepenny bit, a copper penny from 1920 with the head of George V, an Edwardian shilling so worn that its details were barely visible. Perhaps it was a charm or lucky piece. There were three envelopes that bore Dublin postmarks of 1926 and 1927, sent to Liam at different addresses in Dutchtown, their contents removed. Printed on the flap of each envelope was the seal of the Sinn Féin party. A correspondence from the anti-Treaty side about a return to Dublin? Another brown envelope held a small sheaf of receipts for remittances made in the twenties to Michael Patrick Moran, drawn on the Royal Bank of Ireland and payable at a bank in Castlebar, each for one pound sterling, at intervals of about three months. Liam was repaying a relative for his fare to New York and Cincinnati, when he had to escape Dublin in a hurry. I phoned Gretta and asked to see her.

She owned a nineteenth-century house on Elm Street in Over-the-Rhine, restored to single-family use, not far from Music Hall. It was 1964, Kennedy was dead, Vietnam was escalating, and I was worried it might claim me yet. The district was rapidly becoming African American, you could feel anger on the street, but it didn't seem to bother her. Her first husband had been from an old German family who'd made a fortune in riverboat shipping and he left her well off. She admitted that she fell in love with Liam because of the stories of his fighting days in Ireland. She even found his habit of speech charming. I imagined him saying, Gretta, I love you, Gretta, I love you. She met him at Findlay Market – apparently he had a craving for German sausage. She was Desdemona to his Othello but the only tragedy was his early death.

I'm sorry I missed the wake, I said.

We didn't have one. Since he gave up drink he found those Irish wakes tedious. He said he didn't want to be at another.

My grandmother hated them too.

We had a quiet funeral at De Sales and a little reception here. Not many of the Dutchtown crowd came. I think they're afraid of the neighbourhood.

The Cincy Irish can be pretty racist, I said. I was a Berkeley boy then and disdainful of the attitudes of my hometown. I asked if my father had come.

He was here, she said, I was happy to meet him. He told me

a funny joke about two drunks at a wake who take the corpse to the pub, but I can't remember the punch line.

He pulled a knife on me, he did.

That's it. You heard it before?

You could say that. I want to talk to you about Uncle Liam's gift.

Nothing to talk about. He wanted you to have his Irish memorabilia. That's what he called it, and he put the package together himself. He had no children, and he felt you would appreciate it, Dónall.

I was surprised she knew my Irish name; he must have given her lessons. But, Mrs. Moran, I said –

Call me Gretta, she said. She was pouring tea into Dresden cups, looking graceful in a summer dress and silver necklace. I was wearing a Berkeley uniform of jeans and a loose plaid shirt, my beard ragged. She offered some German cookies like the ones Granna Anna used to bake.

I had brought my California book bag, embroidered with bright Indian decoration. This was what Uncle Liam gave me in the hospital, I said, and pulled out the Easter Rising proclamation as she listened politely. I said this ratty piece of paper was like the American Declaration of Independence and worth a lot of money. I'd already checked sale records at the library and phoned a New York auction house. The man there said, Whatever you decide to do, keep it safe and insure it for at least a hundred grand. No, two hundred. No, three hundred.

Liam never showed it to me, she said. He wasn't interested in money. I wonder if he knew how valuable it is.

Well, he knew its historical value. I don't understand why he would give it to me. I hardly knew him. He wasn't really my uncle even, some distant cousin.

Who else could he to give it to?

Well, the Irish National Museum in Dublin, for a start.

Won't it have a copy already? And even if they don't, he had no love for what Ireland has become. He refused to return, though I said I wanted to go and would pay. No, he wanted you to have it, Dónall.

But what should I do with it? It's too precious to keep locked up.

Then sell it, she said. Don't you think that's what he's saying to you? He wanted to help you, and this is how he did it.

By rights it should be yours.

No, it was a bequest before death and I don't need the money. By the way, she said, There's something else I found. She went into another room and came back with a large appointment book or desk diary, well used. The addresses of his relatives in Mayo are here, she said. You might as well take it – I'm not going to Ireland now. It could be useful if you make the trip.

I was twenty-three. When I finally did go to Ireland – Filligí ar Éirinn – I was as old as Liam at his death.

*

People say a boy learns how to be a man from his father, for good or bad. I never managed it. I couldn't mimic his relaxed attitude, free and easy on the draw, like the Lucky Strike ad. After my mother died I was with him so often you'd think I'd have absorbed it like blotting paper. I can't tell a joke to save me from death. He taught me how to throw a ball but when he realized I wasn't any good he stopped. My bungled try-out for the Purcell football team was a last desperate move to fit his notion of what a son should be. Taught me to drive when I was eleven in our prewar Chevy coupe, but I ran the car into a ditch, dented the fender, and the lessons stopped. Wouldn't let me touch the Pontiac Chieftain.

I was away at Columbus when Granna Anna died. I came back for a last visit to Middendorf's in Covington, the terminus of my German line. Dad stayed on in the house on Urine Av alone. I imagine he had girlfriends but we didn't mention them, and he never remarried. If he went to Dutchtown on Saturdays he didn't tell me that either. The district changed, first falling into decay, then sprucing itself up with antique shops and espresso houses. All three of the old bars are long gone, replaced by a faux Irish pub and an over-priced florist.

Gradually our street was transformed as well. As far as black folks are concerned, white people in Cincinnati are border dwellers. There is a deep-seated southern attitude modified by a tentative northern one, and the mix is volatile. My family was uncertain even what to call African Americans. Coloured? Negroes? Most of my relatives stayed unspecific as in, I hear they're moving into Hewitt Avenue. Dad's racial attitudes meshed with the time. He wouldn't hesitate to tell a racist joke, using a ridiculous accent and Stepin Fetchit gestures, but he had nothing in particular against black people and seemed resigned to sharing the neighbourhood with them.

White flight was just beginning. Now that Cincinnati is fifty percent black, it's hard to recapture the combination of fear and hope that marked race relations at the time. Even people in favour of integration had to admit that property values declined when blacks approached a neighbourhood. If this bothered Skip, he didn't show it. Maybe he couldn't bear to leave his mother's home. Maybe he wanted to be with the memories of his wife that remained there. Maybe it was inertia. In any case, he was the last white man on Urine Av, waving to the descendants of a different kind of immigrant.

On one of my infrequent returns to Cincy, I asked him what it was like to live in a black slum. I was joking, because Urine Av never was a slum; it was always respectable and looking up. He took me seriously, though, and defended his fellow householders, saying they were people who were trying to better themselves. They had jobs, they mowed their lawns, they spoke to him on the street. They call me the old honkey, he said, and sounded proud to be recognized as an old-timer.

He died of lung cancer the next year at age sixty, those Lucky Strikes proving not so fortunate. Us O'Daniels don't live long, he said when he was failing, already in Good Sam hospital. I'd come home a week before, when it was clear he wasn't going to make it, and was in the attic when the hospital called. We're all orphans when our parents depart, but it's a special burden for an only child – there's no one left to share the memories. Cousins aren't much help. Mike denies he pushed me off the basement steps, Dottie Sue can't remember Grandpa Luganman's stories. When the phone rang I was going through the attic boxes, incarnations of remembrance, fossil light traveling from the past. And the strange things in the boxes that refuse to conform to memory, the lost things, the orphan things, I kept them all.

The hospital would release the body only to a funeral home but I wasn't about to call the Finnegan boys. I asked around and found an elderly guy with silver hair named Conor McNulty who remembered how things were done in the old days. He was retired and without premises but still had a mortician's license and a scratched-up Lincoln hearse. We brought the corpse to Urine Av and laid Dad out on his bed in a good suit, no embalmment, no makeup, no rosary in the fingers, no sickening flowers. I had the wake there that evening, candles burning around the bed. It was a proper wake, all night, himself lying on his mother's death bed. Cases of beer in the kitchen, Hudelpohl and Schoenling, bottles of Old Grand-Dad and even more of Jameson. It got pretty raucous, the Dutchtown crowd singing Irish songs and the plumbers telling dirty jokes. I'd heard the jokes before, of course, out of my father's mouth. I hoped he was enjoying it.

Some of the new neighbours dropped in. An elderly black lady, obviously church-going, was a bit shocked by the noise and jollity. It's what the Irish do, I said, though the truth was I'd never been to such a wake and what I knew I'd learned from Delia years ago. Why did he die today when he never died before. Flick was there, the plumber from Tennessee. His real name turned out to be Francis Xavier Murphy, and he sang out a limerick:

> A plumber from the town of Dundee
> Was plumbing a lass by the sea.
> Said the lass, Stop your plumbing,
> I hear someone coming,
> Said the plumber, still plumbing, it's me.

Somebody objected that Dundee was in Scotland, not Ireland. Flick said, Limerick is in Ireland, so all limericks are Irish. He gave another:

> A plumber from the town of Adair
> Like to fut-fut on the stair.
> One day in mid-stroke
> The banister broke
> So he finished it off in the air.

In the morning I stood around the bed with the night's survivors, then washed my face and put on Dad's second-best Sunday suit – he was wearing the best one – with a green tie spotted with shamrocks in a lighter shade. He'd worn it once to a Paddy's Day dinner he dragged me to at the Knights of

Columbus hall. It was a horrible tie but in my post-wake condition I thought it appropriate I wear it. In his closet I also found the Yashica camera he'd given me twenty years before. I'd abandoned it long ago, first for a series of 35mm SLRs and lately for a 16mm Bolex for my documentaries. The Brownie box camera was also there; he'd saved them both for me. There was no film in the Brownie, but I stood at the door, focused carefully on Dad's body, and clicked the shutter.

I went to De Sales once more, following McNulty's hearse in Dad's Pontiac. He couldn't stop me from driving it now, and I arrived with tears on my cheeks. Father Mick said the funeral Mass. I was in the front row with Aunt Dot and miscellaneous cousins who complained that I stank of whiskey. The children's choir squeaked out the Dies Irae. I sang along, still half-drunk. Dot told me to be quiet.

I buried Dad in Calvary Cemetery, alongside his mother and father. Standing graveside, I looked back toward our house and could just see my bedroom window over the cemetery wall. I remembered a day long ago, before my own mother got sick. I'd been nasty to her, something smart lipped, and Dad took me aside. He wasn't angry but he was very intense. You have to respect your mother every day, he said, You won't always have her. I'd already apologized for what I'd done, completely ashamed, but he went on. My mother's over there, he said, gesturing toward the cemetery. I'd get down on my knees and dig her up with my bare hands if it would bring her back. The gruesome image stuck with me, dirt under his fingernails, decayed flesh, brown bones. They didn't dig Delia up, but they did open her grave to make room for Dad, her last child, her darlin' Johnny, buachaill, acushla machree.

He might have preferred to be in Covington with his wife but it didn't seem right. I'd forgiven him a long time ago, though to be honest I'm not sure what it was I forgave. I don't believe in an afterlife and it shouldn't matter to me where two corpses rot, but I didn't want him next to Mom, holding her hand, telling jokes.

I sold the old house right away, to a man named Sayed Ali, an unsmiling Black Muslim who wore a beaded skullcap to the closing. My life was elsewhere. But someday I'll go back to Urine Av, jump the wall of the cemetery as I did when I was Little Skip, and pour a bottle of Jameson over Big Skip's grave.

PART THREE

Four Films

9

Flyboy. A film by Rody Moran. Dutchtown Films/Cinema Brazil, 1985. 108 min.

A commercial airline pilot called Nate, about thirty-five, kisses his wife and daughter goodbye and backs his Jeep Cherokee out of his driveway. Suburban house, somewhere in the American Midwest. Completely by accident, he backs over a little girl on a tricycle. He turns in the seat and looks behind before reversing but the girl is coming along the sidewalk, hidden by a tree for a tragic second. We see there is nothing he could have done to prevent it. We hear the thump as the right rear tire rolls over her, then the thump from the front tire, and look from his point of view through the windscreen: the crushed tricycle lying twisted around the body, one little leg up in the air, a red plastic sandal dangling from a toe. He gets out, dressed in his sky-blue uniform, three gold stripes on each sleeve, first officer rank. He bends down and touches the girl's foot. It doesn't move.

Nate is not charged but endures harsh publicity. How can he be trusted to fly a passenger plane if he can't drive carefully even for a few feet? We see his boss place him on temporary administrative leave. Time on his hands. Neighbours avoid him as he mows the front lawn. The police investigation and the loss he caused his next-door neighbour affect the relationship with his wife and his own daughter, aged thirteen. We gather this not from dialogue, but from the looks they give him at dinner one night, when he accidentally knocks over a glass of wine; the dark-red liquid slowly drips off the side of the table onto his white shirt. Music in the background: Marty Robbins singing Streets of Laredo. Sitting after midnight in a dim room, a snifter of brandy on the table, he grabs his passport and some cash and runs away. At O'Hare Airport in Chicago he studies the departures board a moment, then flies to São Paulo, where he starts a new life. Why he chooses that city is not explained. The film skips the details of arrival, apartment hunting, and job hunting; we next see him flying goods up the Amazon valley in a twin-engine prop transport, World War II era, noisy. Beside him is a bearded young co-pilot wearing an automatic handgun in a holster. They unload the cargo at a small airstrip, cardboard boxes taped shut. There are angry words in Portuguese between the co-pilot and the man accepting the goods, wads of money change hands, US dollars. Two tribal men, almost naked, watch through the trees at the edge of the landing strip.

The next scene shows Nate returning to a small apartment in the crowded centre of São Paulo, preparing a meal alone. The sound of the busy street comes through the window. He opens a Brahma beer and drinks from the bottle. The phone rings, he answers in stumbling Portuguese. We hear his side of the conversation only, hardly more than a rumble on the sound track, as he appears to agree to something. There is a framed photo of his wife and daughter on the table.

In the morning he is flying over green hills in the cockpit of the same transport, wearing a quilted flight jacket. He lights a cigarette and seems nervous or suspicious; he glances at the co-pilot's empty seat. We see the route chart, marked to Los Angeles. His American passport peeks from his front jacket pocket. In a repetition of the car accident, he loses control and crashes into a mountain valley – the shots make it seem a strong crosswind is to blame. No dialogue or music, only the naturalistic sounds of the plane and the crash.

His double shoulder belt has saved him, bruised and bloodied in the face, but intact. Limping through the smouldering wreckage, he tears his chinos on a piece of metal, cutting his leg, then discovers the cargo: eighteen boys and girls of eight to ten years old, smuggled aboard in four aluminium crates, now scattered on the ground. He counts the children one by one, his face registering horror. The co-pilot with his pistol is in the destroyed fuselage, his body twisted and bloody. All are dead except for a single beautiful boy, who opens his green eyes as Nate touches his leg.

He radios his location, the Brazilian police and militia arrive, and Nate manages to take the boy back to São Paulo. The story looks as if it will enlarge to deal with international child trafficking. Bandaged and still limping, Nate searches the internet on a laptop in his apartment and we see only glimpses: slum children sold for sex or domestic slavery, kidnapped out of the favelas and expected to live only as long as their childhood. Disgusted with himself, he goes to the police and soon discovers that corruption restrains the authorities from investigating the organizers, who remain elusive. He is told this by a rough but sincere São Paulo detective: They know you know, he says. You must leave. *Agora mesmo.* Now!

Nate takes the boy, whom he calls Afortunado or Lucky, gets air tickets to Mexico City, and after a phone call to an unseen person, again just a rumble of clatter, manages to buy a Mexican passport for the child. We see him collect it in a street of shanties in Saõ Paulo. They arrive in Mexico City, are waved through customs. Somewhere off the Reforma he buys a used Cadillac and the dealer applies Texas license plates. It is all so easy that he smiles for the first time since he kissed his wife and daughter at the beginning of the film. Drive to Juárez, the man tells him in heavily accented English, Cross to El Paso. La Migra is more easy there.

While Nate is out making these arrangements, Lucky is waiting in a comfortable hotel room. He doesn't understand Spanish and gets bored with TV. He goes out, wanders to the Zócalo, bouncing proudly in his new clothes, a fancy Mexican white shirt, black trousers, black Nike shoes. Mariachi music on the sound track. It grows dark. A long aerial shot seems lit by the yellow glow of pressure lanterns. We see the boy stare in amazement at the National Palace and the cathedral, wander through a market, stop at the stall of a woman selling tortillas and beans at a small coal stove. She hands him a tortilla and he smiles in gratitude. She speaks; not understanding her, he shrugs his shoulders and takes a bite. We do not hear the dialogue. In medium shot, the woman suddenly grabs his arm and pulls him down an alley out of sight. The camera moves in slowly as the noise of the great square overlaps the music. The mariachis are brought into the frame, photographed from behind, playing La Paloma. A tenor sings Ay! que dame tu amor! Trumpet accompaniment, baleful. We see the woman's empty stall in a close up on the glowing coals, the tortillas beginning to char.

Jump cut to the hotel room, Nate sitting in a chair, unshaven. Two passports and keys on a table, a bottle of water half empty, a partly packed bag on the bed, the framed photo of his family on top. He is absolutely motionless but it's not a freeze frame, the window curtain behind him is fluttering. He turns his head slightly, facing the camera head on. There is no readable expression on his face or in his eyes, no sound.

The Brazilian countryside, the two giant cities of São Paulo and Mexico City, the site of the crash, even the Midwest landscape in the first scenes, are all photographed poetically but without sentimentality by the Peruvian cinematographer Carlos Vargas. There is one voice-over: as Nate and the boy travel in a police jeep away from the crash site, a woman's neutral voice recites in English an excerpt from Camoens' The Lusiads, the sixteenth-century epic about the Portuguese voyages of discovery. In the passage, Vasco de Gama speaks of his arrival in Calicut and the wonders of the Malabar coast, reflecting the imperialist glory of his king and the heroism of adventure. The relevance of the spoken passage is uncertain.

*

Daniel O'Daniel arrived at Ohio State captivated by mystery. He ignored the football mania, except for the few times his father came up to see a game against Michigan or Indiana, and discovered refuge in the library and the natural history museum. His friends were all anthropology students, mostly tanned year-round from working summers and Christmas vacations on digs in Turkey or Mexico. They included Judy Jensen, a tall woman with a scrubbed face, eleven years his senior. She was a graduate student married to an intern at the university hospital. While Dan was still a sophomore, she introduced him to illicit love one late night in the anthro lab. Her body, normally disguised by an oversized lab coat, turned out to be remarkably soft and pliant when she removed it. Under the vitrines of arrowheads and dancer rattles, she showed him things not usually on display. The affair lasted two years, until she got her PhD and left Columbus. As far as Dan knew she kept him secret from her husband, who worked impossible hours and at home was too tired to notice.

Dan was in love; what she saw in him, aside from youth, was part of the mystery. It was his first real physical relationship, after the false starts in Santa Barbara and high school. Investigating unknown or little known cultures, finding out how they viewed the world and made themselves at home in it, to him seemed the same as investigating the enigmas of Judy's flexible anatomy. Scrutinizing the foreign allowed him to circumvent his discomfort with himself. He thought of other peoples, so-called primitive cultures, as mysteries to be solved. Spying on the Other, engaging with disappearing ways of life, fitting together the pottery shards of thought: he expected to be a scientist of behaviour, shedding light.

He missed Judy heavily throughout his senior year. Women of his own age seemed hollow in comparison. Though he had opportunities, he held himself back from commitment and, with a few exceptions, from sex. He often dreamed of erections, and that disturbed him. He wasn't bothered by homosexuality; he even experimented with a male roommate over a period of months. But the lad wanted more than Dan did, and moved out. If mysteries of sexual preference had been secreted in his youth, Dan was unable to subject them to the anthropological method.

After Judy left he found some comfort in listening to the Reds' games on the radio. Waite Hoyt was still broadcasting, his voice an anchor to childhood and Dan's old crystal set. When he got to grad school at Berkeley he was shocked that he couldn't receive the Reds on the radio except when they played in San Francisco. He objected to the relocated Giants because they disrupted his boyhood knowledge of the National League, and he lost interest in baseball.

The Vietnam problem receded. After his draft board medical he was declared 4F because of a heart murmur. Even money, he thought: one thing less to worry over, one thing more to worry over. He got drunk on the news, and threw up on the street in North Beach, just outside the Condor Club, watching Carol Doda's red nipples flashing on the neon sign.

His own PhD prepared him to study liminal rituals that had survived into the present. The premodern amid the modern and the postmodern. His first book was about wedding ceremonies, followed by a documentary film on the same subject, then he moved to rituals of passage to manhood. He thought that if he presented himself as an objective observer, a simple recorder with no stake in what he was recording, the results would be clean and accurate, dispassionate. But if tribal subjects choose to elaborate or lie, the anthropologist is helpless. Native informants are not subject to the polygraph. Anthropology, already contaminated by colonial biases, the Us and Them predicament, becomes a double falsehood. He began to suspect this when he turned on the camera and watched the participants begin to observe themselves. The longer the camera ran, the more they performed for it, and the ceremonies no longer held the purity he sought to preserve.

He hoped to show how contemporary economics were destroying a traditional way of life: tradition is pure and the modern polluting, the creed of his profession. But he found that his subjects were not ignorant of the world or the politics of Peru and Ecuador. They knew what he knew. The rituals he filmed could never be innocent, precisely because he was filming them. The observer effect. An observer may have idealistic intentions but if a culture is under threat, isn't it already contaminated by the exogenous? Those ideas disturbed his early career. If he was right, anthropology was no solution to the problems it uncovered.

So he gave up that self-promoting ideal and stopped making documentaries. The transition to fiction seemed completely natural, just another step on the same road. Liberation from the actual allows us to investigate life more deeply; he liked to say, more actually. What is fiction but the invention of the real? He quickly learned how to do that with film because he understood that film is about light, not motion. Photography: writing with light. But truth depends not only on light; it also depends on how the light is directed, what shades or filters are applied to record it. It takes a lot of trouble for a film to look untroubled.

To go along with the change in his life's work, he changed his name. No more DanDan. From now on, he said, I will be Rody Moran. Rody, the name his father was trying to call him, from his great-grandfather, and Moran, from his grandmother. His immigrants.

Flyboy followed the new pattern. The image is the narrative, the way the images relate to each other is the story. Not like Antonioni's *Blow Up*, which is a detective tale gradually revealed by enlarging photographs, but by framing the central character's crisis only in visual terms. He cast an actor named James Jackson, then about forty, not well known. His rigid facial gestures, like Clint Eastwood without the penetrating eyes, expressed Nate's inner turmoil with almost no dialogue. Verbal expression of feeling was eliminated; the words characters use are statements of events, not interpretations of them.

He met Carlos Vargas when working in La Paz on a anthropological documentary about football rituals. He was born in Lima; because Dan had spent so much time in the Andes and spoke Spanish with a Peruvian accent, Vargas felt comfortable with him and chose him as mentor. Vargas worked as a grip hired out to TV studios and visiting production companies. He spoke English fairly well and was a quick learner. Dan gave him a chance to photograph a short piece for the BBC on the Urarina people of the upper Amazon, and he blossomed. He had a better eye than anybody on the set.

Flyboy was his third feature as cinematographer. Vargas intuited the camera's intrusions, how they change and direct the scene. He was fascinated by the autumn light in rural Ohio, where they shot what became the opening scenes of the film. In Brazil they photographed densely populated cities and empty landscapes with silent figures walking through them.

Unlike photography, editing is about choice, and choices are always political – choices mean that one thing is more important than others. In editing *Flyboy* Dan began to understand that some truths are better hidden, some spaces better left dark. He found that Vargas had given him enough footage, even on their limited budget, that permitted two different films, one about understanding Nate, the other about not understanding him. The first would be explication, psychological, nuanced, cathartic. It would see Nate as unfortunate but sympathetic, a normal guy who got a bad break and suffered disaster despite good intentions. But the other film, one Dan had not intended to make, would be about the inexplicable, the callousness of the universe, hounding by fate. It would be heartless, merciless, a Greek tragedy. A man pitted against implacable gods who don't give a shit one way or the other. That's the one he released.

Movie makers say there are three films in every project: the one you write, the one you shoot, and the one you edit. If there were remnants in the final version of what Dan had first written, no one seemed to notice. Partly thanks to the lustreless stare Jim Jackson gave to Nate, critics took it as a movie about shame, about a man who cannot escape a sense of doom and feels responsible for what he's caused. But in Dan's eyes – Rody Moran's eyes – it's not about shame at all. It's about the pitilessness of light.

*

Long before he was Rody, Dan knew his relationship to women was flawed. He was hopelessly attracted to women who combined come-hither with indifference, women who were illusive, distant, self-contained. Beauty that reserved itself from allegiance yet seemed to long for defilement. A cool sacrificial offering. Well into his thirties he remained nervous around women, unsure of what to say. His liaison with Judy Jensen at Ohio State, almost entirely sexual and conducted in secrecy, didn't help him to treat women as equals. In fact he thought most women were not equal but far superior to him. He found physical attraction, not to mention love, unsettling, his own position insecure. So he conducted himself poorly, without fashion or flair, often mistaking appearances. He didn't know how women saw him and that unnerved him.

You wouldn't say he was handsome. His boyish cuteness had gone but he was pleasant looking with an engaging smile. He had the face and height of his father, lively blue eyes, long thin lips, uncorrected teeth, and a slightly weak jaw that he began to cover with a beard at Berkeley. His thick dark hair came from his mother. He felt confident in his work and interviews, wearing the clothes of independence, jeans and sweaters and a scarf in the cold. He was completely unfazed by the commercial side of film, the selling and promotion. With journalists he had a habit of telling the truth and admitting failure, which endeared him to some people in the business or on its fringes, primarily women. Sex was never far from his thoughts. He reflexively sized up an actress or a new acquaintance and passing girls on the street, face, tits, ass, legs, then felt guilty about it.

He had excuses, plenty of excuses. His Catholic upbringing in the forties and fifties, where the body, especially the female body, was treated as so sacred it became mysterious. Masturbation was a mortal sin, thinking about sex a sin, touching a girl's breasts a sin. The nuns and priests were crazed about sex, it was never out of their minds, and they took it out on us, he thought. Though no priest ever accosted him. He was grateful to the church for that, if nothing else, to have escaped Catholicism untouched.

But of course he wasn't untouched, no one raised a Catholic is. The nuns at De Sales, the Marxist Brothers at Purcell High, old Monsignor Schengber, Father Mick, they all left their mark, along with the Dies Irae every school day. Doesn't matter if you escape, if you've had ten years of it when young, it's there for life. The Sanctus bell at Mass kept ringing in his head, just as he rang it as an altar boy.

His wife had also been raised a Catholic. Though she was much freer and seemed unmolested by religion, when he looked at her naked body, thin but with full gear, dark skin that shone in dim light, welcoming lips, the slight smile, he said Sanctus, Sanctus, Sanctus.

Her name was Estrella de las Nieves: Star of the Snows. In bed he called her Snowstar. He met her through Carlos Vargas, but she was Mexican, not Peruvian. She was born in Taxco, the silver town between Mexico City and Acapulco, and raised in a middle-class family in Los Angeles. Her father owned a successful handicraft and silver shop on Olvera Street. Rody was still Danny then, Danielito, and met her in a bar in Lima – she was working in television with Carlos. Dan was stunned when he saw her, her magnificent poise, deep black hair, a light blouse with flounces, tight black jeans. Her face, angular, intelligent, conspiring, had been in his dreams before he met her. Did she remind him of his mother? He put that out of mind. He forced an introduction, spoke to her in Spanish. She laughed at him and said she'd gone to Santa Monica High, maybe they could talk in English. As far as Danny was concerned that was it: she was the love of his life. He was amazed when she concurred.

Six months later they were married in LA, at Saint Vibiana's Cathedral to please her mother, who knew a priest there. Dan was almost thirty-eight. He spoke the required words and shut his mind to the rest. Estrella took communion, saying it meant nothing to her. Dan refused, because once it had meant so much. Carlos was his best man. Skip had died three years before and no one from Cincinnati was invited. Dan told her that standing in front of the crazy mixed architecture of Saint Vibiana's, her face looked like snow light. What's snow light, she asked. He couldn't explain because it existed only on film. A blank white light that was soft, bluish at the edges, the full moon on a dark woman in a white dress in the snow, cold and alluring.

There's a poem by Wallace Stevens, he said, about what the snowman sees.

And what does he see?

Nothing that is not there and the nothing that is.

She nodded but didn't understand.

She was fascinating to him, exceptional, and not just because she overlooked his faults. Something about her meshed with his own uncertainties. Though she was sure of herself in public, she was between worlds, two languages, two cultures, two countries. She sometimes felt at home in America, sometimes lost, the traveller's fate. Maybe she found in him what he found in her, the strength that comes from doubt. If they were ambiguous separately, together they were single-minded. They thought of alternative lives, children in America, or a move to France where his documentaries were taken seriously. They didn't fear the future because they could make it suit them.

Estrella was a good writer, better than Dan. She enjoyed writing in a way that he didn't, took pleasure from moving pen over paper, never used a typewriter for first drafts. She had worked as a journalist in Lima for a newspaper and for TV, reporting on cultural affairs and international cinema in Spanish. Since she was completely bilingual, it was natural that Dan would use her for his documentary films. He had begun to move on from the subject of the Andes, and was teaching at UCLA in anthropology and film studies, so they were chiefly in Los Angeles, living in an apartment in Westwood and traveling together when required. She wrote the script for what turned out to be his last documentary, on the survival of the Mexican Day of the Dead in Southern California.

Carlos did the photography, sleeping in the room they used as a study. The apartment was on the third floor and overlooked a small courtyard with a kidney-shaped swimming pool that no one ever used. After dark it was illuminated underwater; it brought in blue light day and night. By then Carlos seemed part of the family, and slept in the blue room when he was in town. He loved Estrella. One evening in Lima, before she married Dan, he tried her out, though it never got beyond kissing and touching. She might have sensed what Carlos had not yet sensed, that he was ready to cross over. Once in California, in the last years before the AIDS epidemic, he freed himself from his upbringing and was exploring the panoramic gay landscape of LA. Perhaps, he thought, his attraction to Dan had been partly sexual, and wondered if Dan felt it too. He came to see Estrella in a similar light, almost a mother substitute. He stayed out late, testing the bars and himself, and sometimes in the morning he was a little too groggy for filming. Dan said nothing but Estrella did, telling him he was losing his eye for shots.

Like most South Americans he was crazy for football. Not US football, which he thought unsubtle, but what most of the world calls football. That evening he'd not gone to a gay joint but to a sports bar that regularly showed soccer matches, a hangout for South Americans in LA that was a little on the rough side. Getting to bed late, he noticed a small stack of pages by the typewriter, a short story in Spanish that Estrella must have typed during the day. *Quizás sí, quizás no* it was called, Maybe Yes, Maybe No. He read it quickly and, still a little drunk, excited by Argentina defeating Brazil, burst into their bedroom. Though it was three in the morning it wasn't unprecedented; he used to do it to Dan in Peru when he saw a new idea for a scene, like a child waking up his father. What is it this time, Dan said from bed. Estrella hid under the covers.

Aren't you tired of documentaries, Carlos said, I'd like for once to be free from *los hechos*.

What do you mean, *los hechos*? The facts?

Your wife there wrote a story. It's great for a movie. He waved the pages in the air.

Estrella sat up and turned on the light. You read my story?

What story?

Esté, Carlos said, *es perfecto para una película. Un film de Danielito y Carlito.* The next day Dan read it, as well as his Spanish allowed. When did you write this, he asked Estrella. It's fantastic. Why didn't you show it to me before?

I didn't think it was any good, she said.

That's why I love you.

Funding proved easy. Around 1980 new money was available for bilingual and Chicano projects and, based on the success of the Day of the Dead documentary, Estrella and Carlos together managed to convince public agencies and private businesses of the worth of the story. It concerned a Mexican woman who comes to LA with her ten-year-old daughter in the hope of a new life. She suffers numerous indignities and almost gives up, but in the end chooses persistence and low-level survival. Re-titled *Forgive Us Our Trespasses*, it did well at small film festivals and in Hispanic communities. It was Dan's first feature film, and his first as Rody Moran. Estrella didn't like the new name – she thought it would confuse his identity. It's confused already, he said, But for you I'm still Danielito.

Six months after it opened they were planning a second feature. It was to be about a character like Dan's German great-grandfather, Arnold Luganmann, who settles in the Over-the-

Rhine district in the 1850s, and would cover the period up to the First World War. Estrella was writing the script after a visit to Cincinnati.

She's beautiful, Danny, his Aunt Peg said, Is she really a Mex?

Aunt Dot, who had always been cynically realistic, told him that she would be difficult to keep. Women like her, other men go after them, you know must that. Men with money and power. She's just too exotic. I've seen it happen. It may be hard for her to resist. Dan couldn't deny that if he found her irresistible others might as well. Then there's your age, Dot said, She's younger than you, ten years maybe? Doesn't matter now, but it will later. What's the matter with American girls?

Out of respect for his mother's memory he never argued with her sister. It disturbed him, though. Dot had put a snake in the garden.

He showed Estrella around: Urine Av, De Sales, Price Hill. At Findlay Market she asked why the district was called Over-the Rhine. German immigrants settled here, Dan said, the other side of the Miami and Eire Canal. It was all German speaking then. When they walked home from working downtown, crossing the canal they said they were going over the Rhine. She asked to see the canal. It was filled in many years ago, he said, to make the Central Parkway, but the name stuck.

They crossed over the Ohio to look at his mother's neighbourhood in Covington, and then to Newport where the whorehouses and gambling dens used to be. The river was high with spring floods and looked dangerous. In bed that night he told Estrella about Dot's warning. He was tracing his finger along her belly from her nipple to her crotch, stopping to draw a circle around her navel.

She thinks you'll leave me for someone else.

Why?

Because you're too beautiful for a plumber's son from Cincinnati.

I am too beautiful for a plumber's son from Cincinnati, she said, but not too beautiful for you.

But I am a plumber's son. That's ambiguous.

No kidding, she said.

Here's the canal, he said, touching her pubic hair. What if I cross over the Rhine? Would that be ambiguous?

Afterwards, lying behind him spoon fashion, she held his cock through the night.

*

They decided to have children but Estrella couldn't get pregnant. She was young so they were not overly concerned but after two years of trying they had themselves checked. Dan called it an anthropological investigation. His sperm count was low. Actually, quite low, the doctor told him; probably just some genetic cock up. He didn't seem aware of the bad pun, and added that it was unlikely Dan would ever father a child. Dan took the news stoically, since a part of him wasn't ready. It was a grave disappointment for Estrella. She talked of adoption. Dan was ambiguous.

*

Forgive Us Our Trespasses won awards at festivals, which prompted the dean of film studies at UCLA to organize a champagne gala, a screening followed by a Q&A with Dan and Estrella. Carlos refused to participate, claiming his English was embarrassing, though Dan was determined to bring him on stage anyway. The event took place off campus in a Westwood art house. Carlos and Estrella were busy that day talking to potential producers and planned to arrive during the showing, in time for the talk. When they didn't appear Dan wanted to delay the interview but the dean insisted they couldn't keep their guests waiting.

On stage Dan kept looking at his watch. Since Estrella was efficient and always punctual, Aunt Dot's warning kept going through his mind. The dean reminded him of the delays of LA traffic, and introduced him.

Do we call you Daniel O'Daniel or Rody Moran, he began.

Both, I guess, Dan said. It's a new name to me too. But it's *MORE-in*, not *Mur-ANN*. My grandmother's name, Delia Moran. She was very insistent about its pronunciation.

Why did you change it?

To make it clear that the films I'm doing now are different from the documentaries I did before. I'm forty now, halfway through life. I've always disliked my name anyway. DanDan, they used to call me back home, or DanODan. Even the nuns. That got a laugh.

A young film student spoke up. I read somewhere that you hate metaphor. Why is that?

I don't hate it, it's just wrong in film. Metaphor, simile, they belong to poets and novelists, that's how they explain characters and ideas, one thing in terms of another, because in reading – as a reader you have to create it all in your head. But film, well, to me film is already a metaphor or a symbol for something else, of the world the film was made in. A film always stands for something else, something actual in the world.

The student interrupted. But doesn't a novel do that too?

Not the same way. When I shoot a scene, the scene is what it is, nothing more. It is its own meaning. That's the way I made documentaries, the way most directors make documentaries, I suppose, but now that I'm making narrative pictures I feel the same. I don't want to release a movie and people go out saying, What was that about? As if it were a puzzle to be figured out. I want it to be about what the camera shows, only that.

The dean said, But is that possible? Won't audiences try to puzzle out things anyway? You have to admit that the film we just saw is not always clear about its meaning.

Dan thought about this, and looked at his watch. My wife wrote this as a short story, he said, and then wrote the film, Estrella de los Nieves. She's supposed to be here, and I don't know why she isn't. She might be able to answer that, I'm not sure I can. Audiences – I guess audiences will do what they do, and I will do what I do. I hope to learn more about that. I don't think we succeeded this time, not fully anyway. If we did succeed a little here and there, it was because of Carlos Vargas, the DoP, who should also be here, I don't know where he is either. He understands how to make light work for us, what it will look like on film. I tell him what I want and he figures out the light.

The event dragged on until almost eleven. The dean concluded by saying that the response showed how powerful the movie was. Dan wasn't listening and rushed to a phone to call home. It rang on in the dark. He called his answering machine. The California Highway Patrol had left an urgent request to contact them. His hands were shaking; he could feel the blood draining from his face and his heart beating faster, too fast, far too fast. He was in some office at the back of the cinema and sat hard on a hard chair, trying to catch his breath. It wouldn't come. He had to dial the number three times to get it right. Estrella and Carlos had been in an accident on the I-10 and had been taken to the UCLA Medical Center, a few minutes away.

It had happened just after seven, almost three hours earlier.

Estrella's parents were already there, her mother in tears, her father looking at Dan in shock, as if he didn't understand why this gringo was there. A young ER doctor had just told them that Estrella was dead. For the first time in his life Dan fainted. The dean caught him, put him on a chair, the doctor revived him with a wet cloth.

What did you say, Dan asked.

Are you the husband? I'm very sorry. She suffered severe head trauma, there was nothing we could do. A semi crossed lanes, trying to make a late exit, hit the side of her car and flipped it over. The truck driver is under arrest.

Why is he telling me that, Dan wondered.

I'm afraid the child couldn't survive, the doctor said.

Child?

Fetus. She was pregnant. Didn't you know? About four months.

Dan's face went white and he put his head between his knees. He thought he was going to throw up. The dean put a hand on his shoulder, a small comfort that had no effect. Talking to the floor, Dan said, Was she driving?

No, the man was – Mr. Vegas, is it?

Vargas, the dean said, Carlos Vargas. How is he?

Beat up. He'll survive. Again Dan wondered why the doctor thought that important. If Estrella was gone, how could it matter?

*

He let her parents arrange the services. Memories of Finnegan's Funeral Home and Middendorf's – he couldn't go through with it, mortician, embalming, casket, sickly flowers, cemetery plot. Thinking about it made him throw up again. He stayed in bed for two days, drinking Jameson, eating only cheese and Knäckebrot. Since he wasn't much of a drinker, he threw up each morning, then started over. He couldn't go to the viewing, the wake, *el velorio*, closed casket anyway because of her injuries. He didn't even know where it took place. He'd heard that Mexican funerals encouraged emotion, but his grief was private, belonged to no one else. He didn't want to see her relatives and friends, some of them his friends, sharing his loss, shaking his hand. He kept grief close to him, a kind of madness. How could she die that night when she never died before?

He managed to stumble in for the funeral Mass at Saint Vibiana's, walking slowly up the aisle just as at their wedding, following her coffin this time, a shiny black thing with gaudy brass handles and a spray of gardenias. He was dressed in black, his tie badly arranged, his hair sticking out at the back from lying in bed too long. Officially he was the chief mourner, but he wore dark glasses and smelled of alcohol as at his father's funeral. The priest ignored him.

But he listened intently to the words of the Requiem Mass, and was not comforted. It wasn't because the words were in English instead of the Latin he knew by heart, the Dies Irae, the Requiescat, and it wasn't that he no longer believed in the life to come. He knew Estrella was not in heaven or hell or purgatory or limbo, he knew she was nowhere. It wasn't that either. What he missed was the condolence of Father Mick and that old kraut Monsignor Schengber, the familiarity of Saint Francis de Sales, the smell of wood polish on the pews, the big organ in the choir loft with its bass reverberation, appalling sounds. All his history, which wasn't her history. He was shocked to realize that California made him another kind of immigrant, cut off from the connivance of the past, unable to find solace in ritual deflection of grief. Outcast. Marooned. Bereft.

*

Carlos was out of the hospital in a week, bandaged but intact. He was under heavy medication and walked with difficulty. Gradually he dropped the pills and the cane, the hurt became an ache, the ache became part of him. The limp never went away entirely; years later, a slight dragging of one foot wore out the sole of his left shoe before the right. The limp was his scar, his memorandum. In the first weeks after the crash, however, much worse than his pain was the fact that Danielito couldn't stand to be near him.

Dan looked in on him in the ICU the night of the crash, saw the bruises and bandages, then rushed to the men's room and was sick in a stall. He knew the crash was not his friend's fault but his guts spoke louder than his brain and for months he couldn't rid himself of the idea that the wrong person had been killed. Estrella's parents felt the same, and said so. Since they also blamed Dan, he stayed away from them as well. Blame is a powerful narcotic, he thought, because it drives away the dread moment when you accept that loss is irretrievable. Despite understanding this, he couldn't bring himself to forgive Carlos. In his despair he concluded that women were the problem: they were creatures who died on him. The two women he loved most deeply, his mother, his wife, gone at thirty-five, gone at thirty-two. Deep love was dangerous. He began to understand that life is a bereavement.

And the pregnancy: had the doctor been wrong about his sperm count? The alternative was intolerable. Los Angeles, a miasma of desolation.

Carlos continued to sleep in the blue room and wrote pitiful notes. Danny, please come home. Danny, *lo siento, perdóname.* Unposted, unaddressed. Dan had flown to Cincinnati. Ostensibly he was researching the new film, but it was pure avoidance.

Carlos guessed he might be there and called every O'Daniel and Moran and Luganman in the phone books from Dayton to Louisville, to no avail. He wanted to go home to Lima – not the one in Ohio – he wanted his mother to take care of him, but the injuries prevented him from travelling. Rehabilitation was slow, life ahead precarious.

Dan was in the Mount Washington district with Aunt Dot, then in her eighties. Carlos didn't know her name was North, her husband's name, dead in the war. Dan had driven Estrella to this house only a few months earlier, up the Columbia Parkway from downtown, as she marvelled at the view of the wide Ohio below. This was when Dot gave him the background about her grandmother who thought her baby was a pig. He lost himself in the archives downtown and in Covington, but the deeper he went the more he realized he could never make a film about his great-grandfather, the traveller from Oldenburg. Without Estrella he had no idea how to write it, and no desire to do it.

He was making work for himself around the city, out most of the time, but one evening Dot cooked dinner and insisted he stay in. She made German potato salad and hot slaw to go with some bratwurst from Finlay Market. It felt familiar, the food of Dan's youth. Dot liked martinis and got a little aggressive after a second one. What are you hiding from, Danny, she asked.

Am I hiding? he said.

She's dead, you can't run from that.

The next day, a Saturday, he borrowed her car and ran off to Columbus, looked over his old campus in the autumn sunlight, heard the distant roar of the football game. College nostalgia and memories of Judy Jensen didn't alter his state of mind. He lingered late, at loose ends, drank too much at dinner, couldn't find a hotel room – the game had been Ohio State against

Michigan, the biggest day of the year. He slept in the car on a residential street and was awakened at four in the morning by heavy rain on the roof. He was cold and groggy and had to pee. He found a secluded spot under a tree and let it out, yellow stream mixing with dark rain, dropping on fallen brown leaves that shrivelled like the pages of a book. He was back in Cincy at dawn on a dreary Sunday and booked a flight for LA leaving that afternoon.

The Greater Cincinnati Airport is northern Kentucky, not far from Covington. He stopped to pay another visit to his mother's grave and to Watkins Street where she grew up. The cemetery looked shabby, the houses run down. Most of the landmarks from his childhood were gone, the store where Granna Anna worked, the saloon on the corner that supplied a bucket of beer for his grandpa. The house next door, where Len Sanger crooned The German Band a cappella, was enclosed by a high chain link fence. No one was on the street. The hollow off to the side, where Gert said she once found an Indian on the ground, dead or dead drunk, she wasn't sure, had been paved over by a new road. On Watkins Street the past was gone. Would Estrella ever be past to him? He couldn't imagine it.

*

They showed *The Shining* on the flight, which seemed an odd choice. Dan admired Kubrick but thought Nicholson over the top and the story ridiculous. He had no sympathy for horror films. Ordinary life was more frightening than counterfeit phenomena. But watching a family disintegrate on screen helped him overcome his antagonism to Carlos. Dan could never forgive him for surviving Estrella's death, that was the turmoil of grief, but Carlos was too valuable to him, as a friend and as a colleague, to remain estranged. Still, returning to the place in

Westwood was impossible; the blue room now reflected only loss. Carlos found a small apartment in Santa Monica, and Dan by then had enough money to buy a small house in Northridge. He spent too many evenings alone there, sitting in the backyard with crickets and Jameson. I'm becoming my father, he said to himself, and raised a glass to Skip. He gave up teaching.

For the next year they were cautious with each other. They never spoke of the accident or Estrella's pregnancy. Once when Carlos had difficulty rising from a chair in a restaurant, Dan pointedly looked the other way. A bond had been broken. Dan made a short documentary for the BBC on a new archaeological discovery in Peru, and collapsing into the selfishness of anger, chose a different cinematographer. He knew it was offensive and childish but couldn't help himself. He felt at the mercy of an irrational power and began to develop heart trouble, skipped beats that plagued the rest of his life.

Carlos found the way out. For the second time he brought Dan an idea, a film about the trafficking in children from Brazil to the US, based on an incident he read about in the *LA Times*. Dan saw its potential but hesitated over the big theme, which seemed too easy. One early morning, feeling terrible after drinking much of the night, he stood in the shower until the hot water ran out, then filled the tub with cold and sat in it until he was shivering and awake. He threw up in the toilet. He drove to Santa Monica, sat on the edge of the pier in impenetrable seven o'clock fog, and worked out in his head the full outline for *Flyboy*. After its release he and Carlos were considered important filmmakers, and people stopped asking why Daniel O'Daniel had changed his name.

10

Lost Time. A film by Rody Moran. Dutchtown Films/ Cinéma du Nord, 1995. 95 min.

The first scene is night-for-night with a film noir sensibility, in colour but with dominant tones of black and grey. It's snowing heavily in a city with high stone walls, Warsaw in wartime. A large 1940s sedan passes, the driver and front passenger in Wehrmacht uniforms. Glimpsed in the rear seat, a general sits next to a woman, large hat, wrapped in a white fur coat. Her face is pale, her mouth determined. Suddenly a van pulls sideways in front of the sedan, while an open jeep blocks it from behind. Two partisans (members of Leśni, the Polish resistance) in civilian clothes place handguns to the heads of the two men in the front seat and fire. It happens so quickly the general is slow to react. He attempts to draw his sidearm, a P08 Luger with a red lanyard attached to the grip. The lead partisan, Michal, breaks the car's window with his pistol, disarms the general, and hands the Luger to the woman. She points it at the general, two hands, both shaking. The general says in German, You know these people, Beata? She says, That's my husband. But she cannot pull the trigger. Michal shoots the general in the back of the head, then pulls Beata out. There are splatters of blood on the fur coat. She screams as he rushes her into the back of the van, which drives off to the sound of tires crunching over snow. The partisans pull the dead Germans onto the road and drive off in the sedan, the jeep following. Beata lies on her front on the floor of the van, her hat lost. Close up on her face, neutral expression. We hear dance music of the period.

Dissolve to an old woman sitting alone in an expensively furnished room, staring straight ahead, a shawl over her shoulders, the same neutral expression. She's over seventy. On her lap is the Luger with the red lanyard, the colour faded. She opens the magazine with a practiced move, checks the load, and replaces the clip. We hear a man's voice off camera: Grandma? She hides the pistol in a bookcase and looks out the window on a park covered with snow. A young man enters, she smiles. They descend in an elevator, dressed for winter. On the street we see that it is New York, Upper East Side. Yellow Cabs silent in the snow. Central Park looks magical: it's Christmastime. They go down the steps to the subway.

Bright filtered light as we see the young Beata come up the steps from the Paris Metro. It's summer, she's in a light green dress, bare arms, smiling. She walks toward the Seine and we see Notre Dame in the distance. Along the book stalls on the quay she meets a man of middle age. They embrace quickly. He says *Beata* in an American accent.

The same 1940s dance music as Beata is at supper in a private room with the German general, his tunic unbuttoned at the neck, duelling scars on his face. They drink champagne. He has a hand between her thighs and she laughs. She is very beautiful. He holds her temples and begins to force her head down to his lap. She laughs a little but resists; he is stronger. Camera up on his face, twisted in pleasure. His head thrown back, he says in German, Does your husband know how good you are at this?

Michal pulls her roughly from the van in front of an apartment building in Warsaw. In Polish he says, You couldn't do it, could you? You actually liked him. She replies, I hated him. In a barely furnished room, dim light, they sit facing each other across a kitchen table. She says, You told me to seduce him, Michal. It's a little late to get fastidious. He says nothing, but his face reveals how trapped he is. Outside we hear drunken German soldiers singing Stille Nacht. Michal quickly turns off the light. We see Beata's white face in the snow light from the window.

The destruction of Warsaw is underway as the Germans retreat, late 1944. Beata is running through rubble-filled streets, smoke and fire in the background, occasional explosions, people in panic. She's dressed plainly in trousers and a woollen coat and hat. She comes upon the van from the first scene, which is smouldering, the roof crushed. Through the window she sees Michal in the driver's seat, obviously dead. She struggles to pull open the door and his head falls gently into her arms. She looks at his bloody face a moment, then pushes him back inside, picks up a canvas bag from the seat, closes the door, and runs on.

It's 1949 in Paris and Beata is a translator in a publishing house. Crowded office, a number of small desks. She is still beautiful but plainly dressed, no items of elegance, a working girl, about age twenty-five. She speaks to her colleagues in French: Hello, How are you. The man from the quay scene comes to her desk, carrying a slender book in Polish. I'm Russell Purling from New York, he says in English. I'm told you know Czesław Miłosz. Forgive my pronunciation. He holds up the book: poems by Miłosz. Yes, I know Miłosz, she says, in a Polish accent, I think he's here in Paris now. Russell says, I want to publish him in English, and I want to take you to lunch. She replies, Miłosz you can have. Mais moi, you cannot. I have a boyfriend. Russell says, Not for long. Beata smiles.

Old Beata with her grandson, who is about nineteen, sitting in a restaurant in a quiet corner, white linen. She says, I have something for you, Michael, now that you're a man. He says, Am I a man? She says, When I was your age in Warsaw, I'd been in the underground for two years. I watched many boys become men. I think I can tell when it happens.

She passes him a manila envelope and he pulls out an Iron Cross medal, first class. You're interested in history, she says. It was around the neck of General von Hoppe. My Michal killed him in 1944. I kept it with souvenirs and put them out of mind, but it's time to get them out again.

Thank you, Grandma, Michael says, what should I do with it?

As you wish. Sell it, keep it. I want to be rid of all that at last.

Who was Michal?

You're named after him. He was my first love. He was ... very brave. I still dream about him. We did terrible things to survive, and for the country. Then the Russians – well, you know about the Russians. She is silent a moment, picks up her cutlery and says, You'd be surprised what you can do with a fork and a table knife. She sharpens the knife blade against the fork, sets them down, smiles at her grandson and says, Happy birthday, Michael.

Paris, outdoor restaurant, bright light, Russell with Beata in the green dress. He says, So you'll come to New York? She looks uncertain. He goes on, New York will be the centre of the world. Paris is finished.

What will I do there?

Translate. Choose books from Poland and France for my publishing house. Have beautiful children.

I'm a European.

So is half of New York.

Are you Jewish, Russell?

Does it matter?

Again she looks uncertain.

Warsaw 1944, waltz music. Beata and General von Hoppe are dancing in a supper club filled with German officers, a few men in business suits scattered around. The women are all good looking: it is a meeting place for adventurous Polish girls. Cut to Michal standing outside, smoking a cigarette, the music muted. Inside, von Hoppe leads Beata to a table. Champagne. I like it that you are Jewish, he says in German, Jewish women are more passionate.

My father's side, she says. According to the Talmud I'm not Jewish.

According to the Führer you are. He's smiling, teasing her: Behave, or I'll send you to, well, you know where.

She's not smiling. Will you do what I ask? he says.

What do you ask?

Ah, I don't know yet. We must see what I can think of.

Cut to exterior: Michal is gone.

New York, 1960, funeral parlour, Russell laid out in a coffin surrounded by flowers. Beata in black looking woeful and worn, now about age forty, holding the hands of a boy and girl, both under ten. A woman approaches them, takes Beata's hand and hugs her. He went so young, the woman says. Beata is silent. The 1940s dance music again, briefly. She turns her stoic face to look at Russell. Music again, briefly. Someone else approaches and shakes her hand.

Warsaw, Christmas 1945, dance music. Russian soldiers on the streets in the snow, drunk, celebrating. Beata is at the apartment window, afraid to go out. She finds the Luger, puts on the fur coat and hat and holds the pistol in a fur hand muff. On the rubble-strewn street the soldiers whistle, she hurries on. A car passes. She arrives at a brightly lit restaurant, is shown by a waiter to a private room. Two Russian officers are there, drinking vodka. What do you have for us, Beata, one says, in Russian.

I have information, colonel, about Nazi collaborators.

Where is the information?

She points to her head.

And what do you want for it?

Dollars, and an exit visa.

Dollars are easy. The visa – you may have to give more than information for that. Both officers laugh. The second one says, Are you prepared to give more? Beata smiles.

Le Havre 1950, from the stern of an ocean liner Beata watches the shore recede. Russell approaches and puts his arm around her. Jump cut to:

New York 1994. Old Beata sits in the same chair in the apartment, the Luger on her lap. Cut to:

Warsaw 1945, hotel suite. Beata completes dressing while the Russian colonel, in a red silk dressing gown, signs a document at a desk and gives it to her. She reads it and nods. She puts on the fur coat and hat, picks up the muff, and shoots him in the chest. He falls. The second officer rushes in from the bedroom, naked, and she shoots him, twice, in the crotch and in the head. Steps over the blood on the floor and leaves. The camera backs out of the room slowly and follows her down the corridor.   Pan to:

New York, 1965, door to Purling Publishers opening. Beata in a private office, *Russell Purling* on the desk plaque. She's on the phone, looking out the window. A secretary comes in, Beata signs some papers. On the phone she says, Yes, yes, we publish Albert Camus . . . no, we can't do that. Cut to:

Warsaw 1945, Beata walking back to the apartment. A Russian soldier shouts something at her from a few yards away. She turns to face him, takes one hand out of the muff and points the muff at him. He laughs, she smiles, turns, and continues walking.

Old Beata in the chair. She puts the Luger to her head and pulls the trigger. The gun clicks but does not fire. She opens the magazine and checks, replaces it, and pulls again. Click. Cut to:

Near Warsaw, Michal and Beata holding hands, skipping through the snow in the country, both laughing. Cut to:

Old Beata in the chair, the Luger on her lap, staring straight ahead.

*

- Allusive to the point of incomprehensibility. A war film without the war. – *New York Times*
- The best independent film of the year. – *Village Voice*
- Bring an airsick bag because it's so difficult to follow it will make you nauseous. – *New York Post*
- Beautifully photographed by Carlos Vargas, there is a delicate sense of absence to the visuals, as if the real story were happening off to the side, just out of reach of the camera's eye. – *The Guardian*
- According to Moran, men are corrupt and women are whores. The director thinks that a beautiful woman has no choice but to prostitute herself in order to survive, then to kill the men who abuse her. The world is misogynistic enough already; we don't need further encouragement. – *Toronto Star*

*

Dan had no experience of actors before he made feature films. Trained in social science, he was used to thinking of tribes or communities, not individuals, much less individuals who pretended to be other individuals. The human subjects in his documentaries belonged to the group under study. Even if they became self-conscious about their roles, they were ordinary folk who had nothing to do with the business of movie making. His transition to feature films proved easy in cinematic terms but actors were a foreign territory he never managed to map. He was an immigrant there. It's a commonplace in theatre and film to say that actors aren't like other people and shouldn't be expected to behave like other people, but Dan supposed the opposite. He asked actors to bring themselves to his films, to create their characters without his assistance in finding an inner life. He gave them words to speak, marks to stand on, told them what he thought the scene should convey, and left them to manage the rest. He didn't know how to guide them psychologically and didn't try; he assumed they knew their own business. He knew it wasn't as simple as that, that acting was dependent on a range of emotion and experience, both true and false, real and invented, that he had no desire to learn, but it helped him to simplify the process. His most common direction was: Stop acting.

His lack of exposure to actors also meant he had no immunity to them.

Irena Woznika was born in Cracow in 1962. Dan saw her in an unsatisfying French film called *Les Assassins de l'Amour*, playing the secret mistress of an obsessively jealous government minister. On screen she looked striking but distracted, long blonde hair and eyes that in close ups seemed unfocused. He met her by accident at a reception when he was in Paris for an award and knew right away he wanted her to star in his next feature, though he had little idea of what it might be. She looked straight at him with deep blue eyes that were intelligent and knowing and he wondered why she appeared so unsettled in the film. She was in demand in France for roles for beautiful women from Russia or Eastern Europe – her French and German were good, and all Poles of her generation had been forced to study Russian in school. She'd learned a colloquial form of English from American films; it was often incorrect and was heavily accented. She agreed to meet him the next day but proved elusive; her French agent couldn't locate her, and admitted she often disappeared, hinting at some trouble. These Poles, he said, very emotional.

She woke him at his hotel a day later, insisting they have breakfast. I'm here now, if you want me, she said on the house phone, without irony. At a café near the Bourse she ordered an English breakfast for both of them – eggs and sausages, toast, marmalade, *café crème* – and said nothing about missing their previous meeting. Dan rarely ate breakfast and felt nauseous when the plates came. She ate hers and most of his. Paris makes me ravenous, she said, it must be the air and, how do you say? The bustle. She pronounced the T. He didn't correct her, already following his directorial habit. She corrected his pronunciation, though, twice, for her home town, *Krakov*, and for her name, *Eeraina*.

In daylight she looked about twenty-six, and on film could pass for younger, though he knew from her agent she was just over thirty. She wore flat shoes and jeans and a sleeveless top, blue as her eyes. Her large face was without makeup, or it had been very artfully applied. In the sun on that warm spring day the lines around her eyes were visible. Laugh lines or worry lines, Dan thought, what you call them is a matter of preference. Her eyes were enormous and would fill up the screen. Her hair was thick, more golden than blonde, pinned carelessly in a bun at the back, her posture upright and slightly disdainful. She gave the impression, and he couldn't figure this out, that she was both slender and full bodied. She was open about herself, unpretentious, blunt. I don't know your films, she said, and I don't like America, what she does to the world, and that Hollywood, I hate, too much money, it ruins. You convince me, if you want me. You tell me about yourself, not cinema self, real self, then you tell me about script.

He told her. His life in Cincinnati, his mother's death, his father, his career as an anthropologist, his documentaries, the mountains of Peru and Ecuador, the madness of cities in South America. He talked about Carlos, the best photographer he'd ever seen, and how they were making a different kind of film, social and political but with images above plots. You don't have to worry, he said, I'm not Hollywood. I'm poor.

You are married?

She died.

Children?

He shook his head and looked away. Irena ordered two more coffees. They waited in silence. She lit a Gauloise, put it out after two drags. He watched her gestures, which were large without being showy. Her fingers were a little stubby, the nails short and unvarnished. He'd never seen an actor like her, full of life, unselfconscious, with an underlying sadness masked by grace. When the coffees came she said, I like you, tell me of this film, Roddy. Again he didn't correct her pronunciation.

It's a war movie, set in Warsaw. You play a resistance fighter who infiltrates the Germans.

How does she do that, sex?

Yes.

They always ask me to do sex roles, as if being beautiful were being one thing only.

You think you're beautiful?

Of course. How could I not know that?

This character – the woman is much more than beautiful. She is real, aware of herself in the world, very courageous.

What is her name, this woman?

What would you like?

I like Beata, the name of my mother.

I like it too, Dan said, from Latin, the blessed one.

So that's settled, Irena said, give the script.

It's not quite ready, he said, which was a serious understatement. I was waiting to finish it until I had the actor.

When will you have it?

Dan took a deep breath. Will Monday do?

Yes. But there is a problem: I can't go to Warsaw. She told a story.

She grew up in a Catholic family who were fanatic admirers of Pope John Paul II when he was archbishop of Cracow. Irena was a contrary child, she said, and hated the empty rituals of the Mass and the bombastic sermons condemning godless communism. Dan thought of his own high school speeches, ghosted by the Marxist Brothers, that did the same. When she was seventeen, in her final year of secondary school, she had an affair with an older man named Mateusz, an artist who was a notorious womanizer. He introduced her to the wide circle of painters and poets that populated Cracow, the old capital and traditional artistic centre of Poland. Her father was a lawyer held to low-level jobs because he once had criticized the Communist Party. Horrified by his daughter's behaviour, he arrived one midnight at Mateusz's studio, banged on the metal door until it was opened, pushed the artist aside, and dragged Irena home by the collar. She cried all the way, though she was secretly glad because Mateusz had begun to abuse her sexually. I was still a child, she said to Dan, and hardly understood what he wanted me to do.

Unfortunately, she was pregnant and was horrified to be carrying Mateusz's child. Defying her parents again, she had an abortion. Then she set her mind to work. Inside of a year she finished school, started acting in small theatres, and took up with a musician who played the double bass in the symphony orchestra and underground jazz clubs. She was soon recognized as talented, worked in two films within months, and moved to Warsaw with the musician, who had switched to an old Fender bass guitar for gigs in the fledgling rock scene. She refused to use his name. Him I have erased, she said. She continued to act until she became pregnant a second time, about eighteen months after the abortion. She was then twenty. I was very fertile, she said, and also naïve. He told me he was taking care of that.

His own career had faltered after leaving the Cracow symphony, and he was jealous of her success. He wanted her to stop working. She refused, and he struck her across the face with the back of his hand, cutting her lip. When he did it a second time, she left him and went home to have the child.

She lit another cigarette and again crushed it after two drags. Why do you do that, Dan asked. She shrugged her shoulders, then continued. Her lawyer father advised her to put the bassist's name on the birth certificate; in his mind that would create less stigma than leaving a blank. Adam was born in 1984, when Poland was a battleground between a lingering Stalinist government and the Solidarity labour movement. Popular demonstrations on the streets were met harshly and the secret police had informers everywhere. The country was headed toward collapse. Despite public unrest, Irena was happier than she'd ever been. Adam changed my life, she said, but not always for better.

The bassist learned he was officially the father and came to Cracow to see the baby and seek partial custody. Irena's father put him off but soon realized that his advice had been mistaken, since the law granted rights to a father, in or out of marriage. In the next few years the demands became intolerable, as the bassist sought some kind of stability amid the chaos overtaking the country. He had a dream of family life that Irena was not about to fulfil. He hired lawyers and threatened violence. Irena began to worry that he would abduct Adam. With her father's help she escaped to Paris with Adam in 1987 and developed a new film career. Six years later she still feared what the bassist might do, and refused to return to Poland.

Don't you worry he'll come here? Dan said. He must know about your film work in France.

He's bad boy with bad reputation. They won't give him passport and he has no money. I'm safer here.

She spoke about Adam, how good his French was, how good in his studies. She showed a photo of a boy of nine or ten, curly blond hair, blue school uniform, sailing a toy boat in the pond of the Jardin du Luxembourg.

Dan, half-listening, was recalculating the film. Can you go elsewhere in Europe?

Where?

I don't know, we'll have to look into it. We'll need stone buildings, snow. Belgium maybe, or Germany. Some scenes we can shoot in Paris.

Will there be German actors?

Definitely – it's a war movie. And maybe Russian.

You know Poles hate Russians.

Then we'll have you kill a few of them.

I'd like that, Irena said.

*

They shot the Warsaw scenes in late February in Aalborg in Jutland in northern Denmark. There weren't many stone façades but there was plenty of snow on cobbled streets. Carlos revelled in the challenge of snow light. Irena looked magnificent in white furs, cold, distant, implacable. Her white face, so different from Estrella's dark broodiness, shone with determination. In scene after scene she brought a killer's energy to the role. Dan and Carlos often worked until three in morning preparing for the next day. With only four hours of dependable light that far north, there was no time to waste. The indoor scenes were shot in the late afternoon when it was already dark. Everything was done in three weeks.

On the last night Dan took Irena to dinner at a picturesque restaurant in the centre of the old town. They ordered fish and it came quickly. They were drinking a bottle of Alsace wine that had a lovely green tinge in the candlelight and a slight acidic taste. Truth wine, Irena claimed it was called in Poland. Have you been avoiding me, she asked. She took her second puff of a cigarette and put it out. Dan was cutting his fish and said he didn't know what she meant, since they had been working together every day.

But you haven't come to me off location, she said. You are first director who not try to fuck me. Except for Dominique Clairant, and everybody but him knows he's the gay. Is that what you say in English, the gay? You're not the gay, are you?

No, I'm not. But mixing with the actors, that's not good. Makes everything too personal.

You prefer not personal?

He took time to chew and swallow. I prefer professional, he said.

Carlos I understand. He's the gay and knows it. Anyway, photographers, they're all voyeurs. Not excited unless through lens. He showed me his photos of Estrella. I think he was in love with her too. Very beautiful. Dark, delicate features. I am not your type, am I? Slavic jaw, blonde hair, big tits.

It's pronounced *Estreya*, her name. In Spanish.

You still think of her all time, that's what Carlos said. You've not been with a woman since, he thinks.

Well, it's not exactly his business, is it? Or yours.

She took a large swig of wine, ignored her plate and lit another

Gauloise. She was mocking him, an undercurrent running with anger. He suspected she was talking about something else, something she was unhappy about in the film, but he had no idea what it might be since she'd been so cooperative on the set. Look, he said, if you want to go to bed with me, I don't know why you would, this is not the way, talking about Estrella and my private life. And we still have another week of filming in Paris.

What's wrong with your, how you say in American, your noodle? Couldn't you relax, just one night? Just be Danny? Is that your real name, Danny? Danielito? He put down his knife and fork and stared at her. His impulse was to go before things got worse, but he was too polite to leave her sitting alone. And he still needed her, to finish the movie.

I wonder why people change names, she said, unhappy with themselves? It's preten-tee-ous, *n'est-ce pas*? Is that the word, preten-tee-ous? She grabbed a piece of bread and tore a morsel, balled it in her hand, and threw it across the table at his chest. She took her second drag and snuffed out the cigarette in her untouched dinner. The butt stood at an angle in the fish like the gnomon of a sundial. Not hungry, she said. Take me back.

Can I finish my dinner?

How can you eat after what I offer you?

What have you offered me, besides trouble?

Nienawidzę głupich ludzi, she said, and stood up. She made a fuss at the door about the white fur coat, which she'd borrowed from the set, along with the fur muff and hat, demanded a taxi, and was gone. Dan tried to eat but managed only a few bites before he paid the bill and walked back to the hotel slowly through the snow, making tracks all the way. Cincinnati came back, trailing home from school the winter after his mother died.

Put that out of mind. He wanted to think of nothing, look at nothing but the snow, and remembered the Wallace Stevens line, Nothing that is not there and the nothing that is.

Irena was sitting in his room with her fur coat and hat still on, shoes kicked off. Can I have coat to keep, she said.

It's rented, it costs thousands. You'd have to buy it.

It is your gift to me.

What did you say in the restaurant, in Polish?

I hate stupid men, is what I said. I'm always stuck with them.

You must attract them, then.

I didn't think you were so stupid.

I'm not stupid, I'm just slow. I'm tired, Irena. I don't want to argue.

She stood, more deliberately than when she left the table, turned toward the door, then turned back and opened the coat. Nothing underneath. She must have gone to her room first to undress. Dan thought of a clichéd scene from film noir in the forties, the femme fatale photographed from behind, holding her coat open like a flasher in the park, about to devour the witless hero. Irena was indeed both slender and full bodied, slim here, expansive there. He moved his eyes away, then moved them back. I am a cliché, he thought, the witless hero. The rest of the night was a cliché too: it's why Dan found porno films so boring.

*

When they returned to Paris Adam was gone.

Irena hated to fly and Dan accompanied her on the train from Copenhagen, which took almost twenty-four hours. They booked a private Wagons-Lits berth and entertained themselves. After his mostly celibate years of mourning, and faced with Irena's inexhaustible spirit, he felt like Little Skip at the plumber's picnic with Helen Leibold, without the interruption.

They arrived at her Paris apartment at about seven in the evening on a Monday, exhausted and happy, to hear the dreadful news. A Polish friend named Jana had been looking after Adam. They got on well, she said, no disagreements. In the last weeks they went to the park, he sailed his boat, he played with a friend. But that day he didn't come home from school. Jana waited a few hours, checked with all his friends, then informed the police. She was overcome with worry.

Most of the conversation had been in Polish, though Dan understood the gist. Irena seemed to enter a nearly catatonic state almost immediately – it was her constant nightmare, suddenly come true. Her shoulders were shaking, she couldn't stop them, she grew even paler. I should not have gone to Denmark, she said to Dan. It's your fault he's gone. You convinced me to take stupid part in stupid film. How could you do this to me?

Can you reach your father by phone, he said. See if he can find out anything about whatshisname, the bassist. I'll go to the police. I hope my French is good enough. He made sure that Irena was competent to telephone. When she reached her father, Dan left with Jana to speak to the detective who took the initial report.

His name was Pierre Gerard, a short man in a dark suit and red socialist tie. He was sympathetic but shook his head. It is difficult, he said, after only a few hours . . . He sat them down and explained how many times a week a young person disappeared. Usually they return, he said, then hinted darkly at North African gangs. We are on the alert, he said. Perhaps the boy is lost and will show up. We pray for that.

Irena was waiting for a call from her father, who had promised to use his legal contacts to investigate. Dan went to his temporary Paris office. Though it was late, Carlos was there, having flown back the day before, along with the local producer. They agreed they might have to delay the Paris shoot, which was due to start Wednesday. It could push them over budget, but Irena couldn't be asked to perform in her current state.

He was exhausted but went back to Irena's place. Her father had discovered that the bassist was in jail. He'd been arrested a week ago in one of the many demonstrations against the government and could not have been involved in a kidnapping. It would have been better if he had, for Adam at least would be safe. Now they were back to nothing, without a trace. Irena thought of the Roma. She hated the Roma and all Romanians too; they were dirty people, she said, not to be trusted. Dan said nothing about North African gangs. He wanted to go to his hotel but Irena insisted he stay with her. I have no one, she said, hugging him desperately. Jana slept on the sofa. Adam's bed lay empty. They were awake most of the night.

At eight o'clock Tuesday morning Detective Gerard arrived with Adam. The boy was cold and hungry but otherwise fine. He had wandered through the Jardin de Luxembourg on the way home from school, as he often did, and stopped to watch the toy boats on the pond. He'd been up late Sunday finishing his math homework and was tired, so he sat under a tree to rest and fell asleep in the late-afternoon sun. It grew dark, the attendants missed him in their sweep of the park, and he was locked in for the night. He was frightened and tried all the exits. He shouted and banged on the iron gates. No one came. He searched the entire grounds and convinced himself he was safe since there was no one else inside. He found a discarded half sandwich in a trash bin and the leavings of an orange drink in another. A pile of raked leaves against a stone wall was a bed; it was a mild March night. At dawn he waited at the gate. The attendant arrived and called the police.

The reunion was tearful. Dan had never met the boy and thought he was immune to such obvious emotions. He looked at Adam, a nearly helpless ten-year old, the age he was when Gert died. Dan was sure he felt older then than Adam seemed to be, but he was just as lost. He was overcome by an unexpected compassion for the boy, the boy in front of him in Paris and the boy behind him in Cincinnati. But Adam had his mother again. Dan thought he'd rid himself of self-pity, another miscalculation.

*

Irena insisted on maintaining the schedule. It will take my mind off Adam a little, she said. They shot the indoor scenes without delay, those set in Paris and those set in New York. She was gripping in them, especially at Russell's funeral, holding the hands of two children, her face made up to age her by ten years. The boy in the scene was played by her real son; she held his hand so tightly he cried out in one of the takes. Dan didn't understand how using Adam would take her mind off Adam, but she insisted on that too. She had the unfocused light in her eyes as in the French film that brought her to Dan's interest. She was physically present, her attention was in the moment, but some part of her was considering an elsewhere. Like a skittish gazelle at a water hole, aware of two spaces at once. The result was magnificent. It was a cruel thought but Dan was glad Adam had gone missing because it had deepened Beata's character in the film. He loved Irena's heavy accent when she spoke the English dialogue, how it carried the loss of her past, marking the character the way accents mark immigrants.

Against his principle he stayed with Irena most nights for the next two weeks, unable to keep away. When he woke one morning feeling guilty about betraying Estrella's memory, he knew he was in love again. He stopped wearing his wedding ring. He also grew fond of Adam, an intelligent kid interested in science. They had conversations about anthropology and Dan's work in South America, though Adam didn't speak English and Dan's French was halting. One time he unconsciously drifted into Spanish when talking about Peru. Adam stared at him dumbfounded. Tu parle en espagnol, Danielito, mon amour, Irena said.

When the time came for the New York shoot he didn't want to go. But the schedule was tight and the actors waiting. Irena kissed him as the taxi pulled up. What do I look like when I'm old, she asked.

I'll tell you when I get back, he said. I've only seen her head shot.

Do I have wrinkles?

Many wrinkles. Your skin is dry, your back aches, and I'm told you walk unsteadily. But you're rich.

And still in love with Michal from the war. How sentimental you are, Danny boy.

*

During the New York shoot Dan rang Irena many times. No answer, even at night, and her agent, Jean-Baptiste Duclos, didn't know where she was. When the crew returned to Paris to begin editing, Dan went to her apartment to find Jana cleaning the place. Irena had given up the lease and gone back to Cracow with Adam. Her father had been pressuring her to return after Adam's all-night adventure and at last she agreed that it was better to raise him with his grandparents and cousins. She left no note for Dan. Jana said she didn't have a phone number or address. Dan didn't believe her, but she held to her story. We have the spring scenes to shoot in two weeks, Dan said. Is she coming back for those? It's in her contract. Jana shrugged her shoulders like a Frenchwoman.

He visited Duclos the next day with the film's legal advisor. Your client is fucking me over, Dan said. I can't finish this project without her. Duclos insisted he had no forwarding address or phone. You better find her, Dan said, or you won't get the rest of her fee. And we'll sue you for breach of contract. I don't have to tell you what bankruptcy laws are like here.

Two days later the agent, after much searching, reached her on the telephone. She said she always planned to return and Duclos put up a bond as a guarantee. Dan demanded her phone number, but Duclos wouldn't give it. Don't you understand, Monsieur Moran, he said, she does not want to talk to you.

Dan thought she was in love with him, at least a little. He lost himself in work but he was uneasy all the time. Forget her, Carlos said. She's not worth the trouble. She's one of those women who have no soul without a man to show it to her.

But why can't she tell me what happened?

What happened is she got what she needed from you, some blood for her veins. She was bored, she wanted excitement.

I feel like she used me up, Dan said.

That's what she wanted to do, so you'll remember her. Not having her anymore, that's her insurance against oblivion. She thinks you would have dumped her soon, when you found out what she really is, so she beat you to it. She's already got another man, over there in Poland.

How do you know that?

I don't, but I know her.

Carlos, you have a low opinion of women.

It's not my opinion of women, Danielito, it's my opinion of her. Your problem is that you judge every woman in light of

Estrella. Nobody is going to come near that.

So what should I do, forget Estrella?

You'd better not, Carlos said.

*

I was a wreck. I was too upset to talk to you.

They were about to film the remaining scenes, Paris in the sunshine, and Irena was apologizing, in her fashion. She looked gorgeous in a sleeveless yellow dress in the early morning light along the quayside bookstalls. Goosebumps on her pale arms from the chill off the river. She shivered and wrapped herself in a cream-colored woollen shawl, which made her seem more vulnerable. How does she do that, Dan wondered, even a simple thing like covering her shoulders is heartrending. But he had set up stone walls against the siege of her battalions.

I was taking pills, she said. I needed help and you were in New York. I felt lost without you, then I realized Adam was the trouble, not you. He needs a father, and you weren't going to help with that.

I like Adam. Very much.

But you can't be father to him. You're too closed up for that. So I went back to Cracow. Jakub came to visit, we'll work something out.

Jakub?

Adam's father.

He has a name now? I thought you hated him. Now you forgive him?

Some things are more important than forgiveness.

Then you won't mind if I don't forgive you, Dan said. Can we get to work? I want to finish this stupid film.

It's not stupid film, it's wonderful film.

You called it stupid yourself.

Did I? I don't remember.

She looked hurt. But when they started shooting she was as magnificent as usual, and continued to be brilliant for the rest of the week. Her eyes were focused again, her mind clear, her face unaffected by anything outside the scene. When they finished, director and leading actor said goodbye, two professionals parting, no passion, no rancour. Dan wore his wedding ring.

11

Playing Soldiers. A film by Rody Moran. Ciste Scannán na hÉireann/BFG/Dutchtown Films, 2005. 93 min.

The camera is rocking gently; we see a blue lake but no shore, Lough Mask in County Mayo. We are in a rowboat with a middle-aged man, Mick, in tweeds and a soft cap, who is fly fishing, half-asleep. The sun is shining, the sky as blue as the lake with pure white puffball clouds. He sets down his cane rod, picks up the oars, turns the boat ninety degrees. Now we see a wooded shore. He ships the oars, retrieves his rod, and casts. Soft plop as the line hits the water and an immediate strike. It's a big trout, fighting hard, the rod bends, Mick kneels to keep the boat steady. He hears gunshots in the distance, little more than the plop of his line in the water, and looks up to see a group of IRA irregulars, variously armed, driving a troupe of British Black and Tans towards the water.

The British reach the edge and the Irish continue to advance, slowly now. The Black and Tans – there are six of them against the ten of the IRA Flying Column – walk into the water, to their ankles, to their knees, then stop and face the enemy. Drop your arms in the water, the IRA commander shouts, Hands up! The British obey. We stay in long shot, Mick's POV, as the irregulars then fire point blank. The Black and Tans fall into the water. Mick drops his pole in the boat and the trout breaks the line. The IRA commandant wades in, unholstering his sidearm. He checks the fallen men, fires a coup de grace into the head of one, then wades back to shore. A young irregular, Kevin Walsh, a boy of about seventeen, looks up at Mick in the boat, now about fifty metres from shore. Kevin holds the gaze a moment, then aims his rifle at Mick. At a harsh command from the commandant, he lowers the weapon and smirks. Medium shot on Mick's frightened face. Long shot on the column retreating, leaving the corpses rocking in the bloodied water. We follow as the soldiers march briskly into the hills. Kevin falls behind, shouts something indistinct, and peels off. The others continue and disappear into the trees.

It's May 1921, evening. A village pub, turf fire, oil lamps, shadowy interior, a girl (Sheila) behind the bar, two men chatting to her in low voices, Mick the fisherman at a corner table, his back to the camera, a pint of stout in his hand, barely touched. Two young men enter, laughing: Kevin and Declan. Kevin sees Mick and stops, smirks again, and cocks his finger and thumb toward him. The fisherman rises quickly and pushes past him, out the door. Mick, Sheila says, You're after leavin your glass.

Kevin says, I'll finish my Uncle's pint, Sheila, never worry, and laughs again. As he sits at the vacated table, the door bangs open and two more men enter: Reardon, in the uniform of the Royal Irish Constabulary, and a Black and Tan carrying a blackthorn shillelagh. In a Dublin accent

Reardon says, So, Kevin Thomas Walsh, you didn't get to the hills with your lads? And to the B&T, Is that two of them? In a tough Cockney voice, B&T says, Only one of them, and hits Kevin across the face with his shillelagh. Kevin falls from the chair, bloodied. The two men at the bar start to creep out but Reardon stops them. Kevin comes around with a shake of his head and says, Are you Irish, Reardon, or feckin English like this cunt? The shillelagh is raised again. No, no, Reardon says, not here. There'll be time for that. And to Kevin, I'm Irish enough. Youse people have still to learn ya won't get what ya want this way, they'll never give it ya.

Then we'll have to take it, the boy says, spitting blood.

Come along now, no more trouble. The intruders pull Kevin to his feet. Behind them Sheila says, Will you take a drink, Officer Reardon, afore ye go? Reardon turns and is saying, I'd not mind a small Power's, if – as she blasts him with a shotgun. The men quickly tie up the B&T and drag Reardon's body out the back. Sheila tosses a bucket of soapy water on the floorboards and begins scrubbing on her knees. Kevin has taken Reardon's handgun, holds it on the Cockney and says, Was it my Uncle?

I've nothing to say to you, you stupid Paddy.

All right with me, Kevin says, with a smirk.

A series of short scenes without dialogue, montage style but with slow editing rhythm, lasting a total of seven minutes, twelve seconds. No music, only a faint drum beat and naturalistic sounds. 1) Kevin, cleaned up and with new clothes, wearing a soft cap, a bruise on his face, sitting on a train in daylight, hard rain on the window; next to him is Sheila, her head in a tied scarf, a small case on her lap.

2) Kingsbridge Station, Dublin: Kevin is met by a man and Sheila by a woman, who escort them hurriedly down the platform, then move them separately into waiting cars. 3) Mick holding a tin mug of tea in front of a small turf fire in a plain cottage room; a knock on the door. 4) A mass meeting in a Dublin square, a speaker holding forth with large gestures on a raised platform in long shot; we hear only the drum, increasing in tempo and volume. 5) The Irish Tricolour flies over Dublin Castle; through an open window we see Kevin in a sergeant's uniform of the National Army (Irish Free State army), at a desk with a bottle of whiskey. The drum stops.

In the room, still shot from outside the window, Kevin is talking to Declan, also in uniform. Christ, Declan, it's not just you, they're letting me go too, mustering out thirty thousand, the lot of us. Youngest first. He pours a drink and offers one to Declan, who shakes his head. Kevin continues: Peacetime. The country's new and it's feckin broke. Declan objects that the soldiers created independence and settled the Civil War: They owe us more than what they're giving. Kevin: What they're giving will just about keep a man in drink. Declan: What will you do, Kevin? Close up on Kevin, no smirk.

Kevin walks unsteadily up Sackville Street at night, looks at the front of the GPO, staggers a moment, then turns towards Henry Street and enters a public bar filled with a rough crowd. He gets into an argument, makes a short speech about the betrayals of the Free State government. A punch-up starts, Kevin's nose is bloodied, he's dragged out the back door to a tiled toilet, knocked down and kicked. One of the attackers says, Don't ya have a mother to go home to? They all leave laughing. Kevin tries to get up and falls again, his head in the urinal. Water splashes down on his face.

A rooming house, Sheila cleaning him up with care, sitting on a narrow bed. This can't go on, she says. He lies down and falls asleep. She lies next to him, eyes open on the ceiling. Kevin snores.

Daylight, long shot, Kevin walking along Talbot Street, mournful uilleann pipes. A man in a flat cap comes up to him, puts his arm around him in a friendly way, and points to a shop across the street. They enter it, the camera follows them to the back. Another man, well dressed, starched shirt, green tie, is at a plain wooden table in a dim room and gestures for Kevin to sit opposite him. Over-the-shoulder shot. The man talks but the only sound is the tune played on the pipes. Kevin rises, the first man pushes him hard, back into the chair. Green tie stares at Kevin across the table, then looks at his helper and nods. The first man puts a large revolver to Kevin's temple. The music stops in mid-phrase and we hear green tie say softly, Your choice, Kevin Thomas Walsh, your choice.

Jump cut to Kevin on an American train. The conductor comes through the carriage, announcing, CINcinnati, CINcinnati, next stop the Queen City of CINcinnati. Kevin rises, looks grim, collects his gear.

Cut to Sheila sitting on the bed in the rooming house, alone, looking at her face in a hand mirror. She turns it sideways. Smiles slightly.

Walking camera into Kevin on a barstool in Donovan's saloon in Dutchtown, staring at the mirror behind the bar with bottles in front of it.

To Lough Mask, an empty rowboat riding high on the current near the shore. Uilleann pipes come up softly, then a bodhran, then a fiddle. Tempo quickens.

Fade.

*

From the *Irish Times* review by Fintan Flaherty:

There exists a long line of Americans who have come to Ireland to stake a claim on their roots. We see them wandering the Ring of Kerry every year starting on the 17th of March, looking cold and disappointed. There is a shorter line of English and Americans who come to tell us that we should be more Irish. Few have the courage of John Ford or David Lean or John Huston, to make movies that represent us better than we represent ourselves. None has had the blatant cheek of Rody Moran, a second- or third-generation Irish American (his real name is Daniel O'Daniel), whose ancestry is half German. Moran is an anthropologist and has come to Ireland to teach us our own history.

It is not a history you will recognize because it is told on the slant. Unlike Neil Jordan's Michael Collins *of a few years ago, this is not a big film on a grand scale. All the major events of Independence and Civil War are omitted. It is a short chamber piece, only an hour and half long, focusing on one man, a half-fictional IRA irregular from Mayo, who becomes a casualty of Independence . . .*

*

Churchfield is a hamlet about three kilometres south of the village of Tourmakeady in south County Mayo. It lies on the R300, a two-lane road that runs along the west side of Lough Mask. When the sun shines on the large lake, you'd wonder why anyone would ever leave the place. But they did, in masses, starting about 1846 with the Great Hunger and continuing well past Delia's day. County Mayo was nearly emptied. The land was too poor to support large families yet the families remained large. Even after the Famine Ireland had the highest birth rate in Europe; emigration was built into the equation.

Tourmakeady these days holds about a thousand souls. The nearest towns are Westport and Castlebar to the north, each about a half hour by car. Galway city is a bit more than an hour to the south. Churchfield itself is a collection of houses and farms spread along the road. With the help of the Family Research Centre in Ballinrobe, Dan found the birth dates of the children of James Moran and Mary Higgins of Churchfield, as registered in the Civil Records of Birth for the District of Cappaghduff, in the Superintendent Registrar's District of Ballinrobe, in the County of Mayo:

John (that's Seán the Mule), 6 April 1866

Ellen (Nellie), 2 February 1868

Catherine (Caty), 24 November 1869

William (Willie), 26 July 1871

Bridget (Delia), 8 January 1876.

There may have been other births, as Delia often said, but if so the babies died before registration. The British colonial administration was efficient but infant deaths were so common parents did not report them. The midwife, if she'd been called in time to witness a stillbirth, probably wouldn't insist. Sometimes the surname is written as Mowhan, sometimes as Moran or Morehan or Morahane. In a time when the majority of the population in the west was illiterate and used Irish as the first or only language, the spelling depended on the clerk's understanding of how the name was spoken to him.

In 1998 Dan was scouting locations for a new project. He

needed a European city with medieval buildings, crowded laneways, and a wide river, but the script was set in the future in an unnamed city and he couldn't use anywhere readily identifiable. Ireland was actively seeking film production and offered tax incentives, so he and Carlos went to Dublin for a look. In the end they couldn't make it work but it changed Dan's life. Unexpectedly, he fell in love. Not with a woman this time, but a place.

Why had he never gone before? He had plenty of excuses. He was busy in South America, had an academic career and a film career, and to him Europe meant looking at museums in Italy or communists in East Berlin. He made many trips to London but never crossed the Irish Sea. Have you ever been across the sea to Ireland, his father used to sing, but Skip had refused to go when his son proposed a trip together. He didn't want to see the poverty his mother had escaped, he said. For thirty years he'd listened to her stories of the bog, the water rising over the floor of the cottage. The stony potato field, the cut turf gone soggy.

One thing, then another, and two years later he decided to make a film about Delia. It was a strange decision. He had little more than a fogged-up glimpse of her passing in a large panorama. The process of immigration, its panic, its tedium, the empty sea, the hardscrabble of resettlement. She might stand for a whole time, he thought, the disruption brought by modernism and the twentieth century, the speed of living, the wars and displacements. A commonplace immigrant, one of millions upon millions, not one who made good or did bad, no Irish gangs or Italian mafia or brutish police or corrupt politicians. No rags to riches. But could an ordinary story bear that much weight? It had to be done on a small scale, a human scale, not a historic one.

What is more human than the places we live in, he thought.

He could start with the houses, to provide a way back to her life. He dug out Cincinnati census records and legal documents to find addresses and took still photos of the houses that survived, where she worked for German families on Dexter Avenue and Cleinview, both still there, and where she'd lived on Cohoon Street (one house pulled down, one standing). That was done in a half-day of driving around the city. He also shot places she would have known, Fountain Square (the Fountain had been moved), Carew Tower, De Sales Church, even Finnegan's Funeral Home, which still made him shiver. The inclines and streetcars are all gone, though the Suspension Bridge to Kentucky is still in use. The riverside was completely changed by Riverfront Stadium and then by its replacements, a new football stadium and new baseball park. He went to Over-the-Rhine to see Findlay Market where she shopped for the Dinkelmanns. He chatted to an elderly butcher who still made sausage the old way, as well as the headcheese the butcher called souse but Gert's German side called *schwartenmagen*. He took pictures of the empty house that had been Jaeger's butcher shop on Republic Street and of Doc Joe's former office on Vine.

Delia and James moved to Urine Av in 1926. Dan stood photographing in the middle of the quiet street and a black man of about twenty accosted him. Hey, man, what you doing? He was dressed well and about to get a car parked in front of the O'Daniel house. Dan explained that he'd lived there as a boy, born there, in effect. When was that, the man asked.

In the 1940s. Dan could see him try to take that in. I sold it to a man named Sayed Ali after my father died.

A Black Muslim, I remember him, the young guy said. My parents bought it from him six or seven years ago. Why do you want pictures?

Memories, that's all. I don't live in Cincy anymore.

There was no point in talking about movies. The street looked bright in September sunlight, the roadway resurfaced, the sidewalks repaired, the front yards mowed and planted with flowers. Many of the houses had been painted in two tones. It wouldn't be possible to use the house or the street in its current condition in a film about the past.

The street's changed for the better, Dan said. Do kids still sled down the hill in winter?

Hasn't been enough snow lately. The man paused a moment and studied Dan. That's a long time ago, he said. You don't look that old. Which room was yours?

That one in the front, on the left. Dan pointed to the second floor.

That was mine too, until I moved out for college.

It's a good room. Is the gaslight fixture still on the wall? It had been there since the house was built, before electrification. When DanDan was six he used to turn it on to smell the gas, until Skip wised up and disconnected the flow.

I don't know what that is, he said. You want to see inside? I don't think my mother would mind.

Dan wanted to go up to the attic – which now had enlarged windows on the street side, double-glazed – and look down at the backyard again, see Tommy Hertz and Charlie Wilson drilling the recruits in the army club, sit on the floor of his mother's closet, wrap himself one last time in her hanging clothes and her smell. But he'd be looking out the window with the wrong eyes, and her smell was dead. Best to keep the past locked up. Thanks, he said, the outside is enough. Good luck to you. They shook hands, roommates across time.

Dan didn't know how to use those photos. They seemed to

lead nowhere. At loose ends, tired of California, he went back to Dublin. Two projects had stalled and he wanted a rest. Property prices were rising fast but he had some cash left after he sold the little house in Northridge. As they say in Hollywood, he was between wives, and thought he might put the money in Ireland as well as anywhere. It wouldn't buy much but he found an artisan's cottage in Stoneybatter he liked, two up, two down, the agent called it. He learned he could apply for an Irish passport because of his grandmother and got the papers together, certificates of birth, marriage, and death from her on down. While waiting for a response he wandered around the city without much to do.

One evening he met a man in his thirties in a pub called the George. Dan didn't know it was a gay place until he saw the decoration. The man's name was also George, though Dan thought he was joking. He gave his name as Rody, said he was a filmmaker. Rody Moran, is it, George said. I heard you were in town. He knew and admired Moran's films. He taught drama at Trinity College and asked right away if Rody would run a course in screenwriting for theatre students.

He had taught before at the big film schools. Twice for a semester at NYU, where all the students wanted to be Scorsese. That was better, he thought, than his time at UCLA where everyone wanted to be Spielberg. Why don't you want to be the next you, Dan would ask, and the honest ones replied there was no money in it. And none in being Rody Moran either. But in Dublin the students were a different breed. They'd seen a lot of films but knew little technically, so teaching was freer – he could start at the beginning without hearing groans. The first assignment was to write a short radio play. They thought this strange but saw the point when the next week he asked them to make it a short screenplay without dialogue or words of any kind, spoken or written on screen. Going from all words and sounds to all images shocked them. He was giving away his own secret; he thought that's what teaching should be.

A student in the class named Kieran Kilbane came from a little place in County Galway, near the Mayo border. Dan was chatting to him after a Thursday class about a scene he'd set there, two old geezers sitting in a car waiting for a third one to show up. Derivative Beckett, one of the Irish diseases, but he'd used the landscape in an interesting way. Dan mentioned his grandmother's origins, and that he'd just received notice of Irish citizenship. I know Lough Mask well, Kieran said. We used to fish for trout there in a little rowboat. It's a beautiful place.

I've never seen it, Dan said.

Ah, you should, so. I'll take you there, if you'd like. You have a car? We can go to my parents' gaff and then to your family home.

It had been so long in Dan's mind it had become mythical, a place to be dreamed rather than seen, a dim vision of Delia's, a memory more than a century old. Now it was only three hours away. I could rent a car, he said.

They left Friday afternoon, met Kieran's parents, who gave them a high tea of chips, egg, and bacon. Dan spent the night in a little B&B nearby, had breakfast of chips, egg, and bacon, and Saturday morning they were on the shore of Lough Mask. It was, as the Irish say, fairly lashin'. In other words, pissing rain. They could barely tell the water of the lake from the water on the windscreen. The wipers couldn't keep up, even when the car was stopped.

They drove on to Tourmakeady, found a little café, and got soaked going the few feet from the car. It was warm inside and the windows were fogged, masking a dreary street of a few shops and a pub. Dan tried the coffee and was sorry, switched to tea, which at least was hot. Kieran was eating chips, egg, and bacon and started to say something – Dan could tell it was going to be one of those Irish silver-linings. He put his palms out to stop the young man from continuing. After an hour they were about to give up when the rain cleared, as smartly as it had started.

On the shore of Lough Mask they watched the storm move along the water toward Ballinrobe. It was still drizzling but Kieran had a hat and said he'd walk along the lake a bit while Dan looked for his relatives. Even then he hesitated. He'd always hated the idea of the returning Irish-American, searching for cousins many times removed as if they were lost brothers. People who were strangers pretending that an ancient bloodline actually meant something. But he did want a photo of Delia's birthplace, and there was only one way to get it. In the diary Uncle Liam had kept, which Dan in turn kept for thirty-five years, he found two Moran families listed in the village. He started with the one directly opposite the lake, walked up the stone path, and knocked on the door.

*

Let me get this right, she said. Your name is Moran, or it is not? They were in her modern kitchen in a modern two-storey built next to the old house, directly across the road from Lough Mask. She was a Moran herself, and married to a Moran. But not related, she added. Some time ago related, maybe. Her husband was from Castlebar and died young, ten years ago, a fishing accident on the lake. She looked about forty herself, in good shape if a little stocky, clear skin, warm smile, intelligent eyes. Red hair like Aunt Peg, perhaps touched up. She was called Carmel and it was her father's property before her. Her father and grandfather were both named Seán Moran, so she was the great-granddaughter of Seán the Mule. Sit there, she said, I'll wet the tea.

She had welcomed him when he gave his name as Rody Moran from Cincinnati. When he tried to explain the relationship, she got a little confused. It's like this, Dan said, I'm the grandson of Delia who went to America with her sisters. Seán the Mule was their brother, and he'd sent them on their way. She married an O'Daniel there, my father was their son. My real name is Daniel O'Daniel.

You're the movie fella, DanDan?

God, he thought, even in Ireland. I use Rody Moran professionally, he said. My passport still says O'Daniel. Who told you?

Somebody called Murray. I think he was a descendant of one of the sisters.

The one called Nellie. The other was Caty. They were older than Delia. Am I in a long line of returning Morans?

No, no. You're maybe the third since I got the house, all from Cincinnati. I even learned to spell it. She counted it out on her fingers, the chant Dan learned at De Sales school, C-i-n, c-i-n, n-a-t-i. So you're a kind of Moran. But why Rody? That's not a name from around here.

He explained that his great-grandfather was Rody O'Daniel from Tipperary, and Dan was to be called Roderick. Delia wouldn't have it, it was the wrong name, Rody is not Roderick, she said, and they chose Daniel instead. Maybe they thought Daniel O'Daniel was clever. My mother went to the court house and changed my birth certificate by hand.

So you've gone back to what they intended, Carmel said. And you're living in Ireland too.

Odd, isn't it?

So many of us escaped.

The rain was coming down hard again. The window was battered by wind from the lake, and Dan suddenly remembered poor Kieran. He found the lad sitting patiently in the car, completely soaked and shivering. It looked like he'd fallen in the water. Dan needed to get him home, so went back to Carmel and arranged to return the next day. I'll be at Mass at ten, she said. Why don't you call in for lunch at half one? Sunday joint? You bring the wine.

She organized a party of Morans. There were three families in Churchfield and two from Tourmakeady, including her son Séan and his wife. Her big kitchen table was crowded with Dan's distant relatives, all Morans or married to Morans. The weather had turned fine and children were inside and out. Everybody was younger than him except one auld fella who claimed to have been to Cincinnati when he was young and met Liam Moran as well as Delia. His name was Luke and if he was telling the truth, it would have been when little Dan was eight or nine and he'd have to be close to eighty himself. Ach, Liam was famous hereabouts, so, he said, and the old folks thought he'd been hard done by, by the Free Staters, hard done by.

Dan wondered whether repetition was a genetic characteristic. He was very good to me, Dan said, and told the story of the Easter Rising proclamation. They were astounded and eager to know what happened to the document. Dan said he kept it for many years in a bank and put it up for auction three years ago. He wanted it to come back to Ireland, but no Irish museum was willing to bid. It went under the hammer in New York to an Irish-American businessman whose name was not revealed.

What's he doing with it, Carmel asked.

He's a collector. I guess he looks at it.

Ah, then, lad, Luke said, you're on the pig's back yourself, are you? On the pig's back.

It's true it went for a high sum, ridiculously high. The money's invested in my film company's name and it's all going to finance a new movie about Uncle Liam. That pleased them enormously – Dan was a fine fella, a true son of the land, a Moran through and through.

What's your company called, Luke asked.

Dutchtown Films. Dutchtown was where my grandmother lived.

It was there I met Liam, Luke said, in Donovan's saloon, I think.

It was more or less where he stayed, Dan said, until he sobered up and married a German widow. Everybody laughed again. Just hearing the name Liam Moran seemed to please them.

Flushed with the food and the wine and the warmth of the room, Dan was accepted as if they'd been together there all their lives. Blood meant something after all. He wanted to believe in the power of connections, that being a descendant of the Morans of Churchfield made him a Moran of Churchfield. Here on the ground of his peasant ancestors, could there really be a belonging, a line of formation, defining himself? It was a dream of his childhood, activated by his mother's death and Delia's stories, the old language, the worn stones of the path to the lake, and the back-breaking toil and hunger that sent her to a distant land.

But he didn't feel at ease. He sensed something false about it. The jollity of cousins seemed superficial, acceptance too easy. Under that was another truth he didn't share, because it was only at that moment he realized he wanted to make a film about Liam instead of one about Delia.

*

People in Ireland called him Rody. He bought one of the new digital cameras, simple enough so he could operate it himself, and came from Dublin to Mayo most weekends to photograph the scenery. He'd kept the old Brownie as well and liked to use it for stills – there was something beyond nostalgia for him in its pictures, something cleaner and more direct than video or photographs through sophisticated lenses. The 620 film was no longer available so he had a studio in LA manufacture some for him and mount it on old spools. He filmed Delia's birthplace, the little cottage to the rear of Carmel's house that was now a storage shed for old farm implements. Two rooms, not large enough for the family that lived in them for so many years. Plaster crumbling with moisture, stone fireplace half collapsed on itself. He started here, one side of him anyway, and he was back without any new insight or understanding. He felt little emotion at seeing the room she was born in. Lucky to escape when they did, those three girls. Houses would never have provided the framework for a film. Houses are objective, callous in the way they outlive their owners. They give up nothing of the occupants whose breaths and deaths they contained.

He sent some DVDs to Carlos, video he shot of Lough Mask, the villages around it, the wild coastline of Connemara, the vertiginous cliffs dropping harshly to the Atlantic, sea spray blowing in his face, wetting the lens. Back in Peru for his father's funeral, Carlos was enthusiastic about the Liam project and longed to confront the Irish light. The money from the Easter Rising proclamation was ready, other funders were ready. Carmel found a house nearby that Dan rented and he began to write the script. He knew he could cast in Ireland; he'd seen good actors and a few almost great ones on stage in Dublin who were eager for film work. He'd selected a fine young man for the main role.

When Carlos arrived with the advance team they set up in an empty church hall in Tourmakeady. Dan's writing had been slow – it was always slow – and he often walked along the lake in the evening to reflect on what he'd managed to get down during the day. He gave Carlos a room in the house and soon they were strolling together, talking about the script, the locations, the light. Sorry about your father, Dan said. They had stopped by a little inlet, mud all around it. He hadn't come that way before and didn't know how to cross it.

He went before his time, Carlos said. Is that how the Irish put it?

My grandmother would say, He got ahead of himself in what he wished for. I think it's a translation from Irish. How's your mother?

She looks old. She says hello. My sister is there. Brother is staying for a while before he goes back to Caracas. Carlos was more contemplative than usual. Damp air slows everything down.

I was in LA for a week after Lima, Danny.

I remember.

You know they let him out?

Who?

José Martinez.

Who's that?

The truck driver, Carlos said. He was in jail eighteen years. The judge hit him hard because his license had expired. Also the truck's permit. And he's Mexican. Reckless endangerment. Culpable manslaughter. I don't even know what that is.

Dan didn't want to hear any of this. In two decades it was the first time they'd mentioned the accident.

You sound sympathetic.

No, I'm angry. I want to kill him. Don't you?

Anger changes nothing. Killing him wouldn't either.

Yes, it would. He'd be dead like her and we'd be alive.

A killing for a killing, the ancient way. They were in the land for it, making a movie about it. They turned around and walked to the house in silence.

Dan hadn't even known the name of the driver. José Martinez. Poor bastard.

*

They hired a producer from London, a man they both trusted, who brought almost everything from England by ferry: actors' trailers, canteen wagons, lights, giant film trucks with their own crews. They overran the village; Connemara speech mingled with English voices. Some residents carped at the number of English working on a film about Irish independence. That war is never over, Dan thought. Shopkeepers were surly, but the publicans were happy.

The actors were arriving, filming was about to start, but in Ireland rain is the scheduler. They planned to shoot outdoors when weather permitted and have the interiors ready for when it didn't. The scene in the pub would require many takes; getting the light right was likely to use half a day. Carlos was experimenting with gels and lens filters and reflectors but hadn't solved it. Dan was always calm on the set and spent much of the time chatting informally with Cathal Driscoll, who was playing Kevin, trying to keep him relaxed. The lad was only nineteen, red hair, freckled, fresh-faced. Hot-headed, that's the key, Dan said. He has no idea from one moment to the next what he'll do. Doesn't think one action leads to another or has consequences.

That was more direction than he usually gave. The actor was respectful, called him Mr. Moran, and more than a little frightened. It was his first major film role. Dan had seen him in a small part at the Gate Theatre in an adaptation of Peer Gynt. They were rehearsing the pub scene. Carlos wasn't satisfied.

Carmel invited them to dinner that evening. Just the three, she said to Dan, two Morans and your shadow. When they arrived Dan asked to show Carlos the cottage at the back. Carmel moved a rake out of the way and unlocked the door. My father once told me, she said, Séan the Mule wanted to add a room after he got married, but the landlord wouldn't allow it. So it stayed the same. His son managed to buy the property at last, when the English were getting out after independence. Instead of an addition he built the new house, and my father added more rooms to that.

And now you have it, Carlos said.

And my son after me.

I've seen a number of plots like this in the west, Dan said, new houses next to the old.

It's the way we do it, keep the old things. Memory of what little we were.

Dan ran his finger along the damp plaster wall, leaving a mark. Decaying memory, he said.

Memory all the same, she said.

At dinner they talked of the movie, how long it would take to finish in the west, then more filming in Dublin. We'll do a rough cut in Dublin, Dan said, see what we have. We'd come back here if Carlos wants to reshoot something. He usually does.

Light plays tricks, Carlos said. Especially this light on the lake. I need to see the whole thing and make sure we have enough footage.

Where will you go after that, Rody?

After Dublin we go to LA for the major edit. Add the music and sound. Premiere at Cannes, I think, then Dublin. You'll be invited.

Your house in Dublin – will you keep that?

I like it there.

Carlos had brought chocolates. Carmel made tea. I went to Galway yesterday, she said. I stopped at the library and looked you up in the reference books, both of you. You've done all your filums together?

All the feature films, Dan said. How many, Carlos?

Twelve, I think. This one should be number thirteen. Most of the documentaries too.

The books there, they say Carlos was born in Peru, but there's no mention of a family for either of you.

Carlos looked at Dan, then said, I'm not married. I'm gay.

Are you? I wouldn't have guessed that.

It was impossible to tell if she was being ironic. There was so much Dan didn't know about her, about the west, about Ireland. He was making a film about things he couldn't possibly understand.

And Rody, she said. No family for you?

Danny's wife was killed in a car accident years ago.

I'm sorry. You had no children before?

The question echoed down the halls of Dan's life, all the way back to his mother. He the only child of her loins and, as far as he knew, of his father's. It would end with him. No, he said, we didn't have children.

A shame. Children – they change everything. What was her name, your wife?

Estrella, Dan said. She was Mexican. It means star.

The most wonderful woman I've ever met, Carlos said.

And she was killed in an accident?

Carlos said, I was driving.

She had no response to that.

It wasn't his fault, Dan said.

It had taken him a long time to say it.

*

As midsummer approached, good light lasted until eleven. A diffused glow in the western sky even after midnight. One warm evening Dan went to the pub for dinner and stayed late talking to the publican, whose name was Pete O'Donovan. Dan told him about Donovan's saloon in Dutchtown where Liam wasted his time. Pete was excited about the film. Will you be using local people in it, Rody, he asked. Dan said they had already put out a call for extras. They needed young soldiers but no one wanted to play the Black and Tans.

When he left the pub he saw that murky clouds were spreading over Lough Mask, spoiling the fine evening. He went along the path anyway, as a soft rain began to fall. There was no moon, though the surface of the water picked up some of the residual light of the sky. He thought he saw a rowboat on the water, close to shore near a clump of trees. He wasn't sure – from the distance in the mist it looked like a dream. He heard a splash and saw the outlines of two men standing in the shallows, guiding the boat to land. They seemed to be unloading something, though he couldn't make out what it was. It was long, wrapped in a canvas tarp, one corner dangling. It seemed heavy. Silence except for the lapping of small waves on the stones of the shore, got up by an increasing wind. Suddenly one of the men shouted Shite! The sound carried across the water and his companion gave a sharp shush, almost as loud. What were they doing so late? Dan could see the two figures, shadows, carry the object between them, about the length of a man, and put it behind the trees some thirty paces from shore. The taller of the two returned to the boat, pushed it out, and rowed away towards Ballinrobe, just dipping the oars. Dan could hear their delicate splash. A creak of resistance from the oarlocks. The other man seemed to have disappeared behind the rocks.

It rained heavily in the night. In the morning Dan went to the clump of trees, still dripping in the weak sun, but could find no trace of what he saw. No object, no tarp, no footprints in the soft earth by the water's edge. Could he ask anyone about it? There might be danger of some kind; it was obvious he was not supposed to have seen it. If he saw it. He hadn't any idea what obligation an outsider like himself would have. He could go the Garda station in Castlebar and report it, but what would he report? If something suspicious going on, it would hardly be to his advantage to get involved in the middle of the shoot.

He brought it up with Carmel in passing, She looked a little worried. Are you sure of what you saw, she said, and Dan admitted he wasn't. Best to forget it then, I reckon. If there was anything, probably it was fishermen. Maybe they used a net or something not allowed and were sneaky about it. Dan knew it wasn't fish, but he let it drop.

That evening old Luke came to his door. He blathered while he sat with a glass of Jameson but as he was on the step leaving, poised between in and out, he finally mentioned what he'd come for. Carmel told me, she did, that you may have seen something t'other night.

It was dark and raining, Dan said, I'm not sure what I saw. Two men, a boat, maybe a long thing brought ashore.

You could be mistaken, then, could you not?

I saw something. What it was or what it means I can't say.

You'd probably be mistaken then, don't you think?

Could be, Dan said. I'm often mistaken.

I'd let it go, then, if I was you, let it go. He turned to leave.

I'll see you past the goose, Dan said, as my grandmother used to say.

She would say that, sure, from around these parts. They strolled together to the crossroads. I like your *geansaí*, Luke said. That jumper was knitted around here, I'd say.

Dan was wearing a heavy Aran sweater, made in the traditional style. I bought it in Sligo last year. It's good for this weather and the damp house.

For the fishermen, Luke said, in the old days the women would knit personal designs for their men. They could use the jumper to identify a body when drowned. You might not tell from the face, you see, after it being in the water a time with the fishes. A fair night to you.

Dan walked to the lake. Again no moon. He wandered for an hour or more along the shore. As he turned toward his house he saw the boat on the lake again. He was sure of it. Though it was a clear night, the boat and the two men in it, seemed surrounded by mist or fog. They weren't moving, just rocking gently on the water, as if waiting. They faced each other from opposite ends of the boat. The rower was held frozen in place. There was a splash from the water – a fish leaping?

He woke with a start. He was in his pyjamas under the covers but didn't remember going to bed. The clock read three in the morning. He was wide awake now. He got up, made tea, looked at the shooting script. We'll have to film from a boat with a Steadicam for the scene at the lake's edge, he thought, when the IRA fire at the Black and Tans. He felt physically tired, as if he had rowed a return journey to Ballinrobe.

Back in bed he lay awake a long time. When near dawn he did sleep at last, he had his regular nightmare, his visitation, he called it. For twenty years it had come the same way. The camera dollies in from above to the rear window of a car traveling fast on the dark freeway, empty of traffic. Estrella in the passenger seat with blood on her lap, holding a tiny baby covered in blood, rocking it and cooing. The camera pans left to see that Dan is the driver. His face is bloodstained, a long gash across the cheek. The screen goes black.

12

The Button Moulder. A film by Rody Moran and Carlos Vargas. Dutchtown Films/Norske Fond for Kino, 2015. 105 min. Music by Edvard Grieg.

Petra Gundersen is in her office on Wall Street. She is an attractive woman of about fifty, tall, commanding presence, dark hair, blue dress, high heels, slight Scandinavian accent. I don't care how risky it is, Benny, she says to an underling, do the trade now, in next three minutes. By the end of the day you'll see I'm right.

She picks up the phone and says, Sandy, cancel my lunch appointment and get me a sandwich. Shot of a busy trading floor, Benny punching a keyboard. In the office, Sandy enters, a young man, deferential to his boss. He hands her a sandwich, an airline ticket, and a US passport. Eight PM from JFK, he says, SAS to Copenhagen, then to Bergen.

Petra is wolfing down the sandwich while checking a computer screen. Sandy says, Take some photos for me. I've always wanted to go to Norway.

Whatever for?

It's romantic, isn't it, mountains and fjords. No response

from Petra and Sandy says, How long has it been for you?

Forever, Petra says. Tinkling piano, Grieg's Norwegian Dance No. 2 (opus 35).

On the plane, first-class bed with sheets, Petra lies on her back, eyes open. Across the aisle an older man is sitting up with a book, lit from above by the reading lamp. He is thin, his face lined, prominent nose, dark circles under his eyes, bony hands. He casts a furtive glance at Petra, returns to his book. In a sudden jolt of turbulence, a serving cart breaks loose and crashes into Petra's bed, hits her on the forehead. She cries out, touches the wound. A little blood on her hand. She seems to faint, her eyes close. The man across the aisle watches. Petra's eyes open wide.

Petra looks tired in the airport, a little bandage on her forehead. A driver with a sign meets her. In Norwegian she says, My brother?

The driver says, He couldn't come.

Inside a black Mercedes, he says to her in the backseat, The fast way or the scenic way?

The scenic way, she says, and stares at the cold light outside. They drive along the edge of a cliff overlooking a fjord. An old red car is parked on the road and forces the Mercedes to stop with screeching tires. A man stands next to the red car, looking at the scenery below. The Mercedes eases around his car. He turns: it is the bony man from the plane. Petra looks at him as they move away. Who is that, she asks the driver.

Never seen him before, he says.

Interior, night, Petra sits with her older brother Kurt in a room with antique furniture and many lit candles. You live alone now, she asks, since Åse died? And your children?

Scattered, he says, Stockholm, London, Canada. Sometimes they come for Christmas.

They're drinking brandy, it's late, she's falling asleep.

Why have you come, sister, after so many years?

To collect my inheritance, brother.

He laughs harshly. You're much richer than me, out here in the wild snow. What do you need you haven't got?

She looks around the room, then at him. I thought I'd stay a while.

How long?

She doesn't answer. The camera closes tight on her face. There is an old scar near her left eye. Sound track: very brief burst of a baritone singing a phrase from *Jeg elsker dig* (opus 5, no. 3).

In the morning Petra is dressed warmly, walking away from the house. Soundtrack: Norwegian Dance No. 4, orchestral version. Long shot: light snow on the ground, moderately sized house, two stories, steep roof, isolated on a rise. In front is an open space leading to the edge of a fjord, a forest behind. She walks with purpose to a forest path, past a small hut that looks abandoned. In a clearing she sees the bony man, who is wearing a small knapsack. The light becomes unreal, both sun and mist. Why are you following me, she says sharply.

I've been waiting for you, he says.

Do I know you?

Probably not, but I am expected. They call me the Button Moulder.

That's ridiculous, she says.

Yes, it is a bit, but it's me all the same.

Get out of my way, she says, and pushes past him.

I'll see you soon enough, he says. She marches on.

Out of the forest she comes to a village and enters a café, a cosy small room. Soundtrack: opening of In the Hall of the Mountain King from *Peer Gynt* Suite (opus 46, no. 4). I heard you were back, the owner says, a man of Petra's age with a smudged white apron and thinning hair.

Do I know you, she asks.

I'm Kai, from school.

Kai Pedersen?

He brings her coffee and sits. Everybody knows about you, Kai says, the famous financier from Trollheimen. How far you've gone. We thought you'd forgotten us.

She drinks her coffee a moment, then says, And Frode? How is he?

Liver trouble. Drinks. He was engaged to a girl years ago but she ran off with a troll. Did him in.

Troll?

You know, a bad boy.

I'm sorry, Petra says, I liked him. He was my –

Did you think he'd wait for you? Things change. He never made anything of himself. Then, neither did I. This is my kingdom, where I serve the trolls. He lights a joint.

Isn't that illegal?

They can fuck off, he says.

POV Petra, quick flash of Kai with elf ears. She blinks her eyes. Hold close-up on her. Tell me something, Kai says. Over there, in America, New York, do they accept you? As one of them?

I never thought about it, she says, I suppose they do. Nobody seems to care.

Close-up on Kai, still with elf ears, who says, We don't get all those black immigrants they have in Sweden. We **do** care, if a person is one of us.

So not everything changes, she says.

Two-shot, his ears are normal. Kai says, Remember when we dropped acid, you and me and Frode?

She points to her eye and says, Still have the scar you gave me.

You moved your head and made my hand slip.

What were you thinking?

Told you, I was making a tiny slit in your eye. People say it's what the trolls used to do. Makes you see the world differently. On the slant. Did it work?

She doesn't respond. He takes a small knife to her face. I could do the other eye.

Get away! You're still crazy. She gets up and takes out some money.

On the house, Kai says. She shrugs and drops a few coins to the table. He throws them back at her; they hit her chest and drop to the floor. Take care on the way, Petra Gundersen, he says.

It's dark in the forest. Soundtrack: opening of Violin Sonata No. 3. She takes a flashlight from her coat pocket, swings the light around, finds the Button Moulder sitting on the ground, his back against a tree, holding a document. We have some business, he says, I'm to collect you tonight.

What do you mean?

He holds out the paper. You are Petra Gundersen, aren't you? She starts off but he blocks the way. He takes out a large ladle from his knapsack. You're to go into my casting ladle. That's what it says here.

What?

To be melted, to make shiny new buttons. That's the Button Moulder's job. We don't like to waste anything. To put it politely, when your soul is really tarnished, off you go into the ladle here with the others, everybody all mixed up, to make a stronger alloy.

I never heard anything so stupid. Souls aren't buttons. You can't put me in there. Anyway, I'm not old, it's not time.

What difference will it make? You've never been anything anyway. All the things you've done, what difference did they make?

They made a difference. I'm Petra, I worked hard, I'm not some failure like the people around here.

Oh, free will, he says, and taps her head with the ladle handle. That's just another illusion she puts in there to keep things running.

She? Who's that?

Or he, if you prefer. You've gone on believing you're you, but there's no you, just more meat for the sausage machine. I melt you down and use you over, that's the real contribution you make.

You're saying the soul doesn't exist.

I'm saying your soul doesn't exist. You're not a saint but you're not a great sinner either, so in the ladle you go.

I'm known all over the financial world. You can't say I'm nothing.

He stands still as she runs away. We'll meet again, he says.

Petra enters the house, out of breath. In the dim hallway Kurt says, Frode came by.

You know him?

He used to work for me. Caretaker.

I met my old friend Kai, she says. He said Frode is sick.

He's in bad shape, but I let him stay on. In that little hut at the edge of the woods. She has taken off her outer clothes and follows him into the living room. Even more candles than last night, a log fire.

So many candles, she says.

They chase away the dark, Kurt says.

I don't see how you stand these black winters.

Dark makes us appreciate the light.

Petra says, So many memories here, more than the candles, it's oppressive.

The dregs of memory stay in the glass.

You're full of epigrams, brother. They are in the positions of the previous evening, now drinking red wine. Do you believe in the soul, she asks.

He pauses a long time, toying with his glass. Then he downs it and says, The self is the soul. But the self, you can't know it. Better to kill it, then you're free. Dinner?

Morning, bright sunlight. Soundtrack: Morning Mood from *Peer Gynt* Suite (opus 46, no. 1). She walks without coat or hat to the hut, knocks, enters. Music ends abruptly. Frode, an old man, unshaven, dimly lit on a cot, lifts his head, smiles. You've come, he says. She goes to him, finds a cloth, wipes his sweaty face. Water, please, he says. She gets a glass, fills it from a pitcher, helps him drink. He lies back, smiles again, strokes her hair.

In a single take, the camera, dolly mounted, pulls back slowly out the door, then leaps up quickly in long shot. Opening bars of Piano Concerto in A minor (opus 16), very dramatic music, loud. The Button Moulder is at the edge of the woods. He walks slowly to the hut, knocks on the door. He pauses, then pushes it open and stands at the entrance, waiting. The camera, still in the same long take, looks past him to Petra sitting by the bed holding Frode's hand. Music blends into a reprise of Norwegian Dance No. 2, lightly on piano. The final shot is held fifteen seconds, then the piano bounces up over the credits.

*

They're not skipped beats, the doctor said, though everybody calls them that. Actually they're early beats, before the heart has filled with blood. A problem with the electrical current. So there's a delay before the pumping catches up, and then you get a strong beat.

Dan was in the office of a consultant cardiologist at Saint James's Hospital in Dublin. Ever since the Mayo project he'd suffered increasing arrhythmia. Dr. McFoyle was in early middle-age, greying temples, a look of detached concern, strong Cork accent. Half glasses hanging from a red neck cord. The heart's just a pump, he said, it's a mechanical thing. Pretty amazing thing, really, but sometimes it goes out of control.

When it happens it's jumping around in my chest, Dan said, like it's trying to get out of its cage.

Let's make sure it doesn't. I'll give you some meds. Cut down on the alcohol and coffee. Stress and anxiety, they'll be bad for you, sure.

I'm in a stressful and anxious business.

Yes, I guess so. You can get dressed now. While he wrote the prescription he said, I liked your Irish film. That boy – a fine actor. He sounds like a Mayo lad. What's his name?

Cathal Driscoll. He's from a middle-class family in south

Dublin. Good ear for accents.

Did it do well, the movie?

It won awards and lost money. Critics said it wasn't spacious enough. It was meant to be a small film, a bit quirky. When you have a big subject like Irish independence, I guess people want an epic.

I wouldn't think you'd read the critics.

I don't, but they're so loud I hear them anyway. They say that no matter what the subject, I always make the same film.

Is that true?

Maybe.

I thought it was a real work of art.

Did you?

You don't?

I don't know, Doc. I'm not sure what art is.

Dan took the prescription and they shook. McFoyle had a big, fleshy hand and a strong grip. What's next?

We're in Norway this winter for a new film.

Good luck. But stay off the ski slopes. The doctor tapped his patient's chest.

I grew up with snow, the patient said. I hate it.

*

In high school Dan acted in the annual operetta, mostly because girls from Saint Mary's were also cast. He usually had a small part but in his final year the director, Brother Martin, who had a good voice and liked to show it off, gave him the leading role. Edvard Grieg in *The Song of Norway*, a pastiche musical that uses Grieg's music to tell his life story. Dan couldn't sing well and one by one Brother Martin cut all his songs. That made the girl who played Grieg's wife the star, dancing at the finale to the first movement of the Piano Concerto in A minor while Dan stood to the side and held her hand at the end. He never did understand why he'd been cast in the role, but on stage he found his mark and spoke his lines with conviction. One of the characters was Henrik Ibsen, played in blustery fashion by a classmate named Jake Jackson. He wore a false black beard that waggled as he talked. Dan hated their scenes together. He found Jake so off-putting that he decided he hated Ibsen and never read his plays.

About a year after Estrella died, a small theatre company in LA asked him to direct *Hedda Gabler*. He didn't feel competent on the stage and turned it down, but he read the play anyway and Jake Jackson disappeared. Dan read all of Ibsen in the next few years, and saw productions in London and New York when he could.

In Denmark on the *Lost Time* shoot, a day when the light was too poor for an outdoor scene, he went alone by bus from Aalborg to the tip of Jutland. He spent a couple of hours staring across the strait toward Norway. The distance was too great to see land, even on a bright day, but he felt closer to Ibsen than ever. He wanted to go to Norway, to see the landscape of Grieg and Ibsen. He found a bilingual copy of *Peer Gynt* in a shop in Aalborg, the original text in Danish side-by-side with English. The bookseller said that in Ibsen's day, when Denmark ruled Norway, Norwegian was considered unsophisticated and Danish was the standard written language. Dan got one of the Danish crew members to recite a bit to him while he followed along in English. They made some copies and had a reading of the last act, using Danish or English depending on who was speaking. Carlos read the Button Moulder in a captivating Spanish accent, breathy and sibilant. Irena insisted on playing Peer, and was very good.

He's not a man, she said, he's really a woman who's lost in

the world of men. He wants to be a man, but can't. Let's make a film of it. Dan said he didn't know how. Do what you usually do, she said, change everything into your own life.

*

After Aunt Dot died, the boxes had been kept for some years in a storage lockup in Mount Washington, everything still in the old cardboard. In the winter of 2010 the roof iced up and leaked, damaging some of the contents. Dan came back to Cincinnati to sort them once again. Some photos and letters had been ruined but a number of things survived intact. He convinced Moira, one of the grandchildren of Uncle Ed, that it was time for her to look after the family effects. I'm not going to have children, he said, and you'll probably get interested in them when you're my age.

How old are you, Moira asked.

Seventy this year, beyond the O'Daniel allotment.

They looked through the pictures and documents, his mother's diploma from secretarial college, the US naturalization certificate of his great-grandfather Arnold Luganmann, who renounced allegiance to the Grand Duke of Oldenburg, a copy of the deed on the house on Urine Av. Moira was bored with the photos of her ancestors, people she'd never met and had barely heard about, but was intrigued by a letter Dan forgotten. It was sent to Ellen in Cincinnati by her brother William Moran. Three pages, handwritten on lined notepaper.

58 Palmer Terrace
Wellington Quay
Tyne – England

April 29th/1924

My Dear Long Lost Sister.
Just a few loving lines hoping to find you enjoying
the best of health as this note leaves me at present thank
God for his kind mercy towards us all. Well Sister you will
be surprised to hear from me but I have been after your
address for years but could not get it until my Brother
John sent it over at last and I cannot tell you how please I
was when I got it so I have wrote this letter straight away.
Well Nellie I can see by your name that you are married I
hope you and your Husbent are in good health you will be
supprised you hear that I am married this 20 years I have
10 of a family 9 of which are alive the oldest is a boy James
18 years he is a fine boy he won the Scholership when he
was 11 years. I sent him to a high School for 4 years were
he passed and won a high class Certifecate and now he is
a pupil Teacher for 12 months reciving £2 a month and in
September of this year he has to go to Collage for too years
that is if I can be able to send him it is costing so much for
him and the work is so bad in this country. I have only done
6 month work in 3 years this country is done. I have to girls
ready for work but there is know work for them. Annie is 17
years and Bridgie is 15 they are very tall it is ashame to see
them wasting there time in this country. I will be sending
there photos through to you now when I got your address.
Well Nellie how long is it since you seen my other two
sister Kattie and Bridgie are they near you if they are give
my best love to them if John son is near I send my best
regards to him. Well Nellie I think I have to you all this thi
time I am that much over joyed at getten your address I
cannot write much more untill I hear from you so good by
at present write streagh back and let me hear from you once
more. from your long

> *lost Brother William*
> *best love from all at home*
> *Wife and family*
> *XXXXXXXXXXXXXXXX*
> *P.S.*
> *If you know my other*
> *too Sisters will you Please*
> *sent them through*

It's wonderful, Moira said. Do you think Nellie answered him?

I just have this letter, Dan said. I imagine she did.

I love all the spelling mistakes, and the grammar. It makes it seem real somehow. Where did he work?

From the address, I'd guess he worked the Tyneside docks. Shipbuilding maybe, or coal loading. The Irish usually got low-paying laborers' jobs in England, just like here.

Did you try to find his children?

There'd be great-grandchildren by now. It's something I should do. Or maybe you should do. I don't even know Nellie's descendants in Cincy. They weren't around us when I was a boy.

The farther you go back, the wider it becomes, Moira said. I didn't know my grandfather at all. What was he like?

Uncle Ed, the electrician. He was very different from my father, sober and quiet. I think he was a contented man. I never heard him raise his voice.

I wish I'd known him, she said.

Some of the boxes were still damp and they decided to put everything into an old steamer trunk Moira had inherited. She was very organized, placing everything in separate envelopes or small boxes, labelled as well as Dan's memory would allow. He was sorry to see the old boxes thrown out, since he'd known their cardboard for as long as he'd known their contents. Their markings in the hand of Nellie or Caty or Delia or his father.

Are you interested in the past, Moira?

When we studied American history in school I used to think of myself living there, with Lincoln in the Civil War, or Jefferson, something like that. But you can't get there, can you?

I think if you went back there, to Delia's youth, say, you wouldn't much like it. Because you'd still be you. These things – keep them safe. They're as close as you'll get.

*

Delia's blackthorn got wet in the leak and the black bark was peeling in places. Dan took it back with him to Ireland, a return Delia never imagined. He knew that she'd hit Skip with it, more than once. The knob was slightly cracked. It was too short for Dan as a walking stick but he took to carrying it around Dublin anyway, ostensibly to fend off dogs, the way he carried it as a swagger stick in his soldiers' club. He knew it gave a false sense of security, but the northside of town where he lived was a bit rough and he thought no one would bother a tall man holding a stick, even if he had silver hair. Skangers, Dubliners call the tough young lads from the impoverished section of the city, or knackers, descendants of a long line of slum dwellers, the underclass. Some were in drug gangs, some were addicts or drunks, most were just poor, living in crowded council flats, with low ceilings and low expectations. They had their own talk, like the Travellers, and a distinctive accent, flat and nasal, consonants slurred even when sober. They were aggressively impolite and quick to take offence. The kids liked to ride horses on the streets. They'd get them at the Smithfield Horse Fair, once a month on Sundays. A horse trader would spit on his hand before shaking to close a deal.

Walking along Stoneybatter one evening, cobbled roadway, little traffic, Dan thought he might give the blackthorn to Carlos, who was short and sometimes still needed a cane when his leg acted up. He was spending much of his time in Lima with his mother, who had declined since her husband's death. Carlos himself had grown thin on the Norway shoot; he didn't like the food and often felt ill in the morning. Dan was worried about him. They had a lot of work to do on *The Button Moulder*, some re-shoots in LA, then editing the final cut.

Carlos was worried about Dan too. He said it on Skype, more than once. Dan didn't like Skype and turned off the video. He preferred the telephone, a simple and reliable technology, but Carlos said it was too expensive to phone from Peru to Ireland. It's not good for you to live alone like this, he said. When's the last time you had sex?

I can't remember.

You have no friends, you're cut off there, in the outskirts of everything.

Joyce called Ireland the scraggy isthmus of Europe Minor, Dan said. Carlos said he didn't know what any of those words meant, and Dan admitted he wasn't sure either. I do have friends, though, Dan said.

Do you go out with them?

Now and then.

How often is that?

Once in a while.

Exactly my point, Carlos said. He made another comment but the connection was poor and his voice broke up. Dan shut off his laptop. It was true, he had to admit. His social life had collapsed in Ireland. There were people he liked but they were busy and they never called him. When he wasn't working he had too much time on his hands. He decided to rent a car and drive north, to Newgrange or the Giants' Causeway, see more of this heartrending country.

From the rental agency he had to get onto the M50, the new ring road around Dublin, which confused him. He took the wrong exit and found himself on the M4, the motorway to Galway, as if the car wanted him to go west only. Like his father, he hated to backtrack and allowed himself to be taken there. It was a Sunday with little morning traffic and in less than three hours he was at Lough Mask. He phoned Carmel on his mobile and she joined him for lunch at the pub. She was still in her church clothes, woollen skirt and jacket, medium heels. She looked thinner, her cheeks red from the wind, her red hair neat under a natty little hat.

You're back, she said, and you're wearing nice clothes. After a lifetime of rejecting traditional men's jackets, he'd recently seen their virtue. He'd always dressed in jeans and sweaters and had a favourite Japanese quilted jacket for the cold, red with blue piping. He still used his trouser pockets in the way of his youth, but now he had to carry reading glasses, pills, notebook, pen, phone, a passport. In the pub he was in a grey tweed jacket with a dark green sweater under it. But still no tie, Carmel said.

I hate ties.

What about when you get an award? Don't you dress up?

The kind of awards I receive, you want to dress down.

They ordered lunch from Pete O'Donovan, who welcomed Dan warmly. It was cosy by the open fire, the acrid smell of the burning turf as much a part of the west as runny noses. How long has it been, Carmel asked.

A few years. I don't imagine they've missed me much, aside from Pete there.

Well, some people liked the filum, especially those who were in it.

And others were offended?

Maybe disappointed, she said. They thought it showed us in a poor light.

It didn't celebrate the glorious dead like the republican songs, if that's what you mean. What did you think?

He was drinking water at lunch these days, trying to follow the doctor's advice, but Carmel had a second glass of wine and got expansive. I liked it, she said, but I thought it was a foreigner's view. Making a nation out of nothing, no money, no resources, after centuries of oppression, that was hard. Having to take what the English gave instead of the full freedom we deserved. The treaty was hated by the Shinners and not liked by many, but it started us on the right road. That's important to people here. Whatever side our grandfathers took in the Civil War.

It's a story about a man, not a country, Dan said.

I know, I know. Your Kevin Walsh, he got a bad deal, but he wasn't sympathetic.

I detest sympathy. It's sentimental, it's like pity, it doesn't change truth. Truth is harsh.

You're harsh, Rody Moran, you are. A harsh man. You were raised a Catholic, you went to confession, told the priest your sins, he gave you penance.

Father Mick. Five Our Fathers and five Hairy Marys, no matter the sin.

Cheap at the price, she said. Your Father Mick then handed over forgiveness, didn't he? You should accept what he gave you.

Dan said, I never thought forgiveness meant anything. Maybe it changes how we feel about ourselves but it doesn't change the world. I don't believe God or the angels keep score.

But then you don't believe in God or the angels, do you?

They were quiet a moment. Dan looked out the window at the lake as the sun broke through the grey clouds and the water was shining, mocking his mood. Carmel toyed with her wineglass. Then she said, What about you? Do you find it hard to forgive?

Forgive what?

You tell me.

What had he forgiven? His father maybe, and Carlos. Irena – probably not. He couldn't forgive his mother and Estrella for leaving him. Affection boxed up in resentment. The acrid smoke of his own deficiency, the deficit of love. Guilt and forgiveness – if you've got the first, he thought, you're a miser with the second. You have to forgive yourself first, they say, the pop psychologists. But he was like a doubting priest who couldn't forgive God for not existing.

I would have made a poor priest, that's for sure, he said. I'd hate to give absolution. I'd want sinners to suffer on earth.

She laughed. You'd be like one of those Orangemen preachers in the north, Ian Paisley shouting No Surrender!

They are great haters up there, aren't they? You have to admire that. You want a coffee?

Come back to the house, I'll make it there. Will you stay the night?

If it's no trouble.

He paid the bill. Walking to her house he asked if she had a boat.

An old rowboat in the shed. Why?

I'd like to go out on the lough. I didn't get the chance when we were filming.

It might need a little work.

The shed was the old house. The boat was there, a wooden one, standing upright in a corner of the room where Delia was born. He dragged it out into the sun, ready for the morning. One of the oars was cracked in the blade, but would serve. He also found some fishing tackle in the shed. He changed his clothes and took a long walk along the lake, two hours or more. Carmel fixed a light supper and he went to bed early, very tired.

The bed was comfortable, the room warm, the sheets cool. As a child he loved the first moments in bed, tucked under the blankets with a book tucked by his side. I have everything I need, he would think, and delayed reading to savour the anticipation. As he would start to drift off he'd wake himself to prolong the delicious sense of falling asleep. He wanted to know what it felt like to pass over into sleep. But you can't know that, he realized, because you're not conscious when it happens and the next thing you'll know is waking up. You can only feel the almost-sleep.

Once after his mother died he had a dream of sleeping, as if he were watching himself from above, dreaming of his dream. What if someone were watching over me, he thought, the way the nuns say God watches us, or our guardian angels. Why would they be watching? A boring thing, just a boy sleeping. Like a camera recording him, keeping track of his life even at night, guarding or spying. Is God a spy, he wondered, like Santa Claus, making a list, checking it twice? The camera always going. So many movies God would have to watch, he'd need lots of help. That's what the guardian angels do, maybe, preview all those films.

Dan smiled at the memory of that boy. No God or guardian watched him, but as he crossed over the unknowable line into sleep he had the suspicion that a camera was somewhere out in the universe, making images no one would see.

*

He woke early, drank his coffee alone, and dragged the boat to the shore. His shoes got wet launching it. He took them off, and his socks, and stored them under the traverse seat with the sandwiches Carmel had left for him, neatly packed in Tupperware. He'd brought the Brownie along too – he wanted to take some shots of the lake with it, a sentimental gesture. So what, he thought, old men can be sentimental, who's to care?

The water was cold and he shivered a little despite his Aran sweater. His *geansaí*, Luke called it. The usual mist drifted from the water as the sun rose. It had been many years since he'd rowed. Decades. He found a rhythm eventually and pulled out into the large lake. He expected blisters on his hands but didn't care. Blisterburn. The sun hit him in the face and he was soon sweating from exertion. He took off the sweater. Sitting with his back to the prow, he hadn't noticed he was pulling to the left – his right stoke was stronger. He turned and looked at the wooded spot where he'd seen the two boatmen unloading that long object. He thought there was a flash in the trees, like the sun striking shiny metal. Some movement in the underbrush, a rabbit, a bird, he couldn't tell.

He rowed further along the shoreline to the spot where they'd filmed the first scene of *Playing Soldiers*. They'd had trouble with the blood in the water; Carlos wasn't happy with the colour, which was first too crimson, then too pale. Stage blood diluted quickly. A crew member knew that pig's blood worked well in fresh water, so he drove to a butcher in Castlebar to get it. Such a strange business, Dan thought, all that trouble to make the false seem true. He pulled away from the shore and got the fishing pole ready. It was an old cane fly rod with a few worn flies with rusty hooks and a rusty reel. He didn't care if he caught anything. It was the emptiness of activity he wanted, the sun, the water, the unhurried day. He made a decent cast with a Royal Coachman, the all-purpose standby.

He'd learned to fly fish in the Sierras when he was at Berkeley but was out of practice and was unprepared for an immediate strike. He'd heard the trout grew large in Lough Mask and the one he'd hooked felt enormous. The rod was bent and seemed about to snap. He let out more line and allowed the fish to run; when it tired he began to reel it in slowly. It splashed three or four times, its scales a lustrous blue in the light, still fighting hard, about thirty feet from the boat. Just then the sun went in and a soft rain descended.

Out of the corner of his eye something else moved in the water to the right. He glanced over to find another boat with a single rower. The man looked familiar. Was it the boat he'd seen at night years before? The rower was sitting still, watching. Distracted for a moment, Dan loosened tension on the rod and the trout ran under the boat, turned quickly and snapped off the line. Gone. The other man seemed to be smiling. He made a gesture that might have been beckoning, or might have been a commiserating wave. Then he said something that Dan didn't understand. Better luck next time? Or was it See you next time?

The rain was falling harder. Dan put on his sweater and waterproof parka and rowed to shore. He stood under a tree, hood up, still barefoot, and ate a sandwich. Cheese and pickle, good brown bread and local cheddar. He wished he'd brought a thermos of tea. Perhaps he'd had the best of the day. He waited most of an hour, thinking about his next film, a crime story set in Dublin during the boom years. Double plot, bankers set beside inner-city drug lords: which was more dangerous? He knew he could get the funding.

The shower gradually blew over. By the time he was back on the water the sun was out again. He repaired the leader on the fishing line and tied on a new fly, a duller one he didn't know. He was about to cast when the saw the other boat again, a hundred yards away. The man was standing now, gently rocking in the boat, and signalling Dan to approach. Come on, his gesture said, come over here. Dan heard the call as well, though again he wasn't sure of the words. What did the guy want? Was it warning? Perhaps he needed help. Dan stood in the boat, hoping to see more clearly. He steadied himself, legs apart. A dark cloud covered the sun and as if from nowhere a sudden wind rose, bringing chop to the water. The boat rocked hard. He stumbled, lost his balance, the keel rose and he went over the side.

The Aran sweater was soaked immediately and dragged him down. People said the water was very deep here, but what does it matter once it's over your head? He kicked hard towards the upturned boat. His shoes would have gone to the bottom, along with the antique fly rod. And the Brownie, all gone. The wind was driving the boat toward shore, a lucky break. His heart had been racing but calmed a little, now that his hands were on the hull. He kicked to push it, feeling a tightness in his chest and an ache in his arm. He felt exhausted already but sooner than expected the upturned gunwales scraped on the stones at the water's edge. He stood up in the shallows, then sat on the hull, panting. He pulled off the sweater. He seemed feverish, both hot from exertion and cold from wind and water. The oars were gone. He'd have to hoof it back barefoot.

He looked out at the lough, which was now covered in light rain. He saw the other boat and thought for a moment the man was coming towards him to help, but it was pulling away to the north. The rower was strong and it was soon out of sight. He picked up his sodden sweater and started back. It took him about an hour and he had to rest twice.

Carmel was working in the garden and saw him cross the road. She ran toward him. I need to lie down, he said.

We'll get you in a bath first. She helped him upstairs. His feet were bleeding from the stones and he worried that he was staining the stair carpet. In hot water the pain in his chest eased. Carmel cleaned up the cuts on his feet and brought him a mug of sweetened tea in bed. Do you want a doctor, she asked. We have one near who'll make a house call.

Dan said he'd be okay after a rest; it was just a spill in the lake. I have to get the boat, he said. Carmel told him not to worry, she'd phone her son to bring it back. She asked what had happened but Dan was dozing off and she let him sleep.

The rower was there. Despite the mist Dan could see him clearly, an older man who looked like Luke, skin drawn tight on his face, prominent nose, bony hands on the oars, dirty white shirt. Next time, he seemed to say, the words an echo across the water. What do you mean, Dan asked. The man rowed away too swiftly, like a scene with skipped frames.

Dan was sure there was a camera attached to the wall at the corner of the room, fixed near the ceiling. He could hear it whirring.

But there was also a screen on the wall opposite the window. It was showing trailers of his films, spliced together so they made no sense, short scenes or just images cut without attention to their rhythm or narrative flow. It offended him that someone would abuse his work like that. It couldn't be Carlos, he knew that. It might have been someone in Hollywood who disapproved of him. The screen went blank a moment – it was an old-fashioned portable screen on a tripod stand, the kind you'd use for home movies in the sixties. Super-eight, not a good medium. Dan loved 16mm, very flexible. The sound of the projector in the room, a memory from school, those rare days when the Marxist Brothers showed a documentary about missionaries in Africa, save the pagan babies, implants in his brain that predicted his own documentaries.

The screen was showing old clips, looked like the forties, men in fedoras, was that his father there, soldiers returning at Union Station, Aunt Peg holding his hand tightly as they waited for her Cliff to come out, back from France, packed concourse, high excitement. Now the old station is the Cincinnati History Museum. He loved that place, they had a huge model of the town in the 1940s, street lights and buildings and hills and working trains, and little streetcars going their rounds. The lights cycle from day to night, it's beautiful, let's go back, hang on, Danny, Peg was saying, don't get lost.

The movie went on but the screen was blocked by people from Union Station surrounding his bed, dressed for 1946, there was his mother coughing into a hankie, and Delia and Grandpa Luganman and also Dot and Mike and Dottie Sue and Skip in the background with a Lucky and a bottle of Hudepohl. Dan reached out for a drink from the bottle but everybody parted for the priest. He thought it was Father Mick but this man was too small, must be Monsignor Schengber but surely he had white hair and this one had no hair at all. It was Sinéad O'Connor coming towards the bed, shaved head, Roman collar and black waistcoat, large pectoral cross around the neck. She got out the home kit for Extreme Unction his mother had, with a crucifix and little candles and holy oil but the crucifix turned into a black acoustic guitar and she began to sing: Why the fuck should I care what happens to you? The band came on, pushing his mother out of the way and somebody set up some theatrical lighting – too much blue, Dan thought, it would come out wrong on film, Carlos always said stay away from blue, it's not natural – and the beat was so loud it took over his heart which shifted in time to the music and stopped being his heart. I can't dance to that, Dan said, two lead electric guitars and a woman on bass and a drummer and a keyboard man who looked like that black French tennis player, what's his name, loose-limbed fellow, but they made a lot of noise.

Then they were playing the Dies Irae, still loud, much louder than the De Sales children's choir and not that simple Gregorian version but Mozart's, from the Requiem Mass in D minor, with heavy bass chords and hi-hat cymbals. Dan's own Doomsday Book, his Doomsday Machine, that sent him back to belief and forward to a Last Judgement, a promise that had been vacated. Did anyone really credit it anymore, Christ come back to earth to judge the living and the dead? Just another myth for the anthropologists, wondering about a tribe that held on to it so long. I'm not getting out of this bed, Dan thought, it's too crowded in the room.

The light through the window seemed to be the light on Urine Av, bouncing across the street from Calvary Cemetery. Funny that Delia is here, he thought, lying in this bed with me. Was it all one after all, no separations, no division, just continuance? It didn't seem possible, it went against everything he knew about the world, about the isolation of individuals and the impermanence of connections, and yet he was filled with the joy of a bond to this place, here in Mayo and here in Cincinnati, all one. He was in the Pontiac with his mother and Estrella and

Skip on the road. Watch out for trucks, Carlos. He understood that the feeling was illusion, the result of illness and crisis, but it was as powerful as real experience, like a film that wraps you so deeply you're not sure of true and false. You go out on the street after a matinee, still inside the dark of the movie, and you're lost between the realm of the one and realm of the other, blinking in the sunlight.

Críochnaigh an scannán, he said to Carmel, but was she there? Maybe in the corner. All these people! And please stop ringing that church bell, it will break the windows.

How insignificant we are.

What was that, Carmel said, finish the filum? The room had cleared, and she stood by the bed, a mug of tea in her hand.

Abair leis an scannán a chríochnú, Dan said.

Why are you speaking Irish? She was confused, and tried to pass him the mug, but he was looking out the window. Tell who to finish the filum?

Carlos. Re-shoots. Cutting. On my thing there, the phone.

Don't you want this tea?

The light was fading outside. From the bed he could catch a glimpse of the lake. He closed his eyes on that. It seemed very peaceful.

*

Carlos made it two days later, weeping across the Atlantic. The coroner said massive heart attack. No one quite knew what to do, then Carmel had the inspired idea to hold a wake in the old house. She and her son Seán cleared it and laid out Dan in the front room, on an old pine table. The surface had been worn thin by scrubbing. There were ancient things there, no one knew how ancient, a broken bed, a chest, farm mud and tool rust, the lingering smell of turf. Few people came but there was Jameson and Murphy's stout and crúibins. Luke was there, and all the Morans nearby. The Jameson reminded Carlos of one of Skip's jokes he'd heard from Dan, about Pat dying, or Fintan, but he couldn't remember the punch line and it fizzled. Seán's wife started an old olagón. Why did he die tonight when he never died before. But her heart wasn't in it. Nobody got drunk.

Funeral Mass in Tourmakeady. Carlos said it was against Dan's wishes but Carmel overruled him. I'm the nearest relative here, she said, and he will have a proper Catholic send-off.

The priest called him Rody. They travelled with the body to the Glasnevin crematorium in Dublin, where Carmel had to hold Carlos up. Burning fiery furnace. Together they cleared out the house in Stonybatter and put it up for sale. They sent a few effects to Moira. Carlos wanted to have the Kodak Brownie as a memento, Dan's talisman. They searched everywhere and couldn't find it. Carmel offered him Delia's blackthorn instead but he said it should stay in Ireland. She took it back to Churchfield and set it on the table inside the old house, as if it had been casually left there after a stroll.

There would be a memorial service in Los Angeles later. First Carlos took the ashes to Cincinnati, holding the urn on his lap on the plane, passengers staring at him anxiously. The cousins and their children and grandchildren insisted on another Requiem Mass at Saint Francis de Sales, the urn on a table in front of the white gothic altar. Dies irae, dies illa, though there was no longer a choir to sing it.

Danielito, he told me, Carlos said, he wanted his ashes in the Ohio. It turned out to be illegal to scatter them in an inland waterway, but they did it anyway, a few miles downstream at a riverside park. The wind blew some ash back on Moira and made her sneeze. Breathing DanDan, she said.

The water took Dan on a trip to the Gulf of Mexico. Él va a casa, Carlos said.

What's that, Moira said.

He's going home.

She asked what home he meant, but he didn't answer.

Acknowledgements

I am grateful to a number of people who made important suggestions: Mary Buckley, Richard Lehnert, Jane Stanford, Lyndsey Stonebridge, Susannah Tyrrell, and a boatload of Kennedys: Annie, Jessica, Megan, Miranda, and Rob. Cathal Ó Háinle aided with the Irish language and the culture of Connacht in nineteenth century; any mistakes are not his. For practical help I thank Anne Ronan, Donna and Joseph Kattus, Michael Kattus, and the staff of the wonderful Cincinnati History Museum.

For the history of Irish emigration I have relied chiefly on Kerby A. Miller's *Emigrants and Exiles: Ireland and the Irish Exodus to North America*. Miller and Paul Wagner's *Out of Ireland: The Story of Irish Emigration to America* was also useful, as was Arnold Schrier's *Ireland and the American Emigration, 1850-1900*. Some details are taken from John Canon O'Hanlon's *The Emigrant's Guide for the United States*, published in Dublin in 1890. On the history of Cincinnati I was helped by Geoffrey Giglierano and Deborah A. Overmyer's *The Bicentennial Guide to Greater Cincinnati: A Portrait of Two Hundred Years* and Robert I. Vexler's *Cincinnati: A Chronological and Documentary History, 1676-1970*.

Printed in France by Amazon
Brétigny-sur-Orge, FR

14786409R00161